Praise for *According to Queeney*

'A s............ .... written wi..... .... return or
the b........ .... of her literary life' Margaret Atwood

'This is a small, wise book of small prose miracles . . . It is a larger miracle in this way: it makes us feel we see Johnson and his friends in unexpected and unfamiliar ways, which are nevertheless convincing and authentic. I did not think anyone could do this, and still have no idea how Bainbridge pulled it off' Andrew Marr, *Daily Telegraph*

'These real people are superbly recreated in fictional form . . . Bainbridge's characters inhabit a world of perpetual farce, punctuated by confusion and misunderstandings. In her hands, bizarre behaviour is made to seem natural. The result is bittersweet; one would laugh if one did not also feel so acutely their pain . . . Bainbridge's spare prose is perfectly suited to her purpose, conveying an immediate sense of experience, in the muddle and intensity of the present. This is a highly intelligent, sophisticated and entertaining novel, which requires reading more than once to appreciate its complexity' Adam Sisman, *Observer*

'To fictionalise Johnson's life is a daring literary adventure . . . The character created by Bainbridge is entirely believable in all his contradictions . . . Poignant, pierced with truth, *According to Queeney* reaches into the dustier realms of history, bringing vividly to life a group of remarkable personalities with all their frailties, absurdities and cruel sensitivities' Kate Chisholm, *Sunday Telegraph*

'Beryl Bainbridge has written many remarkable novels, but none to equal this . . . Extraordinary. It is as good in its very different form as Boswell; it is even a necessary companion piece to Boswell' Allan Massie, *Scotsman*

'Its subjects – guilt, passion, misunderstanding and suffering – are those that she has addressed throughout her career, sometimes as comedy, also as tragedy, but never so perfectly as in this book. Few of us are as selfish as Mrs Thrale, and fewer still as wise as Dr Johnson, but in describing them, Bainbridge illuminates human nature' Amanda Craig, *Express*

'Bainbridge is wonderfully subtle on the sad, attritional, secretly tragic process of life' Anne Haverty, *Irish Times*

Beryl Bainbridge is the author of seventeen novels, two travel books and five plays for stage and television. *The Dressmaker, The Bottle Factory Outing, An Awfully Big Adventure, Every Man for Himself* and *Master Georgie* (which won the James Tait Black Memorial Prize) were all shortlisted for the Booker Prize, and *Every Man for Himself* was awarded the Whitbread Novel of the Year Prize. She won the *Guardian* Fiction Prize with *The Dressmaker* and the Whitbread Prize with *Injury Time. The Bottle Factory Outing, Sweet William* and *The Dressmaker* have been adapted for film, as was *An Awfully Big Adventure*, which starred Hugh Grant and Alan Rickman. Beryl Bainbridge died in July 2010.

Also by Beryl Bainbridge

FICTION

An Awfully Big Adventure
Another Part of the Wood
The Birthday Boys
The Bottle Factory Outing
Collected Stories
The Dressmaker
Every Man for Himself
Filthy Lucre
Harriet Said
Injury Time
Master Georgie
Mum and Mr Armitage
Northern Stories (ed. with David Pownall)
A Quiet Life
Sweet William
Watson's Apology
A Weekend with Claude
Winter Garden
Young Adolf
The Girl in the Polka-Dot Dress

NON-FICTION

English Journey, or the Road to Milton Keynes
Forever England: North and South
Something Happened Yesterday
Front Row: My Life in the Theatre

ACCORDING TO QUEENEY

Beryl Bainbridge

ABACUS

First published in Great Britain
by Little, Brown and Company in 2001
This edition published by Abacus in 2002

12

A CIP catalogue record for this book
is available from the British Library.

ISBN 978 0 349 11447 7

Typeset in Garamond by M Rules
Printed and bound in Great Britain by
Clays Ltd, Elcograf S.p.A.

Papers used by Abacus are from well-managed forests
and other responsible sources.

Abacus
An imprint of
Little, Brown Book Group
Carmelite House
50 Victoria Embankment
London EC4Y 0DZ

An Hachette UK Company
www.hachette.co.uk

www.littlebrown.co.uk

To Andrew and Margaret Hewson,
with affection and gratitude

According to Queeney

PROLOGUE

On the morning of December 15th, 1784, a day of
bleak skies heralding snow, a box-cart rattled into
Bolt Court and drew up outside Number 8. Three
men entered the house and presently emerged
carrying a roll of threadbare carpet as though it
were a battering ram.

Mrs Desmoulins, shawl tight against her,
remained on the steps of the house and forced tears
from her eyes. Though she felt grief, she was too old,
too used to death, to weep without an effort. She
stood alone, save for a black and white cat busy
washing itself. A number of neighbours came out
and waited with bowed heads until the cart had

gone from sight. From the open window of Number 6 could be heard the jangling of a spinet. It was not known whether Mr Kranach, a man who summer and winter wore a coat lined with the fur of a white wolf, was serenading the departed or merely about his daily practice.

The conveyance turning into Fleet Street, a gaggle of urchins ran in pursuit and leapt for the tail-board, at which the driver flicked backwards with his whip. Francis Barber, walking behind, accompanied his master as far as the church of St Clement Danes in the Strand; then, the bitter cold of the early hour getting to his living bones, he ducked away and sought refuge in a tavern.

Arriving in Windmill Street, the cart trundled into the yard of William Hunter's School of Anatomy. The carpet was carried to the top floor and laid on a dissecting table. A fire roared in the grate and the air was filled with an aroma of herbs, that of mint being the most pervasive. In the corner of the cosy room, a dog, half-flayed, hung from a hook in the ceiling; above, the grey heavens nudged the skylight.

Present that morning were the physicians Heberden, Brocklesby, Butter, Wilson and Cruikshank. Also in attendance were Mr Wilson's son, Arthur, and a Mr White, neither of whom was as yet qualified in the practice of medicine.

Mr White unrolled the carpet and removed the winding sheet. Arthur Wilson made the first incision, cutting downwards from the thorax. A quantity of water spilled from the cavity of the chest and dripped on to the floor. Mr White was told to throw more herbs upon the fire to disperse the stink of dissolution.

Dr Heberden made the second incision, this time across the stomach. He was troubled with a cough, and once, bending over his departed patient, the force of his breath fluttered the dead man's eyelashes, at which Mr White turned pale and swayed where he stood. Mr Cruikshank, noticing his pallor, ordered him to swallow a measure of brandy.

Later, under the instruction of his father, Arthur Wilson wrote the following report:

Opened the chest. Lungs did not collapse as they usually do, as though power of contraction lost.

Heart exceedingly strong and large.

Abdomen appeared to have incipient peritoneal inflammation and ascites.

Liver and spleen firm and hard.

A gall stone size of a pigeon's egg removed from bladder.

Pancreas enlarged.

One kidney (left) quite good. That of the right entirely destroyed.

Left testicle sound in structure but with a number of hydatides (cysts) on surface. Right

testicle likewise. Spermatic vein leading to it
exceedingly enlarged and varicose.

Body, large in life, now somewhat shrunken,
save for left leg swollen from the dropsy. Right
leg recently stitched following self-inflicted
wound.

Left lung removed for perusal of John
Hunter, also slice of scrotum and gall stone.
Specimens transferred to jars. Mr White
pricked his middle finger when sewing up
body. The following day had red lines running
up arm and was laid low with slight fever.

Afterwards, the fire dying and the candles lighted,
Mr Hoskins of St Martin's Lane, sent to Windmill
Street at the request of Sir Joshua Reynolds,
mounted the stairs to undertake a death mask.
When the wax had cooled and he pulled away the
cast, the eyelids were dragged open; he was too
engrossed in scrutinising the imprint of the face to
notice the staring aspect of the original.

The candles extinguished and the door locked,
the dead man and the dead dog waited in darkness,
gazing upwards to where snowflakes, star shaped,
now fell upon the skylight.

CRISIS *n.f. (κρίσις)*

The point of time at which any affair comes
to its height

This hour's the very crisis *of your fate;*
Your good or ill; your infamy or fame,
And all the colour of your life depends
On this important now.

Dryden's *Spanish Friar*

Solitary nights were to be feared, for when darkness fell, the mind, like the eye, saw things less clearly than by day and confusions and perversions of the brain manufactured black thoughts. Which is why he contrived to stay out into the small hours, to shrink the time left until the light came back.

He was fortunate in that he had acquaintances who were willing to sit up with him, some of whom considered it a privilege to do so. He knew this to be the truth, not vanity. His introduction to the Thrale household had been made a year before, in gloomy January, through the offices of his old friend, the Irishman Arthur Murphy. 'They keep high company,' Murphy had said, by way of inducement, 'and an excellent table.'

He had known nothing of his host beyond he was a prosperous owner of a brewery in Deadman's Place, Southwark, and but recently married. There was also a mansion in Streatham with hothouses and chickens.

Murphy thought he had caught him by mentioning the expected attendance of the poetical shoemaker, James Woodhouse, the literary sensation of the moment, but, truth to tell, it was the promise of a fine dinner that led him to accept.

On his return home he had found Mrs Williams waiting up for him, the kettle on the boil. She led, of necessity, a reclusive life and was eager to hear his impressions of the wider world.

'Was it engaging?' she had asked. 'Was it worth the effort?'

'At least we were spared musical entertainment,' he replied and then, in spite of himself, blurted out, 'Mrs Thrale is an unusual woman.'

'How so?' countered Mrs Williams. 'In looks or in intellect?'

Had he thrown aside caution and spoken the words in his head, he would have confided that Mrs Thrale had sparkling eyes, narrow shoulders, penetrating wit, scholarship of the female kind, a favourable interest in himself and a leakage of milk from her right breast.

Instead he said, 'James Woodhouse has an impediment of speech, which is all to the good, as what he has to say is of little importance. Though a poor versifier, it is probable he's a competent maker of shoes.'

'How many at table?' probed Mrs Williams. 'What order of placement?'

'From an upper window,' he said, 'Mrs Thrale pointed

out the site of Shakespeare's theatre. She maintains there are several timbers still standing.'

'And you saw them?' cried Mrs Williams.

'I saw nothing,' he said. 'The night was too black.'

After no more than a quarter of an hour, fearful of betraying himself, he had feigned tiredness and announced he was for his bed. A disappointed droop to her mouth, Mrs Williams preceded him up the stairs; theirs was an example of the blind leading the half-blind.

Now, the new year well advanced, his visits to the Thrales' house in the Borough had become regular, namely every Thursday in the month. Since last September a coach had been sent to fetch him, and as the light waned and the weather worsened he had half a dozen times been persuaded to stop the night. Mrs Thrale had even marked for his particular use a room above the counting house, and had shelves built to accommodate his books, should he wish to bring them.

He was not a fool. He knew full well his presence drew others to Southwark, and if the circumstances had proved different he might have absented himself, in spite of the fine dinners. The satisfaction, however, was not all on one side, for the Thrales had a child, a daughter not much above twelve months old. One afternoon, coming face to face with his boots on the bend of the stairs, she had neither screamed nor scrambled past, simply stared gravely up at him. She wore a bonnet, askew, from which a tuft of hair, the colour of damp sand, stuck out above her ear.

'Sweeting,' he had said, and bowed.

'Da-da,' she had crowed and crawled onwards on hands and knees.

Until that auspicious moment he had always thought of

himself as a member of clubs; now he was inclined to believe he was part of a family.

And then, on the Wednesday evening of the third week in April, climbing to his bed in Johnson's Court, he became aware of the Black Dog crouching on the landing, the shadow of its lolling tongue lapping the staircase wall. The stench of its hateful breath seeped into his chamber. He wrenched up the window to let in the night air, but still the rank odour swilled about the room; he propped himself upright and dozed with his hand clamped over his nostrils.

The following morning he woke out of sorts. He would have stayed where he was and distracted himself with arithmetic if Mrs Desmoulins hadn't clamoured for his attention; yet again she had fallen out with Mrs Williams. His head ached and he had difficulty in breathing, but he calmed himself and spoke rationally.

That afternoon Thrale's coach waited for him in the alleyway. Twice he went out of his front door and came back. The third time, Frank Barber, spying him hovering on the top step, his books spilled from under his arm, took him by the elbow and forcibly thrust him into his seat. Dog-tired, he would have clambered out again, but already the carriage was bowling into Fleet Street; besides, his belly was growling.

He arrived and regretted it, for he did not acquit himself well. When Thrale's mother-in-law began her tiresome and habitual questioning, this time pestering him to give an opinion on the riots in Spitalfields occasioned by the imports of French silk, he'd lost his temper and answered harshly. Though in the right of it, he felt vexed at his lack of restraint; he'd brought himself down.

Midnight having passed, Mrs Thrale urged him to stop

until morning. She mentioned the new hangings, green in colour, she had bought for his bed. 'Dark green rather than bright,' she elaborated, 'with an elegant display of tassels.'

He refused to stay with more vigour than was necessary. 'You do not look well,' she persisted.

'Madam,' he countered, 'I have not been well these last fifty years.' When he went out into the dark, he heard the child crying in an upper room above the courtyard.

In spite of the hour, his household was still at war when he let himself in. It appeared Mrs Williams had taken a tumble and hurt her knee, a mishap caused, so she said, by Mr Levet leaving his bag of medical instruments at the foot of the stairs. Frank Barber swore that Levet couldn't be the culprit, on account of his coming in by the cellar door past one o'clock and falling face down on the scullery table.

'I am not given to untruths,' huffed Mrs Williams, fierce as a bantam cock.

'He is there now,' Frank persisted. 'Bag at feet, head on arms.'

Then Mrs Desmoulins had put her oar in, crying out that such recriminations served no purpose, that it was beholden upon them all to be kind to one another . . . in a general pursuit of happiness.

At which he had lost his composure still further and thundered, 'Enough, Madam,' and given them all a piece of his mind before stomping off to bed.

Alone in his room his rage subsided, to be replaced by an all too familiar lethargy of spirit in which his thoughts drifted like feathers caught in a draught. This near somnolent state – he was staring fixedly at the coarse hairs of his wig flung down in the window recess – was shortly followed by physical stirrings of an unmistakable nature.

By a supreme effort of will he fought off his torpor, striking his forehead repeatedly with his fist to beat away a loathsome descent into sensuality. Sufficiently recovered, he occupied himself in mending his coal box, which was split; in this he was not successful and succeeded only in splintering it further.

The following Thursday he sent a note to the Brewery by Frank Barber, pleading a prior engagement. It was a lie, but then, had the truth of his indisposition been spelt out, he might have been thought deserving of pity. He had been an object of that detestable sentiment throughout his childhood and shrank from the recollection.

It was unfortunate that Mrs Desmoulins let in Dr Adams that afternoon, for he was no longer able to control his agitation of mind. He was aware of Adams regarding him as he walked restlessly back and forth, but remembered nothing of their conversation beyond his own assertion that he would consent to an amputation of a limb if it would lead to a restoration of spirits. As from a distance, he heard himself groaning, weeping.

When Dr Adams had gone he placed half a grain of opium on a spoon and, holding it against the rim of a cup filled with cold tea, carried it down. He thought of dear, dead Tetty and how he had berated her for the same indulgent practice.

That night he dreamt an old dream, one in which he crouched beside his mother on her bed in the room above his father's shop. His infant brother lay sleeping in the crook of her arm. Mother was turning the leaves of a child's book on the doctrine of universal salvation. She said there were two places where people went after their death, a fine place called Heaven and a sad place called Hell. When she began to read, her finger under each word so as to keep pace, he knew the sense of the letters before she did, but pushed their meaning from his mind. On the opposite page was an engraving of devils toppling small figures into the eternal flames. 'The Lord hath made all things for Himself,' Mother read, 'yea, even the wicked for the day of evil, for the wicked shall know the wrath of God and be punished everlastingly.'

He cried out in terror and woke instantly, his big toe throbbing with heat. It was the gout, yet he shuddered. Then it was that the Black Dog, scenting fear, burst into his chamber and leapt upon his chest.

'I cannot bear it,' Mrs Williams said, slopping her breakfast dish of tea down the front of her gown. She was putting it about that she was the most affected by the atmosphere in the house. Both women had risen shortly after dawn, though in the circumstances neither had reason to leave her bed. Mrs Desmoulins, smarting from an earlier encounter, remained silent. The altercation had concerned a half-loaf of bread. 'You forgot to cover it against the mice,' Mrs Williams had scolded, sightlessly raking her fingers along the scullery shelf. Crumbs, pretty as snowflakes, sprayed the floor.

Mrs Desmoulins had denied all knowledge and blamed Frank Barber. 'It was him,' she blustered, pointing a finger, but he, motionless at the table, had stuck out his pink tongue and stayed mute.

Mrs Williams's shortness of temper, in evidence at the best of times, had increased tenfold. Even Mr Levet, with whom she often and perversely saw eye to eye, had fallen from favour. Three days ago, coming across him lying in his customary position at the bottom of the scullery stairs, she had kicked him awake. She hadn't caused him an injury, but it was an indication of her agitated state. He, ignorant soul, had crawled on his knees to the fire and, murmuring the word 'Mother', dozed off again with his arms about the coal scuttle. Some minutes later, contrite, Mrs Williams had asked where he was. 'Gone,' Mrs Desmoulins had lied, and embroidered, 'he was bleeding at the mouth.'

'I cannot bear it,' Mrs Williams repeated, but now her voice broke in her throat and her hand shook.

'You are not the only one bent under a burden,' Mrs Desmoulins told her. All the same, she reached out to cover those fingers trembling upon the tablecloth. In doing so she was conscious it was Samuel's influence that guided her; left to herself she might have resorted to spitting.

'My hearing, at least, is unimpaired,' snapped Mrs Williams. 'Your constant wailing and sighing scarcely go unnoticed'; none the less, she allowed her hand to be stilled.

Presently Mrs Desmoulins went out into the little garden beside the house and sat on the bench beneath the sycamore tree. The air was cold, which suited her mood, for anger warmed her blood. From the dwelling next door she could hear Mr Phipps berating his wife. His was a house riven with discord . . . but then, wasn't that a condition common to all?

Phipps kept a mistress in Clerkenwell. Once, when Mrs Phipps had been away in the country undergoing the lying in of her sixth infant, he had brought home his flighty woman in broad daylight and escorted her for all to see across the Court. There had been a boy child born between them who had died in his third year, one with the same beady eyes and cleft lip inherited from his father. Sometimes, the child, aided by his legitimate siblings, had been seen in the adjoining yard attempting to spin a top.

Samuel, hearing of the child's death, had called on Mr Phipps and offered his condolences. Returning, he shed tears. He said Phipps had cared for that lost boy more than all his other offspring put together. Mrs Desmoulins had adopted a serious look. 'The poor dear man,' she wailed. Inwardly, she felt exultant, seeing her dead husband had been just such a one as Phipps, and one she hoped still roasted in Hell.

Sitting there, her feet turning to ice, she fretted over how much longer Samuel would stay in his room. His self-imposed confinement had begun five weeks before, on his return from the Thrales'. In the morning he had seemed his usual self. She'd had occasion to speak to him at mid-day owing to Mrs Williams accusing her of extravagance in the matter of candles.

Samuel had urged her to be charitable. The pernicious effects of education, he explained, namely that the world had a great deal to offer, an expectation taken from fiction rather than fact, had left Mrs Williams under the delusion she could ride the rainbow. Mrs Desmoulins had protested she was talking of wax rather than the colours of the spectrum. In vain: he and Mrs Williams were two of a kind, both dazzled by words.

That night, returning from his customary visit to the Brewery, he'd raised a storm over some remark she herself had made. To the best of her recollection she had been trying to still a quarrel between Mrs Williams and Frank, and had simply observed that a desire for happiness was human. In this she had blundered.

'Happiness', he'd bawled, 'resides in self-reliance. A man
should never depend with certainty on anyone but himself.'
In an aside, for he was always scrupulous in regard to
sources, he acknowledged he was paraphrasing Aristotle.
Crushed, it had none the less occurred to her how curious
it was that, in order to express themselves, great men constantly relied on the thoughts of those long dead. He'd said
other things as well, wounding things, but she'd fancied
they were directed at Frank and Mrs Williams rather than
herself.

The next morning he'd risen early, which was a bad sign,
he being awake and it not yet noon. None of them had
slept well, for he had shattered the early hours with a persistent hammering. Frank, impudently entering his room,
had found him engaged in carpentry. Though worn out,
Mrs Williams agreed it was fortunate he hadn't started on
one of his electrical experiments, for then they might have
found him crackling in his bed.

They heard him striding backwards and forwards all day,
but he didn't appear, not even for his rolls and butter. Mrs
Williams said he hadn't yet recovered from his recent
labours in putting Shakespeare to rights.

Then, later that afternoon, she'd remembered they were
approaching an anniversary of Tetty's death, and indeed,
that very evening, interrupted by groans, a recitation of
prayers broke out in the room above the parlour. Mrs
Williams winced at this audible show of suffering and
stuffed her fingers in her ears. Mrs Desmoulins felt impa-
tience, Tetty having been gone a good ten years, but held
her tongue and endured. In her opinion, Tetty's demise had
been a merciful release rather than a matter for regret; she
had been tired of life and fuddled towards the end, and he

who now groaned so loudly had been shockingly absent during her fading.

Since that display of grief, if such it was, he had kept to his room; nor would he see anyone, not even Mr Murphy or Mr Reynolds, whom he loved and in whose house he had always been welcome. Once, Mr Hawkins had called and, resolutely mounting the stairs, thumped on the door with his stick and demanded to be let in, at which Samuel, overheard by Mrs Williams, had cried out, '*Etiam oblivisci quid sis, interdum expedit.*' Mrs Desmoulins had no idea of what this might mean, but had observed Hawkins come down quite pale and depart without a word.

As for Mr Thrale, he had sent several notes, all left unread. There had been a break in the friendship some time past, when Samuel, invited to their summer residence in Brighthelmstone, had arrived to find the house shut up and its occupant returned to town, but Mrs Williams held this lapse had been forgiven following Mr Thrale's explanation that he'd hastened back to London upon a sudden decision to stand for Parliament.

Bird droppings splattering the garden bench, Mrs Desmoulins went back into the house and loitered on the landing outside Samuel's room. Suddenly, too abruptly for her to hide, his door opened and he thrust out his chamber pot. He was dressed, though without shoes and stockings, and she noticed the angry redness of his feet. He looked her full in the face, yet he didn't see her. The sight of his stubbled cheeks, brow furrowed and eyes circled with darkness, filled her with terror. He retreated in an instant; the thud of the bolt as he secured his door echoed throughout the house.

She ran downstairs, calling out for Mrs Williams. It no

longer mattered who had the greatest influence, who was deemed closest. Mrs Williams was sat half-asleep in her chair by the parlour fire.

'You must go to him,' Mrs Desmoulins shouted. 'He is not himself.'

'He has often been so,' Mrs Williams retorted, 'but he always returns. A woman's pleadings at this juncture will only add to his anxiety.' Her round face remained placid; she was so fair in colouring she had no eyebrows to raise.

It struck Mrs Desmoulins how useless learning was in times of crisis; Mrs Williams knew French and Italian and scribbled poetry, yet failed to recognise madness. 'He is not anxious,' she screamed. 'He is out of his mind.'

'It is not our function to interfere,' pronounced Mrs Williams and closed her eyes, though they saw nothing when open.

Mrs Desmoulins scurried frantically up and down the passage, wringing her hands and keening. As she confided later to Levet, a man she did not usually address, she had been tormented by a dreadful vision in which Samuel wrestled with the Devil. 'If', she said, 'Mr Delap hadn't chosen to call at that particular moment, we might have lost him for ever.'

Mr Delap, arriving so opportunely, listened to her hysterical outpourings and was wary of intruding. He said Mr Johnson had always been subject to hypochondria and no man liked to be seen at a disadvantage. He spoke to her bosom rather than her face, but then Samuel had the same habit. Mrs Desmoulins pleaded with him; she went so far as to bar his way as he attempted to leave. Reluctantly he ascended the stairs.

To her astonishment, no sooner had he knocked than she

heard the bolt being drawn. The door opened and remained
so, but for some time the voices scarcely rose above a buzz
and she could make nothing of the exchange. All at once
Samuel spoke up, though in a manner so disturbed and
with such a gabbling of words that sense was lost. Above his
wild utterances his companion could be heard entreating
him to be calm. Then Samuel shouted out, '*By Heaven, I'll
hate him everlastingly that bids me to be of comfort any more,*'
and moments later, loudly and with great solemnity, Mr
Delap began to declaim the Lord's Prayer – at which
Samuel mercifully fell silent.

Mrs Desmoulins, crouching by the banisters, joined in
the recitation, to be interrupted during her whispering of
Give us this day our daily bread by a rapping at the street
door. Almost immediately Frank ushered into the hall a
tall man with a florid complexion and a small, pale woman,
whose eyes glittered. Awake at last, Mrs Williams came out
from the parlour and greeted Mrs Thrale by name.

There followed a most distressing scene, witnessed by
all. Mr Delap appeared at the head of the stairs, followed
by Samuel, who cried out pitifully and repeatedly. There
was nothing human in the sounds he made. Mrs
Desmoulins was reminded of the chained and tormented
bear tethered in the square on market days in Lichfield –
and on the instant, the sufferer dropped to his knees and,
bear-like, swung his head from side to side.

Appalled, Mr Delap tried to drag him upright, but the
distraught man was too heavy; he crouched even lower and,
clutching Mr Delap about the legs, began to entreat God to
help him. 'Merciful Lord,' he cried, 'grant me the continued use of my understanding.' Below, the stricken watchers
stood as though turned to stone.

Mr Delap, finding himself under scrutiny, shook free as best he could and hurried down the stairs. His white stockings had been pulled from his breeches and lay in folds about his ankles.

Lurching upright, Samuel lumbered in pursuit. Unaware of those others who stepped backwards at his awful approach, he reached out and caught Delap by the coattails; again he sank to his knees, again he beseeched God to save him from a leaving of his senses. Mrs Desmoulins was not alone in fearing it was possibly too late.

And now began a demented outpouring of self-condemnation, a listing of sins accompanied by such a savage beating of the breast as to shake his very frame. The terrible emotion in his voice, the fearful despair in his eyes as he shouted aloud this litany of misdemeanours, was too much for Mr Thrale; stepping forward, he clapped his hand over Samuel's mouth. Mr Delap, hindered by his fallen stockings, made his escape and hobbled out into the Court.

Mr Thrale departed soon after, either from weight of business or from delicacy. Mrs Williams said it was the latter; no honest man cared to gawp at the derangement of a friend. Before he went he urged his wife to carry Samuel to Streatham, where he might have her full attention and be away from the strains of city life.

Mrs Williams busied herself making up a small bundle of clothing; there was nothing beyond a nightshirt and a Sunday coat with candle grease hardened on the buttonholes. Flustered, she excused the lack of clean linen, explaining Samuel had locked himself in his room for so long she hadn't been able to bring out things to be washed.

Mrs Thrale said it was of no importance, that garments

quite suitable for use had been left behind at Streatham by numerous guests, among them Mr Langton, who, though thin to the point of emaciation, was not much above Mr Johnson in height.

While these domestic arrangements were being completed, the sick man sat in the parlour, watched over by Frank. He now appeared composed and wore a somewhat bashful look. Studying his swollen toes, he wriggled them, like a child paddling in sea water, and chuckled. Mrs Williams went up to fetch his discarded stockings, but found them much holed.

When all was ready, Mrs Thrale's coachman was sent for to assist him into the alleyway; he went barefoot and didn't look back. At the last minute Mrs Williams remembered his wig and sent Frank running.

Mr Levet came home early that evening, sober. Mrs Williams and Mrs Desmoulins vied with each other in giving an account of the happenings of the afternoon. Mrs Williams described how she had been busy dusting the breakfast room when voices from overhead disturbed her. 'I recognised Mr Delap's voice,' she said, 'and thought nothing of it, beyond being surprised, and relieved, that Mr Johnson had admitted him.'

'You were asleep in the parlour,' Mrs Desmoulins objected. 'You only showed when Mr Thrale arrived.'

'I could scarcely have slept,' countered Mrs Williams, 'considering the noise made by yourself.'

'I was on the way to my room', Mrs Desmoulins said, 'when Mr Johnson came out on to the landing. He cried out, "*I am in torment. You alone can help me.*" At that moment Frank let in Mr Delap. It was only natural I should give way, he being a man of the Church.'

'Natural indeed,' agreed Mrs Williams, and smiled without humour.

'If he hadn't come,' continued Mrs Desmoulins, 'the Devil would have conquered.'

She proceeded to describe how she had crouched on the stairs and accompanied Mr Delap in the reciting of the Lord's Prayer, and how, in the middle of the line *Give us this day our daily bread*, the Thrales had called – here she knocked on the table with her fist, causing Mrs Williams some alarm.

'A providential interruption,' Mr Levet remarked, 'for Sam last ate on Tuesday.'

Before retiring, Mrs Desmoulins crept into the empty chamber. The bed was rumpled and a squeezed-out orange sat on the pillow. On the table by the window, arranged along the margin of an open book, lay curls of peel cut into segments; she put a piece in the pocket of her gown, for comfort. Climbing the stairs she spied the cat, mewling on the second landing. She kicked out, from jealousy, not malice; often the animal, seeing Samuel immersed in his books, leapt on his lap and purred away the hours. Soundlessly, the cat fled higher. I live, thought Mrs Desmoulins, among people unworthy of my companionship.

A tree grew close to the window of her garret room. When the wind whipped its branches against the glass she fancied its scrapings echoed her own internal scourging. Lacerated both within and without, she sank into sleep.

Almost at once she felt his arm across her shoulder, one brown hand pressed against her nightcap so that she lay imprisoned on his breast. He said little that was intelligible, yet his chucklings and gruntings were proof of his regard. He was clumsy in his fondlings, but what did she care? She breathed in the bitter-sweet odour of his skin and thought her heartbeats would wake the household.

And then she woke to the small hour chiming of the clock of St Bridget's – a dismal awakening, for now he lay under another roof and all those tumblings of years gone by were but the stuff of dreams.

To Miss Laetitia Hawkins,
2 Sion Row,
Twickenham

Sept. 21st, 1807

Dear Miss Hawkins,
Your kind letter arrived on the 18th of the month, a
birth date which, though he preceded my entry into
the world by more than fifty years, you suppose –
through no fault of your own – that I share with Dr
Johnson. To the best of my belief, I was born on the
17th day of September, it being my mother's later
conceit to pin my arrival to the more auspicious date.

Yes, I do indeed recall the supper given by your
father, Sir John, to celebrate the Doctor's 65th year.
It was held, if I remember, three days early as my
father and Mr Baretti had planned a visit to Paris on
the 16th. You and I were much frowned upon for the
unseemly giggles that burst forth at the sight of Dr
Johnson dropping to his knees the better to examine
Miss Reynolds' new shoes. That same evening I fell
into a sulk provoked by a frank observation made by
your good self. Admiring our childish reflections in
the hall mirror, you declared my face handsome but
'chubby'. The years fly by, but some events – vanity,
all is vanity – remain engraved on the mind.

Your present intention of putting pen to paper
regarding the *Johnsonian Circle* is one worthy of

success, yet I fear I can be of little help. I was not a
year old when Dr Johnson first came to dine at the
Brewery in Deadman's Place and scarce a twelvemonth older when my father afforded him sanctuary
at Streatham Park. Though reluctant to answer
questions of a speculative nature – I have no wish to
revive memories which, owing to circumstances,
arouse in my breast none but melancholy thoughts – I
will do my best to reply to your more factual queries.

The cabinet you mention is in the possession of
my mother, Mrs Piozzi, as is the globe bought by Dr
Johnson to instruct me in Geography. There is a
scribble in the region of the Americas executed by
my brother Harry, for which my mother whipped
him cruelly. Dr Johnson was away at the time, but
upon hearing of the punishment said it was *not well
done*. Mr Baretti, being present, was bolder. I recall
he seized the rod from the nursery shelf and stamped
it underfoot.

Though Mr Boswell and Mrs Piozzi have
frequently asserted that the pet name of Queeney
was given me by Dr Johnson, it is my belief that it
was my dear father who first called me so. First I was
his Queen Esther, then his Hetty, then his Queeney,
the change taking place in about my third year.

The dog seated in front of my Grandmother
Salusbury in the painting by Zoffany was called Belle,
on account of her beauty, though she was stout and
by temperament irritable. It was she who committed
the offence of devouring the Doctor's buttered toast
while he was engaged in slurping his tea.

The titles of the books you refer to, also in the

keeping of my mother, are as follows – the *Poems of Metastasio* in six volumes, the *Comedies of Terence*, a Latin Grammar and a Virgil. As to Mr Baretti's *Dialogues*, it did indeed commence with an eight-page dedication to myself, the concluding sentences later rendered into English verse by Dr Johnson. Modesty prevents me from repeating the lines in full, sufficient to say it began, *Long may live our charming Hetty* . . . In her *Anecdotes*, Mrs Piozzi quotes the verse while omitting any reference to its origin. As we bear the same name, this has led many to suppose the dedication was intended for herself.

Queeney's Covenant is in my possession, but I would not wish it to appear in print. It is in the form of a promise dictated by Dr Johnson, that I would come down promptly every day to be taught Italian . . . *I will be in the very best of humour, nor will I look about me with a vacant and weary expression*, etc., etc. It was signed by myself and witnessed by Dr Johnson.

My sister Mrs Mostyn is well in health though alarmed at the prospect of my mother moving closer. It had been hoped she would be living at Streatham, but news has come that she is thinking of letting. Having her as a near neighbour would be irksome indeed. As somebody has remarked most truly, a fair proportion of the unhappiness of life consists in recollections of past, or dread of future, miseries.

Adieu, my dear Miss Hawkins,
Sincerely yours,

H. M. Thrale

REÍNTEGRATE *v.a. (reinteger,* Fr. *and integer,* Lat.
It should perhaps be written redintegrate)

To renew with regard to any ſtate or quality; to
repair; to reſtore

The falling from a diſcord to a concord hath an
agreement with the affections, which are *reintegrated*
to the better after some diſlikes.

(Bacon's *Nat. Hiſt.*)

Mrs Thrale rose early, on Queeney's account, and spied
from her bedroom window a lawn sparkling under
dew. The dogs, loosed from their chains, scudded across the
grass, spattering diamonds.

When she went to the nursery Queeney was still sleeping. Her mouth lay open and sweat glistened upon the
bridge of her nose. Old Nurse said the child's breath still
smelt sour. She had passed stools twice in the night, though
without discomfort.

'And the pustules on her chest?' enquired Mrs Thrale.

'Now scabby,' Old Nurse said, though her eyesight could
not be relied upon.

Mrs Thrale examined the child's arm and was relieved to

find it less swollen than before. Queeney had jerked in shock when Dr Sutton had made the puncture and the resulting scratch had turned angry.

The haze had lifted from the beech trees in the Park when Mrs Thrale came down to breakfast. The rays of the sun caught the scarlet hangings on the second landing and splashed the stairs with crimson.

It was noticeable that both her husband and her mother had fallen under the influence of clear skies. Mrs Salusbury announced her intention of delaying her return to town, and Mr Thrale, having first visited the kitchens to give final instructions to the cooks as to the advancement of the dinner planned for later in the day, was moved to part from his wife with less reserve than usual.

'I shall return at four o'clock' was all he said, then, bringing his melancholy face close to hers, pressed dry lips against her cheek. It was the merest peck, yet it was not his habit to kiss her and never when sober.

'Four o'clock,' she echoed and, neither raised nor lowered by his gesture, wiped her face with her sleeve. He was a good man, one she had come to like, not love, a sentiment she felt contrary to the proper order of affections existing between men and women. Her mother, who lived on a diet of vegetables and water and could not be accused of emotions disturbed by either spirits or meat, often referred to the dead Mr Salusbury as a 'monster she had been fond of to distraction'. At such times Mrs Thrale, observing the light of passion in her mother's eyes, felt envy. On Sundays, in church, she sometimes prayed, without fervour, to be persecuted by love.

At noon, Queeney awake and the weather still balmy, Mrs Thrale told Old Nurse to carry the child outdoors.

Mrs Salusbury and she were about to follow when Mr Langton came downstairs. After standing in the porch for some considerable time, languidly waving his hand back and forth to test the temperature of the air, he agreed to accompany them. By the time they set foot on the gravel Old Nurse and Queeney were nowhere to be seen.

Walking with the extremely lofty Bennet Langton was tiring. In order to remain at his side his female companions, both short of stature, were forced into an unseemly trot. There was little opportunity to remark upon the heavenly blue of the cloudless sky, the glittering reflections of sun on foliage, to breathe in the sweet perfume of the full-blown roses lolling on their mound above the ice house. Each inhalation was vital to sustain motion, if not life. True, Mr Langton checked his loping stride from time to time and sought to regulate his step, but all too soon forgot. Peering upwards at him, the cloth of his hat mottled by the shadows cast by the beech leaves, it occurred to Mrs Thrale that, should such an unlikely situation arise, she would be well prepared to keep pace with a giraffe.

Perhaps he read her thoughts, for presently he launched into an anecdote concerning himself and Mr Garrick, who was expected that afternoon. 'It was winter', he began, 'and Davy and I had been invited to take dinner at the house of a mutual acquaintance. I was late . . . the weather was very inclement—'

Here Mrs Salusbury exchanged sly glances with her daughter. Bennet Langton was always late for appointments. Those who knew him wisely took it into account. If guests were expected at five o'clock, Langton was told he would be required at three.

'When I entered the room Davy leapt on to a chair and asked me how I did. It was quite comical.'

'And uncivil,' cried Mrs Salusbury, puffing.

'No matter. I believe I got the better of him. "Thank you," I replied, "I am quite well . . ." then no sooner had Davy got down from his chair than I knelt in front of him and held out my hand.'

'He is, of course, on the small side,' observed Mrs Salusbury. 'And conscious of it.' She came to a halt; holding her finger to her chin as though thinking the matter over, she fought for breath.

Mrs Thrale remained silent. She had heard the story many times, indeed fancied she had been present on the actual occasion. To the best of her memory it had been Garrick who had turned the tables – quoting from *The Tempest*, he had promptly retorted, '*Give me thy hand. I do begin to have bloody thoughts.*'

At the recollection, she grew agitated, her own thoughts being far from serene. Not a twelvemonth had passed since the funeral of her second daughter, and though it was true the sickly infant had not lived long enough to leave any lasting impression, the experience had caused upset. Now, four months gone with a third child, she often tormented herself with gruesome images. She was sure Queeney had scrambled free from Old Nurse's arms and was at this very moment tottering towards the lake. Old Nurse, blinded by age and sunlight, mistakenly took her to be sitting at her feet, tearing the heads off cowslips.

'Queeney is now on the mend,' she announced aloud, to reassure herself, and fairly scurried off along the path, although not ahead of Mr Langton. Mrs Salusbury gave up the race and coming to an upturned bucket left by workmen engaged in extending the stables, collapsed upon it, back to the sun, eyes closed and hand pressed to her thudding heart.

Mrs Thrale, thoughts jumbled, had no sooner descended the steps that led between the lilac bushes than she saw Mr Langton and Old Nurse, the child in her arms, coming towards her.

'Queeney, Queeney,' she called out, and ran to clasp her close. She met with resistance; no amount of tugging, or pinching, would budge the child. Face flushed with resolve, Queeney stared defiantly and tightened her grip about Nurse's neck. Her bonnet had slipped off and the glitter of the lake tipped her curls with silver. Relief replaced with anger, Mrs Thrale would have slapped her into submission but for the lofty presence of Bennet Langton.

'The bond between nurse and child', he observed unwisely, 'is often stronger than the natural one we suppose to exist.'

'The sun is too hot,' snapped Mrs Thrale. 'We shall all be more comfortable indoors.' Retracing her steps, she snagged her dress on a lilac bush and could have wept with vexation.

Mrs Salusbury, dozing on her upturned bucket, was disturbed by the sound of footsteps on gravel. Opening her eyes, she saw in the distance the portly figure of Mr Johnson rounding the wall of the pigsty, an addition caused to be built by the pork-loving Henry Thrale to house a Cheshire hog, recently slaughtered on account of its being virtually wild, without fat and so savage as to be a danger to all within reach.

Mr Johnson's advance along the path, though no less erratic, was more convoluted than usual. He had abandoned his rolling gait in favour of a zigzag progression, each diagonal embarked upon the moment the appropriate foot met the grass verge. Several times it was apparent he had turned too imprecisely, for he walked back and started over again. But for good manners Mrs Salusbury would have swivelled the opposite way, to avoid confrontation.

Mr Johnson and she were not friends. When first he had come to her son-in-law's table in the Borough, she had been delighted to make the acquaintance of such an enlightened man. She had so many questions to which he alone, being so learned and yet so lacking in cant, would be able to provide the answers. From the very beginning – she had sought his opinion of the silk riots – he had put her down and continued to do so. His residence at Streatham Park, his every need catered to by her daughter, Hester, had restored his health but failed to improve his temper. Though he no longer woke the household in the dark hours with his mumbling perambulations along the corridors, excursions which drove the befuddled servants from their beds and obliged them into nightly stalkings for fear he put his candle down beside a curtain and set the house ablaze, he was still fiery in regard to herself. She had caught him out more than once in the invention of answers to her numerous enquiries as to his opinion of this or that political conundrum. At first she had laboured under the delusion that the chuckles that punctuated his replies, the frequent glances he cast around the table, the throwing of salt over his shoulder, were no more than displays of eccentricity. No longer; she now thought him ill-bred.

Her daughter held that the antagonism between them

was the result of jealousy on his part. He needed her undivided attention, seeing he was beset by demons and had not had the advantage of a mother's love of the sort she herself had known. Mrs Salusbury knew this was sincere; she loved her daughter and to the best of her ability had not tried to mould her. Even so, she kept hidden her own feelings of jealousy occasioned by the encroaching influence of the ever-present Mr Johnson, who at this very moment, burbling to himself, was on a zigzag collision course with her person. She shut her eyes once more and slumped lower as his mutterings grew louder.

He came so close that his sleeve brushed her bonnet – she distinctly heard the curious words, *October good blast to blow the hog mast* – and then he veered to the right and was gone. She had taken the precaution of tucking her feet out of reach, though even if he had trodden on them he would not have noticed, of that she was sure. It was not poorness of vision that rendered her invisible, simply that she was of no more interest to him than the stone urns set at frequent intervals along the way. Turning, she saw his stout white calves were devoid of stockings and that he wore slippers. The slip-slap of his feet as he veered down the path grew fainter and faded altogether as he entered the shadow of the oak trees and melted from sight.

Gradually she became aware of other sounds, the shrill barking of Belle as she raced alongside the poultry yard, the hum of bees in search of roses, the rush of air as birds swooped overhead. She dozed again, hearing in the swish of wings an echo of the waves lapping the shore at Pwllheli, where once, her shoes laced with salt, the argumentative Mr Salusbury had knelt in the damp sand and asked for her hand. If one is not caressed, thought Mrs Salusbury, one develops thorns. She was not entirely thinking of Mr Johnson.

He, finding the grounds deserted save for Mrs Salusbury, whom he had stumbled upon squatting on the path in the act of passing water, felt he had been abandoned. Rising from his bed, he had come downstairs to a house empty of all but the servants, and now rehearsed in his head in what manner he would reproach Mrs Thrale when next they met.

Dear Mistress, he would say – smiling to soften the rebuke – *I thought to see you at the breakfast table.* She: *My dear friend, the sunshine called me, seduced me, etc.* He: *My dear Madam, the sun will burn everlastingly. Our little illumination, I fear, will be extinguished in the time it takes for a leaf to fall from the tree.* Far from satisfied with this exchange, he lunged at the oak leaves with his stick.

Four months had elapsed since the day when, like sweet bells jangled, out of tune and harsh, reason had forsaken him and he had been brought to Streatham Park. For five long weeks he had remained closeted in his room, seeing no one but Mrs Thrale. They had neither nature nor nurture in common, yet in her alone had he confided the thoughts that caused him such unease. Not quite all . . .

Since that enforced seclusion he had sufficiently mended to resume his old way of life. Though he now spent the better part of each week in the country, he tried, whenever possible, to return to London on a Friday evening to give both companionship and succour to the troublesome occupants of Johnson Court. There, on Saturdays, he received callers and dined with friends. Sundays, he made sure the members of his household ate a hearty dinner, after which, gathering them around the coals in the parlour, he endeavoured to convince them of the common vicissitudes that bound them together.

Mondays were fraught, for at noon Thrale's coach arrived and either Mrs Desmoulins or Mrs Williams, often both, contrived to delay him by a listing of Dr Levet's numerous faults. He fought to be without prejudice but his sympathies lay with Levet rather than with the blind Mrs Williams and the all-too-seeing Mrs Desmoulins. Levet never resorted to tears.

He returned *home* – he had come to think of Streatham in no other light – to a flattering regard for his well-being. He had no sooner to mention that a broiled lobster or a game pie was to his liking than it appeared on the dinner table. If, in an aside, he remarked that the writing table in his chamber was good but small, a more commodious one was placed at his disposal within the hour. Aware that on such a bed of roses the weeds of indolence flourished, he dropped to his knees every night and resolved to mend his ways and rise early – so far without success. Mid-day generally found him still abed.

A stone having lodged under his heel, he stopped on the path to shake it loose and was surprised to see that he was wearing slippers. He supposed he had prudently left off his shoes on account of the silver buckles Henry Thrale had provided him with three weeks before.

He had cause, beyond footwear, to respect Thrale, who had recently shown him drawings of the library he planned to build on to the west wing of the house. 'Its design, Sam,' he had said, 'will be mine . . . but I depend on you to choose the books on its shelves.'

Thrale's honesty, his lack of affectation – he was that

contradiction in terms, an educated man who cared little for reading – was to be admired. Many wealthy men had been known to furnish a library and later blame others for its lack of excellence.

The task would require patience and diligence, a *Gothick* rather than a *Modern* library was desirable, but the request was only reasonable considering the hospitality, tempered with affection, so lavishly bestowed. No man loved another without expectation of returns.

Standing there, it occurred to him that he was feeling in excellent bodily health. His breathing was sound, his stomach easy, and he was free of those pains which afflicted his groin.

On an impulse, and to test his lungs, he lumbered into a run, which he sustained until he reached the lake. A solitary duck flapped its wings at his approach. Breathless, but not unnaturally so, he dug into his pockets and skimmed orange peel across the water, promoting ripples. The duck, obedient to natural laws, swam in widening circles.

He was about to turn back in the direction of the house when his attention was caught by an object trapped in the rushes. He took it for a log of wood, but closer scrutiny revealed it to be a roll of canvas tied with twine. Using his stick, he attempted to poke it loose, at which it cast off and began to bob away.

Without a moment's thought, he tore off his clothes and plunged into the lake, only to find the water came no higher than his knees. He was in time to pluck out the package before it sank. Climbing on to the bank, he examined the contents, which proved of no great interest, being but an ancient fan set with glass panels in which were embedded three round objects. He fancied they might be coins, until, rubbing off the mud, he saw they were buttons, each one engraved with the image of a leaping dog.

He was wiping himself dry with his shirt, the beams of the sun striking fire from the gold amulet hung about his neck, when he spied someone advancing along the path. At this distance, judging from the pace, he thought it to be one of the elderly Southwark workmen employed on extensions and improvements, yet, even as he watched, the figure turned tail and retreated with speed, arms flapping the air as though pursued by wild beasts.

I am not alone, he told himself. The world is full of madmen.

From London that afternoon came Mr and Mrs Jackson, Miss Reynolds, Arthur Murphy and the Jesuit, Dr Fitzpatrick, the last being an old friend of Henry Thrale, as was Humphrey Jackson, the chemist. Both had known him from his fox-hunting bachelor days when he'd kept a pack of hounds at Croydon. Garrick was to have brought Miss Reynolds, but at the last moment he had been delayed and Murphy had obliged. The reason for the delay, when explained, caused merriment all round.

'At three o'clock', Murphy said, 'the manager of Covent Garden sent word to Drury Lane that Davy was to come immediately owing to Mr Quin having suffered a calamity in the middle of his denouncement of Desdemona.'

'What sort of calamity?' asked Mrs Salusbury, who until that moment had been leaning back in her chair and wishing herself in bed.

'The comical sort,' said Murphy.

'Tell, tell,' squealed Mrs Jackson.

'It appears', continued Murphy, 'that for some years past Quin's gums have been in a diseased state . . .'

'Which is why Mrs Ford waves her fan so vigorously,' put in Mrs Thrale.

'He had enunciated with admirable restraint, *Iago, All my fond love thus do I blow to Heaven*, yet when the time came for him to make his exit such was his feeling for the drama that all caution left him and he fairly bellowed, *Damn her, lewd minx! O, damn her!* . . . at which exclamation his few remaining teeth lost their hold and flew across the stage.'

'Flew,' echoed Mrs Salusbury.

'Like crumbs,' said Murphy.

The laughter was prolonged, Mr Johnson, in particular, positively shaking with mirth. Indeed, the story tickled him to such a degree that he strode about declaiming Othello's words several times over. He had caught the sun and his face glowed. Even Miss Reynolds allowed herself a half-smile at Quin's expense. This was unusual; due to domestic circumstances she generally leant towards the underdog. In spite of the hilarity, Mrs Thrale was aware there wasn't one among them, herself included, who wasn't secretly engaged in running their tongue along their gums.

She was pleased the party was proceeding so well. It was not always easy to promote a convivial atmosphere before the wine had taken effect, and well-nigh impossible if Johnson happened to be out of sorts; when he was in a gloom the whole company fell under his shadow.

Bennet Langton not yet come down and Mrs Jackson politely enquiring after the health of Queeney, Henry Thrale demanded the child should be brought from the nursery. When she came he sat her on his knee, where she perched quite contentedly and accepted the attentions of the company with composure. She even allowed her mother to dab the perspiration from her scarlet cheeks.

'The inoculation against the small-pox is a success,' Mrs Thrale announced. 'Dr Sutton assures me all danger is past.'

The compliments on her daughter's prettiness – such lovely eyes, such a winsome curve to her mouth – provoked her into boasting of Queeney's more important attributes. She said, 'She knows the compass as perfectly as any mariner upon the sea, is mistress of the solar system and the signs of the Zodiac . . .'

'What a little marvel,' babbled Mrs Jackson.

'. . . and is thoroughly acquainted with the difference between the Ecliptick and Equator. She is also able to pronounce the names of all the capitals of Europe, recite the paternoster, the three Christian virtues in English . . .'

'A little marvel,' repeated Mrs Jackson, who had no children of her own, and was glad of it.

'. . . also the four Cardinal ones in Latin.' Mrs Thrale's last words were rendered almost inaudible by a tremendous clearing of the throat executed by Mr Johnson. She looked at him and saw that he was frowning, and knew the cause, for he had once told her that as a clever child he had suffered much from being put on show by his father. All the same, she saw no reason to subdue her own motherly pride. Raising her voice, she said, 'In the last few months she has learnt to recount, with near perfect accuracy, the Judgement of Paris and the legend of Perseus and Andromeda.'

At this Mr Johnson gave vent to what could only be described as a warning growl. The dog Belle, wheezing at Mrs Salusbury's feet, struggled upright and waddled to the door. Taking a book from his pocket, Mr Johnson turned his back on the room.

'Do please get the child to read to us,' pleaded the silly Mrs Jackson.

'She cannot read,' Mrs Thrale admitted, and called for Queeney to be returned to the nursery.

At half-past six o'clock, an hour later than planned owing to the tardiness of Langton – he protested the servants had failed to knock on his door – the company went in to dinner. Thrale had ordered the windows to be left open and flies swarmed above the table. There was discussion as to whether the windows ought to be closed, but most held it was better to have air and, besides, there were sweet perfumes drifting in from the darkening garden.

Miss Reynolds said there was a positive plague of insects in town, and Mrs Jackson said, '*Yes, yes, indeed there was,*' and tittered shrilly. She couldn't keep her eyes from Mr Johnson, who, standing up and wildly dashing his glass back and forth in an effort to disperse the flies, spilled lemonade on to the cloth.

Mrs Thrale felt a grudging sympathy for Mrs Jackson, who was openly chewing on her nails. It was obvious she had not been prepared for an encounter with Mr Johnson, and though her husband may have explained to her that she was to rub shoulders with a great lexicographer and poet, it was doubtful if he had thought to paint a true portrait. The reality of Johnson, in appearance and behaviour, the scarred skin of his cheeks and neck, his large lips forever champing, his shabby clothing and too small wig with its charred top-piece, his tics and mutterings, his propensity to behave as though no one else was present, was at variance with the elegant demeanour imagined to be proper to a man of genius.

It was left to Mrs Thrale to direct the conversation

during dinner. At the best of times her husband was a man of few words, and of none at all with a dish set in front of him. Nor could Johnson or Langton, beyond a monosyllable, be depended upon to make a contribution until the serious business of eating was got through. She looked to Arthur Murphy for support, he being a man of the theatre and fond of his own voice.

True to form, he launched amusingly enough into gossip concerning the Reverend Mr Dodd and his scandalous affair with a woman who owned a pie shop in Frith Street. Mrs Jackson screamed satisfactorily at each twist of the story. Dr Fitzpatrick, at its conclusion, observed that Dodd would end badly, and would deserve as much.

'Not so, Sir,' barked Johnson, but added nothing more.

To cover the sudden lull occasioned by this savage interjection, Mrs Thrale asked Murphy if he was engaged in writing a new play. He replied he was not, which she already knew, but confided that only the night before he had finished reading an extraordinary comedy written by a young man living in a remote village near Dover.

'In what way extraordinary?' enquired Humphrey Jackson.

'Why,' cried Murphy, 'because he has never been to the city, is the son of a clergyman and by all accounts has led a sheltered life.'

'There is humour enough to be found in the countryside,' protested Dr Fitzpatrick.

'And none more so than in this play,' Murphy said, 'for it is in seven acts and all the characters are slain in Act Three.'

'Out of the ordinary, indeed,' agreed Jackson.

'Death by the sword, poison and strangulation,' Murphy elaborated.

'How can that be?' asked Mrs Jackson, baffled. 'Who is left to speak the lines?'

'In the next four acts', Murphy said, 'they appear as ghosts. The final mode of death is particularly horrid . . . by a heated prong thrust up the nostril to the brain.'

'Enough,' said Mrs Thrale sharply, for the colour had drained from Mrs Jackson's face and Mrs Salusbury was sitting bolt upright, fork suspended in the air. Beyond the open windows pink clouds rolled through the blackening heavens.

Some minutes after nine o'clock, by which time David Garrick had arrived, the ladies went into the drawing room. The doors on to the grounds being flung wide and the lanthorns lit, the gentlemen gathered on the terrace to applaud Garrick's exuberant re-enactment of Mr Quin's dilemma.

Mrs Thrale noticed her mother was staring fixedly in the direction of the garden; her expression was watchful, as though she saw in the flickering night something other than shadows. Alarmed, she confided in Frances Reynolds. She said, 'The brightness of her eyes when listening to Mr Murphy disturbed me. Her own life has not been free of torment, my dear father being wild to the point of cruelty.'

Miss Reynolds replied that perhaps she stood too close for impartiality. 'To my mind,' she said, her eyes watching the moths that spun above the candle flames, 'Mrs Salusbury appeared more *drawn* than terrified.'

Mrs Thrale trusted Miss Reynolds, whose manner, though friendly, was always tinged with melancholy, like that of someone who had suffered a great deal. The blame lay with her brother, who was in the habit of making her the butt of his caustic wit. Johnson liked her too, though for different reasons, namely that she had shown kindness to Mrs Williams, his poetical friend.

Just then, Mrs Salusbury said loudly, 'Hester, I am not deaf. I assure you it was not the prong up the nose that affected me, rather the talk of ghosts . . .'

'Such things are mere superstition,' cried Mrs Thrale.

'No less a person than Mr Johnson thought otherwise,' retorted Mrs Salusbury. 'He was gullible enough to investigate the Cock Lane Ghost.' She was referring to the unquiet spirit of one Fanny Lynes, which, some years before, had supposedly manifested itself to an eleven-year-old girl residing in Smithfield.

'It's true he investigated,' Frances Reynolds protested, 'for his mind is always open, but it was at the insistence of the Rector of Clerkenwell.'

'He could have refused,' countered Mrs Salusbury.

'It is not in his nature to stand aside,' Miss Reynolds said. 'A curious mind must always be in search of the truth. Besides, he found the scratchings and knockings heard by the child could only have been made by herself.'

'I heard no scratchings or knockings,' said Mrs Salusbury. 'My ghost rose out of the lake, naked save for a shimmer of light that near blinded me.'

Neither Hester nor Miss Reynolds heard her, for just then the gentlemen came in, Mr Garrick riding on Bennet Langton's back. In the ensuing uproar Mrs Salusbury, unlamented, retired to her bed.

Towards midnight games were played, a favourite one being the choosing of a colour that might best express the character of each of those present. Miss Reynolds knew it to be a cruel entertainment and steeled herself.

Mrs Jackson was pronounced scarlet by her husband and pink by Henry Thrale, who, in sentimental mood, trapped her hand in his and now and then leant his head on her shoulder. Mr Johnson, by common consent, was dubbed purple, of the darkest hue, until Mrs Jackson changed her mind and bravely declared him brown. 'Of the lighter shade,' she said, 'like curled autumn leaves or the spots on speckled eggs.' Johnson was so taken by this that he came and stood extremely close to her and fingered the stuff of her gown.

Thrale chose yellow-green as most befitting his wife, a shade vigorously disputed by Johnson, who held it to be sickly.

Next, they played the fool as to what plant or flower each most resembled. Mr Thrale named Mrs Jackson as an orchid of the rarest sort and Hester a dog rose. Mrs Jackson was both flattered and disturbed by the comparison; she had no wish to cause discord between husband and wife. Blinking the powder from her eyes – in studying her dress Johnson had twice jolted her hairpiece – she stole a misty glance at Mrs Thrale and was astonished to see she was smiling. Either she is deaf, thought Mrs Jackson, or else saintly.

'Samuel is a nettle,' Murphy said. 'And Hetty a sprig of myrtle,' inspiring Johnson to add gallantly, '. . . which the more it is crushed the more it discloses its sweetness.'

Later still, by which hour Henry Thrale had slid under the cloth with a saucer of ices melting on his chest, Mr Johnson announced that earlier that afternoon he had come across two items of small significance caught in the rushes of the lake. He and Davy Garrick would mime what he had found and the company would be allowed two questions each to guess what they might be. Accordingly, Garrick, hand on hip, minced up and down the room, waving his hand back and forth. At his side, on all fours, pranced Johnson, kicking up his heels, his wig falling over his eyes.

Observing him, Langton shouted, 'Richard III . . . deformed, unfinished, sent before his time.'

'That is a description, not a question,' opposed Johnson.

'Is it Mrs Ford attempting to be rid of Quin's breath?' asked Mrs Thrale.

'It's that woman in Cheapside,' cried Miss Reynolds. 'The poor soul who set fire to the orphanage and danced among the flames.'

'Wrong, wrong,' sang Garrick, peeping at her through spread fingers and fluttering his eyelashes; all the same, he stood on his toes and pirouetted.

No correct answer being forthcoming, and Johnson finally collapsing on to his back – legs, beetle-fashion, feebly waving – the fan and the button were produced and passed from hand to hand. Mrs Thrale argued that in mentioning Mrs Ford she had been almost right, but Garrick said he couldn't allow it, at which moment Henry Thrale, emerging from beneath the table and staggering upright, demanded to see the button. First he examined it and then, striding to the open doors, flung it out into the darkness. Of a sudden, he jerked backwards; a gust of wind swept in from the terrace and sent the shadows racing. Mrs Jackson clutched at her husband, mouth open in a silent shriek of alarm.

When Thrale turned back to the room he was rubbing the palm of one hand violently up and down his coat as though to relieve some irritation. All were startled at how diminished he appeared; a long shadow cast by the candle-light hollowed his cheeks and turned him old.

Garrick and Dr Fitzpatrick helped him to a chair and a glass of brandy was fetched. Restored, though constantly scrubbing his hand across his knee, he attempted to explain, in his usual stilted manner, what troubled him.

A hundred years before, he told them, a young woman had been seduced by one George Farthingale . . . the heir to a fortune . . . and then abandoned. 'She had a little dog . . . followed her everywhere. Weeks passed . . . young woman vanished. Little dog found trotting up and down beside the lake holding fan in its jaws.'

'Bow-wow,' barked Garrick, and hopped about, hands held up like paws.

'Rich man come to his senses,' continued Thrale, 'returned only to learn that the woman had drowned herself. Full of remorse . . . had buttons made for his coat with the image of the dog upon them. No sooner stitched to the cloth . . .'

Here Garrick, who in lightning fashion had transformed himself from leaping dog to floating body, features first distorted in agony and then smiling beatifically, sprang upright from the carpet and began to thread an invisible needle with imaginary thread.

'. . . than the man . . . in period of weeks . . . sickened and died.'

'And I suppose, Sir,' said Johnson, 'that the dog, snatching the coat from the corpse and wearing it, flung itself into the lake.'

'Of the dog . . . nothing known,' Thrale said.

Soon after, Johnson, looking sombre and placing his feet as though the ground was unsafe, walked out on to the terrace.

'Why did Mr Garrick look so merry when drowning?' whispered Mrs Jackson to Miss Reynolds.

'Possibly out of perversity,' Miss Reynolds replied tartly.

There is always something behind what they say, thought Mrs Jackson, and quivered with excitement.

Presently Mrs Thrale went in search of Johnson. He was standing at the far end of the terrace, emitting strange hooting noises. At her approach he held up his hand for silence, head cocked to one side. Beyond the buzz of voices coming from the drawing room she heard nothing, and said so.

'Shhh!' he bade, and out of the darkness came the answering call of an owl. Beside himself with delight, Johnson clapped his hands and did a jig on the spot.

When he grew calmer, she asked, 'What did you think of the tale of the button?'

'Why, I thought nothing of it,' he said, 'for there was nothing in it that would engage the thoughts of a *sensible* man.'

'My master thought different,' she snapped. 'It has made him quite ill.'

'His illness is caused by an over-burdening of the stomach,' Johnson said.

'There is a distinct swelling on his palm where he held the button.'

'A swelling no doubt caused by the sting of a drowsy wasp. It is that time of year. As for his fiction, there was no lake here thirty years ago, let alone a hundred. It was an excavation begun by your father-in-law and only recently completed by Henry.'

'There is a pond in the field beyond,' she said. 'What difference does it make . . . lake or pond, this year or last?'

'Tolerance,' he chided, 'in regard to matters of truth, merely pardons the weakness in ourselves. If you excuse the folly, instead of condemning, you will begin to imitate it. Dear Mistress, one must always be on one's guard, for, as the Spanish proverb observes, a clattering hoof signifies a nail gone.'

'Pf!' she exclaimed. 'There are nails enough in this world.'

He touched her cheek with his finger, as though ready to impale an unspilt tear, and gazed at her so fondly and with such compassion that she trembled; in his large eyes leapt the reflection of the lanthorn flame. 'It is of small comfort,' he said, 'but it should be remembered that misery is an affirmation of life.' Cupping his mouth in his hands, he emitted a low and tremulous hoot.

Save for Bennet Langton and Miss Reynolds, the guests left Streatham Park a quarter after three o'clock. Before being helped into his coach Garrick took Johnson in an embrace. They swayed together on the gravel, the small man pressing his cheek against the big man's chest.

'Sam, Sam,' Garrick moaned, and for once was lost for words.

'There, there, dear Davy,' soothed Johnson, 'God bless you,' and stood waving until the carriage had crunched from earshot.

The noise of wheels woke the child in the nursery; she cried out, but Old Nurse slept on.

When Johnson went up to his room he shut the curtains against the light that was already spreading above the fuzz of the trees. He lay down and almost immediately fell into a dream in which he and Davy walked home from school across the Market Square in Lichfield. A cabbage lay in the gutter, leaves splayed out like wings, and he kicked it clear across the cobbles and over the railings into the basement of the bookshop. Descending the steps, he spied through the window a man, head in hands, sitting at a table untidy with papers. Rubbing at the glass, he peered closer and knew it was his father. Behind him stood Dr Swinfen, practising the violin. He rapped on the window to make Father glance up, and when he did so his eyes were those of a dead man. He ran back up the steps and told young Davy to go home; he didn't want the boy to see those eyes. And now, the whine of the violin grew louder, intensifying in pitch until it resembled a long-drawn-out scream.

He woke on the instant, gaze fixed on the shelf above the fireplace; the spines of his books were stained with blood. The cause of such a delusion, he told himself, springs from an inward morbid discontent. Turning towards the window he observed how the sun beat against the curtains.

A shocking incident took place two days later, an hour before Johnson left for London. Mrs Thrale was coming down the second flight of stairs when she saw Queeney standing on the landing with Belle at her side. Something in the child's strange rigidity of posture made her pause.

'Queeney,' she called, but the girl stared past her, eyes popping, face darkening. In a flash Mrs Thrale remembered just such a distortion on the face of a cooper's boy who had choked on a fish bone. Terrified, she ran forward and bending the child double smacked her violently about the head. Suddenly Queeney coughed, then spat, then screamed; the button that had caused Henry Thrale so much perturbation flew from her mouth and fell to the rug. Overcome, Mrs Thrale sank to the floor and burst into tears. Still screaming, Queeney scrambled up the stairs, the dog snapping at her heels.

After some moments, anger replacing fear, Mrs Thrale sought out Old Nurse and boxed her ears, at which Queeney, restored save for an attack of hiccoughs, rushed from a corner and kicked her mother on the ankle.

'Wicked, wicked girl,' wailed Mrs Thrale, limping from the nursery.

She was sure Johnson must have heard the hullabaloo and would be waiting anxiously in the hall, but found him instead in the breakfast room, his wig perched beside the butter dish. 'Such a fright,' she shouted. 'My heart was in my mouth—'

'There is something I must tell you—' he said.

'If I had not been there . . . if I had not come down at that exact moment—'

'Of the utmost importance,' he persisted. 'It will not have gone unnoticed that I have not been myself these last few days.'

'There are many things that pass unnoticed,' she snapped. 'Some of them considerably more important than others.'

Pushing back his chair, he told her it would be best if they spoke outside. The weather still uncommonly warm, she protested it would be less tiring if they stayed where they were; he shook his head peevishly. All at once she wanted him gone. He wore her out with his daily demands on her time, his nightly insistence that she sit up with him into the small hours, pouring his tea.

'You cannot begin to imagine what I have just endured,' she said.

'A man indulges his imagination while it is pleasing', he replied, 'till at length it overpowers his reason.' Brushing the crumbs from his mouth he left the room. Was there ever such a man for weighty pronouncements, she wondered, and was obliged to follow him.

Once on the gravel path, he said, 'There is something of mine in the bottom right-hand drawer of my desk which I wish you to take into your care . . . it is for your eyes alone. Nor do I wish you to refer to it on my return . . . or indeed at any other time . . . not unless I broach the subject.'

'What is it?' she asked, but he only entreated her most solemnly to swear she would never divulge his secret, a secret which soon she would share.

'I give you my word,' she said, perspiration darkening the armpits of her gown.

Seizing her hand, he covered it with kisses, looking up at her all the time with such distress in his eyes that immediately she forgot how troublesome he was and remembered only in what affection she held him.

When at last he had gone – the groom was sent back twice, once for his wig, and again for the basket of peaches left in the porch – she went into his chamber. A wasp was burrowing into the flesh of an over-ripe fig on his pillow. On his desk lay a single sheet of paper festooned with orange peel.

With difficulty, for his handwriting was disordered, she read – *Madmen are all sensual in the lower stages of the distemper . . . but when they are very ill, pleasure is too weak for them and they seek pain.* Beneath this was a space and then a single line of Latin, scored through – *De pedicis et manicis insana cogitatio.*

Thrusting open the window – the departed occupant of the room held to the notion that fresh air belonged on the outside – she hurled the orange peel into the stifling day, then, half alerted to what she would find, pulled out the bottom drawer.

To Miss Laetitia Hawkins,
2 Sion Row,
Twickenham

Dec. 3rd, 1807

Dear Miss Hawkins,
I am at a loss to know how best to reply to your
most recent letter without causing offence. Believe
me, my dear Miss Hawkins, I have no wish to incur
your displeasure, but it cannot be repeated too often
that circumstances surrounding my early life were
such that certain events cannot be recalled without
grave disturbance of spirits.

For that reason alone I must pass over your first
two queries, and supply but a sketchy account of
Mrs Salusbury's supposed sighting of a ghost in the
vicinity of the lake at Streatham Park. She had, so I
was told, fled into the Park after a disagreement with
my mother, and was therefore understandably prone
to fancies. Her emphasis on the halo of fire
surrounding the apparition was later ascribed by Dr
Johnson to a trick of the light, the illusion being
caused by the rays of the sun striking the amulet –
given him by Queen Anne when he was touched by
the scrofula – worn on a chain about his neck. That
same night, woken by what I curiously took to be
the sound of a violin, I crept down the stairs and was
leapt upon by my mother. She, as I afterwards

learnt, jealous of my father referring to one of his guests as an orchid of the rarest kind, underwent a storm of the brain and, accusing me of stealing a button from his coat, set about me most roughly.

As you rightly observe, my mother was indeed diligent in regard to the education of her children. The weight of such instruction fell most heavily on myself, my brother Harry being less compliant. I have come to believe that my studious disposition as a child arose not so much from natural curiosity but rather from a fear of the whip.

Dr Johnson often remarked that endeavouring to make children prematurely wise was useless labour. Suppose, he said, that they have more knowledge at five or six years than others of that age? What use can be made of it?

In his own early years he read very hard, and held it was a sad reflection, but a true one, that he knew almost as much at the age of eighteen as he did at fifty. I fear he was right, for it does not seem that I have learnt anything new these last thirty years.

I have no very strong opinions on the character of David Garrick. As a child, the animation shown on his face, and its quick changes of expression, confused me. One was never sure as to his exact feelings. He could make one laugh, but tears were not far behind. I believe that on stage he was considered natural, simple, affecting; it was only when he was off that he was seen to be acting. It was also said that he hated lending Dr Johnson a book, for it was always returned in an unreadable condition, the pages turned down and the print discoloured from the juice of oranges. That he continued in the lending of them says much for his generosity of spirit.

I am sorry to hear of the death of your aunt. Generations, my dear Miss Hawkins, are but like leaves, and we now see the faded leaves falling about us.

I am obliged for your felicitations concerning my forthcoming marriage to Admiral Lord Keith, and remain, for one month more,

Yours sincerely,

H. M. Thrale

I believe I do remember Mr Goldsmith showing me how to play Jack and Jill with two bits of paper stuck to his fingers. Alas, I never liked him, his posturing being so extreme.

SWEETING *n.f.* *(from Sweet)*

1 A sweet luscious apple
2 A word of endearment

Trip no further pretty sweeting;
Journies end in lovers meeting.
    Shakespeare's *Twelfth Night*

The child ran out into the gardens beyond the stables and, fleeing some way towards the mud banks of the river, whirled round with such vigour that her bonnet flew off. Cross, she wanted to put the world in a spin; if she twirled fast enough she might be rid of the image of her mother, spoon digging into a breakfast egg, the scar, caused by a fall from a horse, reddening above her top lip. When Mamma was in a temper the mark became prominent; sad, it whitened.

For two weeks their departure to Streatham had been delayed. Mamma had promised they would leave at the beginning of June, but only that morning she had announced it was out of the question on account of Sophy having sprouted a boil on her neck.

'It needs to be lanced,' she'd said, belly bulging against the table, tongue flickering out to lick the egg yolk from her chin. 'I'm advised it would be foolish to undertake a journey, however short.'

'Then I advise you to leave Sophy behind,' Queeney had retorted, 'for you have abandoned me often enough,' and jumping up from her chair had fled the room. She knew she was in the wrong, but it was hard to be polite when Mother thought so little of keeping her word.

For a full month the atmosphere within the house had been discordant. Mamma spent most of her time closeted in the counting offices with Perkins, the chief clerk, or else sitting at her writing desk scribbling notes to Mr Johnson, who was away in Ashbourne staying with Dr Taylor. Not an hour passed without Mamma commenting on how sorely he was missed. She didn't miss Papa, who hardly ever came home, not even for church on Sundays. New Nurse said he was too busy playing cards and living the gay life.

Outside, though the air still hung heavy with the sour-sweet odour of fermenting grain, the thunderings and clatterings of the yard had stopped, and now, where once a dense head of steam had billowed to the city skies, only a thin scribble of vapour rose from the giant coppers of the Brewhouse. Even Papa's barges had ceased to move with the tide; empty of merchandise they sat idle upon the black jelly of the Thames.

Dizzy from spinning, Queeney sank to her knees and tugged pettishly at the grass. She did not care for Southwark; there were few trees to climb and the kitten Grandmamma had given her had chewed off its blue ribbon and turned into a wild cat, who now stalked the barley stacks in pursuit of rats. There was no one to play with, not

of her own age and interests, and the Italian teacher, Mr
Baretti, whom Mr Johnson had found for her, had not yet
begun to give her lessons. Mr Baretti had a gruesome past –
he'd been had up for murder by a stabbing with a fruit
knife after undergoing the provocation of having his testicles tweaked, and had only cheated the hangman through
the intercession of Mr Johnson and his friends.

Curious as to what it would be like to be hanged, she put
her hands about her throat and squeezed as hard as she was
able. It had little effect, for her chest continued to rise and fall.

Soon, she knew, someone would come in search of her.
Found, she would be lectured on insolence, then kissed,
then, like as not, slapped. Mamma was contrary in all
things. Sometimes Mr Johnson held it was because she had
so many things to worry about, at others that she had not
enough to occupy her. Once, during some disagreement
over the correct treatment for Lucy's ears, he'd likened her
to a rattlesnake – because she hissed so. When I am grown,
the child thought, I shall coo like a dove.

Presently, engaged in making little nests out of grass, she
heard Muggeridge calling her.

She had been christened Hester, after Mamma, but was
always known as Queeney. Mr Johnson, her teacher, often
addressed her by another name, one which showed his
tender esteem – she was his Sweeting. He'd told her it was
an old endearment, one first used when she was but an
infant on the crawl.

'How?' she had asked, for the past mattered to her.
'Where . . . at what time?'

'On the stairs at Southwark,' he replied, 'as a sunbeam
pierced the window.'

'Did I understand?' she had wanted to know.

'But, of course, Miss,' he said. 'You winked.'

He liked her better than her three sisters, of that she was sure. Lucy was quite ugly and cried incessantly from a discharge of both ears, Susannah was clumsy, and Sophy, in spite of her boil, too young to be of interest. As for little brother Harry, why, he was in fear of Mr Johnson because of the noises he made when deep in thought. Mamma had assured him that such whistles and groans were common to men of intellect, but he had nightmares in which Mr Johnson, hooting like an owl, pursued him down a dark tunnel. Besides, everyone knew it was Harry who, leaping downstairs too boisterously and colliding with Grandmamma, had bumped her into the cancer.

'Miss Queeney,' Muggeridge shouted again. He had been employed at the Brewery in her grandfather's day. When young he had worked in the mill house as a grinder of husks; now old, his nose blue and corrugated, he emptied chamber pots, trimmed candles and trailed children.

At his approach – he was dangling her bonnet by its strings – Queeney cried out imperiously, 'Go away, I shall come back in my own good time.' Then, watching his shambling retreat, she remembered Mr Johnson's observation that no one lowly or lacking in education was ever treated with disrespect *except* by the truly ignorant. Belatedly, she called out, 'Please.' She wasted her breath, for his hearing had gone.

A half-hour later, fully expecting chastisement, she returned to the house to be met by New Nurse, who said that if she would be a good, *silent* girl the Mistress was prepared to take her across the river to visit Mrs Salusbury.

'I will be good,' the child babbled. 'Very, very good and very, very quiet.'

The rosy prospect of time spent with Mamma free of the younger siblings scratching round her like chicks about a hen filled her with such joy that she stood perfectly still and uttered scarcely a squawk while New Nurse wrenched the tangles from her hair.

It was raining when they drove out of the gates of the Brewery. Such were the potholes in the road on the approach to Pitt Bridge that by the time the toll house was reached the windows of the coach were splattered with mud. Nothing could be seen through the pock-marked glass save for a glimpse of grey river beneath a rind of weeping sky.

Aware that earlier in the day there had been a falling out between Queeney and herself – though for the life of her she couldn't recall the precise cause – Mrs Thrale endeavoured to engage her in conversation.

'Mr Johnson', she said, 'is thinking of buying you a cabinet in which to store curiosities, such as animal bones and shards of pottery. There is a monkey's paw, mounted on a base of silver . . .' Here, noticing Queeney's hand peculiarly clamped over her mouth, she anxiously enquired if the girl was afflicted with the toothache. Queeney shook her head, but kept her hand in place.

'Grandmamma has the paw in safe keeping', Mrs Thrale continued, 'and does not care for it. It would look well in a collection . . . Mr Hogarth gave it me . . . for sitting still while he painted my portrait.'

She was met with silence, and tried again, this time seeking a considered estimation of young Harry's intelligence. Queeney's opinion, in spite of her tender years, was not without weight. Why, when she was but six summers in age, having been tested on the works of Dryden and Pope, no less an authority than the headmaster of Abingdon grammar school had acknowledged that if the examination had been conducted in Latin she would have qualified for a degree from the University of Oxford.

'To my mind,' Mrs Thrale prattled on, 'Harry lacks concentration. His pursuit of knowledge takes second place to his sword fights with the stable boys. You', she flattered, tapping her daughter's knee, 'veered towards books from infancy . . . though it must be admitted you sometimes tore at the pages.'

Still Queeney uttered not a word. Mrs Thrale's heart fairly thundered in her breast. Heaven help me, she thought, I am intimidated by my own child.

She said, 'It's as well we are not at Streatham Park. I am informed that the dust rising from the building of Papa's library would silt up one's lungs. The feathers of my bantams are turned grey and the goat is heard sneezing.'

Eyes like winter glass, Queeney stared straight ahead.

Losing patience, Mrs Thrale tugged away the hand covering the girl's mouth, and, after administering a spiteful squeeze to the fingers, kept silent for the remainder of the journey.

Their progress to Dean Street was hampered by the number of troops patrolling the streets in response to an alleged Jacobite plot involving the Bishop of Rochester. Twice the carriage was halted, once by a fresh-faced upholder of law and order – his mouth was damson coloured and his manner offensive – and next by a ruffian with a patch over his eye. Of the two, Mrs Thrale was inclined to think the latter more human, for, pulling open the carriage door and observing Queeney, hand yet again guarding her mouth, One-eye had promptly stepped back and ordered the coach to roll on.

Mrs Salusbury's house had a front garden surrounded by paling. The border flowers, foxgloves and the like, were sadly neglected, and cow-parsley ran riot. In the window boxes, primroses wilted.

Entering, Mrs Thrale found her mother lying on a couch in the downstairs room, the dog, Belle, enthroned on a silk cushion, curled across her feet.

Mrs Salusbury claimed that though poorly she was not in pain. 'It is one of my good days,' she asserted, albeit in a weary tone of voice.

Distressed, Mrs Thrale pulled the bell for the housekeeper. The room was cold due to the fire having sunk to embers. When her summons was answered, she ordered the scuttle to be filled with coals and that a basin of warm water be fetched; the corners of Mrs Salusbury's lips were encrusted with spittle.

Queeney stood at the window, face pressed into the curtain. Last year Old Nurse had given up the ghost, along with Didcot, the under-gardener, and a kitchen maid who had purged herself too strenuously in an effort to do away with an unwanted child.

Mamma had taken her to see Old Nurse in her wait to be transported to the grave, lying in her burial shroud in high summer on a trestle table in the storeroom at Streatham Park, a bluebottle spiralling above the black wart on her chin. Breath stopped, Old Nurse was but an empty vessel, cracked in places like the broken vase that nudged the scant hair on her shrunken skull. Past mending, Mamma had murmured, though she was referring to the pot rather than Old Nurse.

'Kiss Grandmamma,' Mrs Thrale urged. Reluctantly, the child approached and pecked the air above the sick woman's cheek; then, falling to her knees and seizing the dog in her arms, she smothered its snout in kisses. Belle smelt sweeter than Grandmamma, whose odour was that of death.

There followed a conversation between the two women concerning bank loans and chemical liquids. According to Mrs Thrale, Mr Perkins had behaved in a most exemplary manner, instructing the men to stop work until matters were taken out of Mr Thrale's hands entirely. It was Mr Johnson's considered opinion that but for Perkins's prompt grasp of the situation they would all be facing ruin. Things were bad enough, but at least the ludicrous attempt to brew beer without the addition of either malt or hops had been brought to a halt.

'Such a foolish enterprise,' sighed Mrs Salusbury. 'One wonders what possessed Mr Thrale to go along with such a notion.'

'Perkins has also insisted on the immediate sale of the land in East Smithfield purchased for the benefit of that wretch Humphrey Jackson and his costly experiments—'

'I never cared for him,' Mrs Salusbury said. 'His wife was an exceedingly vacuous woman.'

'Indeed she was,' agreed Mrs Thrale. 'Had Perkins or I been consulted we would have argued from the start that the preserving of bottoms by such means was doomed to failure—'

She was interrupted by Queeney, overcome by giggles. Exasperated, yet pleased the child was in a less sullen mood, she said, 'The bottoms I am referring to, Miss, are those of ships attacked by worm . . . and it is scarcely a laughing matter, for the scheme has brought your deluded father to the edge of bankruptcy.'

Still Queeney snorted.

'I would have thought', her mother said, 'that you, more than most, would not find worms a fit subject for mirth.'

Mortified at the mention of her affliction, the child turned scarlet. Dr Sutton held she got too close to animals and that she should not let the goat eat from her hand or the cat lap from her cup, but what did he know? Whenever Mamma caught her squirming on her chair she dosed her with senna, which only succeeded in giving her an unpleasant taste in the mouth and a looseness of the bowel. When I am grown, she thought, I shall see-saw as much as I like.

At that moment there came a knocking at the street door, and shortly Miss Reynolds was shown in. Amid the exclamations of surprise and delight, the kissing and exchanging of compliments – a trifle forced on Mrs Thrale's part, owing to the food stains on her mother's gown and the dull aspect of the furniture – no one noticed Queeney sidling into the hall.

Miss Reynolds was in some agitation, her carriage having being surrounded by a mob on its way to the Tower of London to protest against the arrest of George Kelly. Did Mrs Thrale know Mr Kelly, secretary to the unfortunate Bishop of Rochester? He was a popular man afflicted with a frightful irritation of the skin . . . talking to him was unnerving because of his constant scratching. The cuffs of his shirt were often speckled with blood. She had met him when he had accompanied the Bishop to her brother's studio in Leicester Fields. Joshua had abandoned the sittings because he too had begun to suffer from an itch and feared for his hands.

'My coach was stopped too,' said Mrs Thrale. 'Fortunately the presence of Queeney secured our safe passage.'

Mrs Salusbury falling into a doze, Miss Reynolds confided it was her third visit to the house in as many days. As
she informed Mrs Thrale, with much hesitation and alteration of words, she had grown alarmed . . . worried . . . by
the behaviour . . . attitude of the housekeeper, Mrs
Mountjoy . . . and the signs of neglect . . . lack of care . . .
shown to Mrs Salusbury.

'I see it, I see it,' moaned Mrs Thrale, pounding the back
of the sofa on which her mother lay and watching the rise
and fall of the dust.

Eyeing Mrs Thrale's monstrous belly, the well-meaning
Miss Reynolds assured her she was in no way to blame.
'What with the problems of the Brewery,' she murmured,
'and your present condition—'

'There is nothing of more importance than the happiness
of my mother,' cried Mrs Thrale. 'It is my intention to take
her to Streatham as soon as the business with the bank is
settled. Please be so good as to sit with her while I speak my
mind to Mrs Mountjoy.'

She had no sooner quit the room than Mrs Salusbury
woke; struggling into a sitting position, she said, 'Hester
means it kindly, but Mrs Mountjoy and I understand one
another. We are both past the age at which the shine on a
table can bring ease to an ailing body.'

How right she is, thought Miss Reynolds. The pain of
existence could not be removed with a dusting cloth.

Having let herself out into the street, Queeney had no clear
idea of where she wanted to go, save it should be as far away
as possible from Mamma, who had so cruelly taunted her
on the subject of worms. Though the rain had stopped,
the thoroughfare was pitted with puddles and in no time at

all the yellow fabric of her shoes had turned the colour of mustard.

She had been to Dean Street many times, but not for some months, and was astonished at the number of old houses half pulled down and new ones half built up. There were ladders everywhere, and carts full of bricks, and on what had once been the pampered grass of the bowling green a boy was selling flat fish from a stall anchored in mud. At Number 29 the branches of the mulberry tree, snapped by a fallen scaffold, hung in dripping rags. As for the windows of Sir James Thornhill's elegant house, why, they were quite clouded over and, peer as she might, the parrot with the blue legs was no longer visible on its perch behind the glass.

Mamma had taken her to visit Lady Thornhill one morning in summer. She remembered the occasion because Papa, some days before, had given her an amber necklace, the very same which now lay upon the black lace mantle she wore about her shoulders.

When shown into Lady Thornhill's drawing room, the parrot had rocked along its perch and squawked out she was a pretty girl. It had been caught in a jungle place in Brazil by a traveller paid to fetch exotic creatures for John Hunter, the medical man who, curious as to what constituted life, was forever anatomising them into death. Even he had admired the fiery plumage of the bird and, laying aside his dissecting knife, allowed Sir James to buy it from him.

Other visitors had tried to get the parrot to talk, but it had opened its beak only for Queeney. This, she reasoned, was on account of her not joining in the general pestering; she herself grew stubborn when put on show. Mamma, of course, had swelled with pride at its croaking declaration of regard, which only proved how ignorant she was, seeing Mr Johnson held that birds saw only colours, not faces.

She was crossing Compton Lane when the rain fell once more. Had she not been wearing her straw bonnet with the scarlet ribbons she would have retraced her steps and returned to Dean Street; the bonnet was new and Mamma would be displeased if it grew sodden. Sighting the arched doorway of St Anne's, she hurried to find shelter.

The interior of the church was dark, owing to brick dust powdering the windows. A dozen candles did little to disperse the gloom and at first Queeney thought she was alone. She didn't venture in too far, both on account of the darkness and because often such places gave shelter to poor people stricken with disease who had nowhere else to go. Once, taken by Papa to St George's church, she had witnessed an old man, crazy with the fever, attempting to climb on to the marble lap of a sea captain swooning in the arms of an angel. Too weak to reach his goal, he had slid off and hit his head on the stone step below. Papa said the old man would be taken to a hospital and made well, but she had seen how motionless he lay, chest no longer rising beneath his tattered shirt, and that pool of blood, cherry-red, spreading between the angel's toes.

When she had confided the happening to Mr Johnson, enquiring whether it was not wrong of Papa to tell untruths, he said he had come, late in years and against former prejudices, to believe that it was a father's duty to shield his children from the horrors of life. Man, he told her, keeps the prospect of death forever in his thoughts, but is comforted by the hope of some future state. In this he differs from the brute, for whom hope is absent and who endeavours to avoid death instinctively, without ever knowing what it really is. 'Without a knowledge of hope', he concluded mysteriously, 'sorrow is unknown. Papa did right to protect you, for the miseries of existence will crowd upon you soon enough.' After which dismal lecture, dashing his sleeve against the water that threatened to spill from his eyes, he had challenged Harry to a barefoot race across the grass.

She had taken scant notice of his words, it being her experience that even when the sun was a golden orb in the heavens and birdsong girdled the Park, old people took a bleak and melancholy view of the world.

Becoming accustomed to the dim light, she became aware of a figure seated further down the nave, crouched small and still. Dead, she thought, struck down by Providence, at which moment it rose upright and, stepping from the pew, skipped with outspread arms towards the altar. She took the figure to be that of a boy, for its hair was cropped, but when it spun round at the rail and began a jigging return she saw it was a girl, not above ten years of age, her face round as the moon and vacant of expression. One eye was set lower than the other, and as she advanced up the aisle her open mouth emitted gurgling noises, as though she sucked from a cup that could never be emptied.

Queeney wanted to run, yet her legs refused to obey; nor could she avert her gaze from that lopsided countenance. She knew it was ignorant to stare so, but something within her had locked fast and her head wouldn't shift. I am a pillar of salt, she thought, a pillar of marble . . . and now she and the idiot were level. From somewhere outside she heard the sound of hammer blows, and at that instant the amber necklace was plucked from her throat. Clutched in that fierce grip the circlet came away entire, then, as the creature put its fist to its mouth as though ready to munch on an apple, the string broke; beads popped from those clenched fingers and bounced like pips upon the stone flags of the porch.

For what seemed an age, heart pounding, Queeney waited in the shadow of the church door. Her fright was occasioned by what Mamma would say when her absence was discovered rather than by her encounter with the lunatic. She made no attempt to pick up the scattered remains of the necklace, and instead thought frantically of how best she might deflect her mother's anger. Perhaps she could relate, in a dull voice – as though her wits had gone – how, driven from the house by Grandmamma's sickly aspect, she had crossed the street to wave to her friend the parrot . . . just as the mob had surged round the corner. Distracted, she had fled in the opposite direction. If she kept her face free of expression, similar to that of the idiot dancing through the church, surely Mamma would quite pass over the matter of the lost necklace and instead spill tears of joy at her safe return.

Full of resolve and practising in her head the persuasive words she would employ, Queeney hurried back to Dean Street, and was standing on tiptoe reaching for Mrs Salusbury's rapper when the door opened and Mrs Thrale, noticeably animated, swept out.

'Make haste,' she ordered. 'Miss Reynolds tells me Mr Johnson returned last night from Ashbourne.' Propelling her daughter before her, she leapt with such vigour down the path that her skirt beheaded a foxglove lolling beside the wicket gate.

*

Mr Johnson lived in Johnson's Court, off Fleet Street, but a short distance from the house in Gough Square in which he had laboured over his *Dictionary*.

Mrs Desmoulins opened the door to Mrs Thrale and kept her on the step. She said Mr Johnson was away again, at which moment Mrs Williams, recognising the voice, cried out that Mrs Thrale was most welcome and ushered her into the hall. Mr Johnson was indeed not at home, having gone to his bookseller, but he would be back within the hour; Mr Goldsmith and Sir John Hawkins were already waiting on him in the parlour. Smirking, Queeney trailed behind her mother.

Mrs Thrale tolerated John Hawkins and thought Oliver Goldsmith clever and absurd by turns. Hawkins was dry and reserved, Goldsmith showy. Both men inhabited the room according to their character, the former remaining rigidly upright, stiff as the sofa he perched upon, the latter posturing at the fireplace, breeches strained across his nether parts.

It was in Mrs Thrale's nature to put a company at ease, for she could not abide an atmosphere. Within minutes she had softened John Hawkins by kissing him on both cheeks and assuring him of the delight felt by his friends at the recent knighthood conferred upon him by the King. She was not being false; though a bore, Hawkins was an honest magistrate and a musical man to boot. As for Goldsmith, she coaxed him out of his affectations by appealing to his droll sense of humour. In no time all three laughed a great deal and imagined themselves the best of friends.

Mrs Desmoulins, seated in a corner of the room and saddled with the child, could not take her eyes from Mrs Thrale. The woman's wit and intelligence, so often

remarked upon by Mr Johnson, were not strikingly evi-
dent, for her conversation consisted entirely of gossip.
Speaking of Joshua Reynolds, whose unfortunate sister she
said she had been with earlier that morning, she brought up
the perishable nature of the colours it was rumoured the
artist used, and quoted an epigram told her by Arthur
Murphy.

> *The art of painting was at first designed*
> *To bring the dead, our ancestors, to mind,*
> *But this same painter has reversed the plan*
> *And made the portrait die before the man.*

The gentlemen applauded, which Mrs Desmoulins considered cruel, seeing both had been the recipients of Sir
Joshua's famed hospitality. Nor did she think Mrs Thrale
good-looking, her complexion being far from clear, her eyelashes sparse and her upper lip adorned with a scar. And
yet . . . and yet, there was no denying she possessed a certain
winning intensity of manner capable of seducing the
onlooker. Sir John and Mr Goldsmith, wearing foolish
smiles, could fairly be described as spellbound. Mrs
Desmoulins felt her own mouth curving upwards, and
despised herself for it.

Soon Mrs Williams ushered in Frank Barber carrying
the tea urn. Queeney didn't care for Mrs Williams, who,
dressed in a scarlet gown fashionable in a previous age and
wearing a lace cap showing two stiffened wings of hair at
the temples, appeared old and pale and shrunken. It wasn't
nice being stared at by someone who couldn't see; it made
Queeney feel as though she herself had disappeared.

She had never encountered Frank Barber before, though

she knew he was servant to Mr Johnson. He had come on errands to Southwark many times, but always at night, which made him difficult to be seen from the nursery window. As a child, at Mr Johnson's expense, he had been educated at a school in Bishop's Stortford. He hadn't proved to be clever, but Mr Johnson loved him all the same. When he let go of the tray she saw the palms of his hands were the colour of her damp shoes.

Just as Barber was leaving the room, a fearful scream rang out from below stairs. Sir John, guiding Mrs Williams to a chair, jerked in alarm. 'It signifies nothing,' Mrs Williams said. 'It is only Poll Carmichael.' She gave no further explanation and commenced to pour out the tea, the tip of her little finger dipping into each dish to ascertain the level of the liquid.

Mrs Desmoulins made an effort to be cordial to the child, Queeney, whom Mr Johnson spoke of as a prodigy. The little Miss was very much the offspring of her mother, being both plain and mightily assured in spite of her limp bonnet with its bedraggled ribbons. When addressed she responded politely enough, but her eyes were mocking. On being asked if she had enjoyed her visit to town, she said, 'Very much, thank you. Grandmamma is soon to die, but I am prepared for it.'

Presently Mr Johnson returned. He came in clutching a twist of bloodstained newspaper. On Mr Goldsmith observing it was a strange parcel to bring back from a bookseller, he said his errand had been concerned with victuals for his cat; he did not wish Frank Barber to demean himself scurrying about on behalf of a quadruped. Mrs Williams, chin in the air as though scenting smoke, told Mrs Desmoulins to take the entrails down to the scullery.

Mr Johnson fussed over Queeney, patting her hand and expressing the hope he found her well, before turning to his other guests. He embraced first Goldsmith, then Hawkins, after which, without looking directly at her, he bowed to Mrs Thrale. Queeney, watching her mother, noticed how pale she became and how she played with her gloves, first crumpling the fingers, then smoothing.

Mr Johnson's conversation had to do with the hospitality he had enjoyed at Dr Taylor's, who had once been his schoolfellow at Lichfield. Dr Taylor had deer in his paddock, pheasants in his menagerie, the largest horned cattle in England and possibly the biggest bull in the world.

'He is, by all accounts, a man of eccentric habits,' Sir John said. 'Proceedings in Chancery found his moral character not entirely consistent with his profession.'

'Pff!' Johnson snorted. 'I take him as I find him, and like what I find, though it is true, Sir, that he and I disagree on most subjects.'

'How can that be?' asked Goldsmith. 'One cannot form a true friendship with someone who has likings and aversions dissimilar to one's own.'

'It would be difficult—' began Mrs Thrale.

'Why, Sir, it is simple,' scoffed Johnson. 'You must shun the subject on which you disagree. For instance, I can mix well enough with Burke . . .'

'He is indeed an extraordinary man,' put in Mrs Thrale, and was again cut short.

'. . . for I love his knowledge, his genius, his diffusion of conversation, but I would not talk to him of the Rockingham party.'

'When people disagree on matters not to be mentioned,' argued Goldsmith, 'they will surely arrive at that situation in the story of Bluebeard, *You may look into all the chambers but one.*'

'I am not saying that *you* could live in friendship with a man from whom you differ as to some point,' shouted Johnson, 'I am saying only that *I* could do it.'

'Will anyone take more tea?' asked Mrs Williams, and received no reply, not even from Mr Johnson, who had been known to drink fourteen cups at a sitting.

After some moments of silence, Mrs Thrale remarked, 'Your stay with Dr Taylor does not seem to have rested you, Sir.'

'Madam,' he retorted, 'it was not rest I sought, simply diversion, and was not disappointed. Dr Taylor's generosity far exceeds that of *any one* I know.'

Queeney was startled at this implied criticism and even more surprised at its effect on her mother. Far from appearing crushed by such rudeness, she ceased fiddling with her gloves and gazed at him with the utmost composure, and now it was he who seemed unsure of himself; turning away, he gave a bellow of laughter, of the sardonic sort, and banged his fist repeatedly against his breast.

Before he departed, Goldsmith stuck two bits of paper on to his thumbs and waggled them about for the benefit of Queeney. She giggled her appreciation, but was not diverted, being of the opinion that a game of Jack and Jill was best suited to those still in the nursery. Also, she did not like sitting next to a man whose parts bulged so obtrusively.

When the playwright had left, Sir John Hawkins said, 'He is a great one for argument.'

Mr Johnson said, 'Goldy talks so much merely lest one should forget he is of the company.'

'For my part,' countered Sir John, 'I like well to hear him talk away carelessly.'

'Why yes, Sir,' Mr Johnson agreed, 'but he should not like to hear it himself.'

When Sir John too had taken his leave, Mrs Thrale pressed Mrs Williams to take Queeney to seek out the cat. 'She is very fond of cats,' she enthused. 'She has one in Southwark and three at Streatham Park.'

'I prefer dogs to cats,' Queeney said. 'They are less independent and do not grow up so fast.' She did not want to go off alone with old Mrs Williams, who was possibly a witch, but she could tell Mamma wanted her out of the way. She had the curious conceit that there was no ceiling to the room, and above that no roof to the house, and that she sat beneath a sky whose whirling clouds constantly changed shape. Mr Johnson stood at the fireplace, head swinging from side to side as though trying to clear his mind; Mamma was smiling. Neither spoke, yet thoughts passed between them. On the floor, like fairy footsteps, Mr Goldsmith's bits of paper pointed to the door. Defeated, Queeney rose from her chair and reluctantly followed Mrs Williams into the hall.

The stairs to the basement were narrow and twisted. Mrs Williams descended the steps sideways, one hand stretched out, gown whispering as it brushed the wall. Mrs Desmoulins was in the kitchen below, seated at a table opposite Frank Barber, who was scraping mud from a pair of boots, a lit candle at his elbow. In the fireplace corner an old man crouched coughing on a three-legged stool.

Mrs Williams, smelling the burning wax, approached the table and blew out the candle. Mrs Desmoulins pulled a rude face, but said nothing. The old man, now invisible, coughed again; the coals hissed as he spat out his phlegm.

'I have Miss Thrale with me,' announced Mrs Williams.

'So we saw', replied Mrs Desmoulins, 'until you dropped us into the dark.'

'We are looking for the cat,' Mrs Williams said.

'My mamma wished me to see it,' said Queeney, disconcerted by the shouts and hysterical laughter coming from the scullery beyond. 'Then Mamma must be obeyed,' murmured Mrs Desmoulins, a note of sarcasm in her voice. All the same, Queeney liked her best, for she was the most ordinary, being neither blind nor black, nor prone to spitting; she was relieved when Mrs Desmoulins left the table to join in the hunt for the cat.

The animal was run to earth in the scullery, preening itself some yards distant from a young woman in considerable disarray, who was dashing her head against the area door and wailing.

'Kitty, Kitty,' called Mrs Williams, sniffing the air, at which moment the young woman uttered a piercing scream, causing the cat to streak away down the passage.

'Poll,' Mrs Williams cried. 'Behave yourself, we have company.'

Poll took no notice; sticking out her tongue she again dashed her forehead against the door, and now the skin on her forehead split open and blood trickled down the side of her nose.

'What is wrong with her?' asked Queeney.

'Toothache,' said Mrs Williams tersely.

'Drink and men,' contradicted Mrs Desmoulins, eyes glittering.

Prodding Queeney in the back, Mrs Williams propelled her from the room.

There are more ways than one of banishing bad memories, reasoned Queeney, fingering her throat in search of the amber necklace.

Two days before Queeney's birthday Mrs Thrale was delivered of her eighth child. Though shut in the school-room, Queeney heard her mother squealing on the floor above; the sounds were those of a sow caught by the hind leg. Bent over her Italian grammar, Queeney promised God she would be a patient girl for ever if only Mamma wouldn't die. Mr Baretti, noticing the child's pallor, sang very loudly a Corsican ballad about a milkmaid seduced by a goatherd.

At three o'clock Mr Thrale came home, by which time the infant was two hours old. It was a girl, black in the face and unable to breathe properly, and it died before midnight. Mr Baretti said it was not to be wondered at, given the worries Mrs Thrale had been burdened with in the preceding months. 'Your mother', he told Queeney, 'has had the mending of the Brewery to contend with, the discharge from Lucy's ear and the nursing of your grandmother. You must endeavour to be thoughtful to her and not cause her agitation.'

Queeney took notice of his words, for generally he was critical of Mrs Thrale, thinking her too severe with her children and too frivolous in every other respect. Accordingly, when allowed to see Mamma, she had crept into the bedroom and kissed her most tenderly. Mamma smelt bad, but she stroked Queeney's cheek and murmured she loved her more than all the world. The dead infant, sprinkled with herbs, lay in its crib at the end of the bed, face covered with a muslin cloth. It was to have been christened Penelope, but would never hear its name.

For a full week afterwards Queeney was kind to her brother and sisters, even Susannah, who had crooked legs and an umbilical rupture which rendered her so irritable that she was known as Little Crab, though Papa, on account of her pointy nose, called her Gilly, from Gilhouter, the Cheshire word signifying an owl.

Mr Johnson stayed away at Lichfield, mostly, so Mrs Thrale said, because he reckoned she would be too weak to give him her full attention, but Mr Baretti said he was working on a revised edition of his *Dictionary*. He did, however, dispatch Frank Barber to Streatham with the cabinet intended for the storing of curios which he had long promised his Sweeting.

It was a splendid piece of furniture comprising four large drawers within a door, topped by a smaller cabinet containing twelve compartments. Queeney had to stand on a chair to reach the upper cabinet; she filled two of the little drawers with shells gathered from the shore at Brighthelmstone. Mamma had not yet fetched the monkey's paw from Grandmamma's, but Papa gave her a tuft of hair believed to have belonged to Mr Pope, and Mrs Williams sent a poem written without the help of Mr Johnson.

Queeney didn't care for either the poem or the snip of hair, the former being all about a sunset and relying too much on the colour crimson, the latter having the appearance of being plucked from the rump of a squirrel. After some thought, she rummaged in New Nurse's work-basket and taking out a length of ribbon labelled it as belonging to *Frances Thrale, born September 1765, died October 6th, 1765*. Once, she had indeed had a sister of that name, but so long ago that she now qualified as a curiosity.

In November Mr Johnson wrote Queeney a letter, in which he asked after the health of his pet hen and acquainted her with the death of Miss Porter's black cat. *So things come and go*, he mused. *Generations, as Homer says, are but like leaves, and you now see the faded leaves falling about you.*

When Mamma read the letter she said that Mr Johnson was merely being civil. Guests, she said, frequently engaged in correspondence with the children of their hosts; it was a means of conveying gratitude without too explicit a show of subservience. Strenuous expressions of gratitude implied need, something which no gentleman cared to demonstrate. His letter, she explained, was therefore to be taken as addressed to herself, in appreciation of the care he enjoyed under her roof. He would not expect a reply, far less want to be troubled with the scribblings of a child.

Mrs Thrale having gone up to town to discuss Brewery business with Perkins, Queeney approached Papa in his study and enquired if it was not impolite to ignore letters from Mr Johnson. Papa, purple in the face, two bottles of port at his elbow, was slumped over the remains of a large turkey; she knew it was the trouble caused by the bank that made him so hungry.

'What do you wish to tell Samuel?' Papa asked.

'That I am sorry about Miss Porter's cat,' she said. 'And to ask for things for the cabinet.'

'And why is Mamma against it?'

'On account of his being important.'

'No more than the truth,' Papa said, wiping the grease from his mouth.

'So I should not send it?'

'On the contrary,' said Papa, 'it could be that you are of

equal importance . . . which Mamma knows,' after which he smiled, though his eyes did not look merry. Telling her he would see to it that Mr Johnson got her letter, he filled his glass with wine and gulped it down as though but recently returned from a desert; it was the trouble caused by the bank that made him so thirsty.

Two weeks later a second letter arrived for Queeney. Mamma was displeased at its contents, though she pretended otherwise. Mr Johnson complained that Mrs Thrale had used them both very sorrily when she had hindered Queeney from writing to him. He wrote that when he came home they would all have good sport playing together and that none of them would cry, not even Lucy, and ended by declaring himself to be her most humble servant.

In December Johnson left Lichfield and came back to London. Though he dined at Southwark with Henry Thrale and sometimes stayed the night in his old rooms above the counting house, he was not encouraged to return to Streatham. On the few occasions Mrs Thrale visited the Brewery she seemed pleased to see him, yet did not suggest he should come home and he was too proud to ask. He had to be content with her letters, which told him that Mr Baretti and Queeney were the best of friends and that the Italian lessons went forward with satisfaction to both sides. At first Queeney had been given vocabulary lists – nouns, verbs, adjectives, prepositions and articles – but so rapidly had she improved that her teacher had now embarked on a series of dialogues to do with imaginary discussions between the goats and hens in the barnyard. On Baretti's calling these dialogues 'bubbles of air', Queeney, wicked child, had promptly bested him and proclaimed them 'empty bladders all'. The letter also told him that Lucy's ear was worse and that Mrs Salusbury was now so ill she could no longer be left in the house in Dean Street and must be cared for at Streatham Park. He took this to mean that his presence would be an added burden and was envious of Baretti for so quickly assuming importance.

His lot in London was not a cheerful one, for his frequent absences from Johnson's Court had made him less tolerant of its bickering residents; Mrs Williams hated everybody, Levet despised Mrs Desmoulins and did not love Mrs Williams; Poll cared for no one and was a stupid slut besides. In such company, as the weeks passed, his spirits sank and his temper worsened. His one solace was Dr Levet, who, detested by all three women, sat with him while he took his breakfast. Neither bread nor tea passed the gaunt doctor's lips, his stomach generally in a turmoil after imbibing the liquid recompense he received for his nightly ministrations to the wretched inhabitants of Houndsditch. He was not required to stand out or to make conversation, his purpose being closer to that of an old and once useful piece of furniture, which, settled in a fixed position and gathering dust, had become so familiar as to fade from vision.

Johnson's visitors, those who called at the prescribed hour, did not find Levet so easy to ignore, his appearance giving every indication of a man scorched by life. Indeed, as Mrs Desmoulins once acutely observed, he could have sat for the portrait of an alchemist's apprentice, his complexion mottled as if he had breathed in the fumes of the crucible, his clothes singed as though exposed to the sparks of a furnace. For a medical man, his rasping cough fell short of inspiring confidence; nevertheless, Johnson was fond of him. He was poor yet honest, which, as Goldsmith reminded the perplexed members of the Club, was recommendation enough for Samuel.

One particular mid-day, noting Johnson's gloomy countenance and listening to his oft-repeated sighs, Levet enquired if he was dissatisfied with the book he was perusing.

'I cannot tell,' came the reply, 'for I am unable to take in its meaning.'

'I have heard that knowledge can sometimes be a source of unhappiness,' Levet said. He was not often stirred into speech, but concern forced him to find words.

'That knowledge in some cases can produce unhappiness, I allow,' said Johnson, 'but upon the whole, knowledge *per se* is certainly an object which every man would wish to attain, although, perhaps, he may not take the trouble necessary for attaining it.'

'Why cannot you take in the meaning?' persisted Levet.

'Enough, Sir,' shouted Johnson, 'let me be,' and almost on the instant jumped up from the table and, patting Levet on the shoulder, apologised for speaking so roughly.

'Write to her,' urged Levet. 'Tell her it is important you return.'

'You talk in riddles,' bellowed Johnson, and glowered with such lasting severity that Levet fell silent, and shortly after went about his business.

For a further month Johnson waited for a summons from Hester Thrale. He spent his days in the company of Hawkins and Arthur Murphy, or else supped at the Mitre tavern and did battle with Goldsmith and Bennet Langton. He was not feeling well and fretted over an infection in his good eye. Besides, he was enraged by a scandalous item in the newspaper on the tables of the Turk's Head, which stated that an *eminent Brewer was very jealous of a certain Author in Folio, and perceived a strong resemblance to him in his eldest son.* Not one of the members of the Club was reckless enough to comment on this slander, not even the tactless Goldsmith, but he boiled within. Three rainswept nights in succession he perambulated about the town with James Boswell and saw nothing in the crowded streets that did not provide proof of the misery and decadence of humanity.

On the fourth evening, dining with Boswell at the house of General Paoli, he became entangled in a discussion as to whether the state of marriage was natural to man. It was his opinion that it was not, and he expressed it with some force, declaring that of the two inducements to marriage, the one being love, the other money, the first was unwise and the second ignoble. The General then proposed that the union of a man and woman in a state of nature would be more conducive to happiness than one conducted in a civilised society, for it would be free of the restraints deemed necessary to hold it together. This foolish supposition so irritated him that he cried out, 'A savage man and a savage woman would be so unrestrained, Sir, that when the man saw another woman that pleased him better he would leave the first forthwith.'

He was aware of the glances exchanged between Boswell and the General, and fancied they took his outburst to mean that he had been dissatisfied with dear, dead Tetty. In speaking so fiercely it was Levet he had in mind, who, following a dusky courtship in a coal-hole in Fetter Lane, had shackled himself to a woman later arrested for the picking of pockets. Lacking neither patience nor inclination to set his listeners straight, and angry both with himself and them, he quit the table immediately.

In Fleet Street he was overtaken by a horse ridden at such speed and with such disregard for those in its path that he was forced to jump for safety. Unbidden, a memory surfaced of his wedding day and of the ride to the church with his bride. Tired of her controlling the pace, first trotting ahead, then lagging behind, he had booted his horse's flank and, galloping out of sight round a bend in the road, waited in the shade of an oak tree; a gnat had bitten him on the little finger of his left hand. When Tetty caught up with him he had seen the shimmer of tears on her sun-dappled cheeks.

Pondering on the sensitivity of women, he continued on his way, and soon the image of his wife receded, replaced by thoughts of Hester Thrale.

Arriving at Johnson's Court, he stood for a while on the steps of his house, peering upwards at the smoke-filled heavens. At Streatham Park the night would be full of stars, bright as the shine in his dear mistress's eyes. How he longed to bask in the light of her smile.

A cat, not his, stalked the Court in pursuit of a rat, belly scraping the cobblestones. With a sudden surge of terror he remembered what he had once written for the final issue of the *Idler* on the subject of endings: 'In every life there are pauses and interruptions . . . points of time where one course of action ends and another begins; and by vicissitude of fortune, or alteration of employment, by change of place or loss of friendship, we are forced to say of something, *this is the last.*'

Entering the dark house, he climbed the stairs to his chamber, where, abandoning pride, he put pen to paper and begged Mrs Thrale to receive him. He could not wait, he wrote, to be with his Dear Lady, and hoped to give her some little comfort and amusement. A sudden draught extinguished the candle on his desk. He took it for an omen and paced his room in torment.

Not for the first time, it weighed on him that his progress through life had been ill directed, that he had disappointed himself more than others. Fame would not be heard beneath the tomb. His days and years had leaked away in common business and common amusements, and he had suffered his purposes to sleep until the time of action was past. When he compared what he had done, those articles, poems, that poorly received play which Davy Garrick had struggled to promote, his criticism of Shakespeare, the compilation of his *Dictionary*, with what he had left undone, he felt the effect which must always follow the comparison of imagination with reality – contempt for idleness, disgust at lack of resolve.

He would leave behind him no evidence of his having been, nothing which could be added to the system of life, had glided from youth to age among a flattering crowd, without any effort for distinction.

Worse, he had disregarded his father's wishes, squandered his time at Oxford, ignored his brother's pleas for help, spent Tetty's money, failed to attend his mother's funeral, allowed his mind to be polluted by impure thoughts, doubted the existence of a life beyond the grave.

Even now, as he got to his knees in an attitude of prayer, his body betrayed him and he experienced a stirring of lust he was powerless to subdue. Excitement mounting, he conjured up a flurry of skirts, a bulge of thigh, the exclamation mark of a scar above a pouting lip. As he gave way to this compulsion, raised hands lowering to pleasure himself, he discerned that it was not so much madness that disordered him but rather the human condition. Man's spiritual self, he reasoned, panting, trailed far behind the physical.

Mrs Thrale sent her coach for him the following week.

Mrs Salusbury, though weak, her breast horribly swollen and black in hue, insisted on coming downstairs every day, an unsteady descent she often accomplished without the help of the servants.

'I am not yet helpless,' she told her daughter, who, considerably alarmed and stepping backward, went before her with arms spread wide. Twice Mrs Salusbury fainted, though fortunately on the lowest step, where she was caught in the embrace of Mr Baretti.

Johnson was not present on these tottering occasions, being abed until noon. He was suffering from a persistent cough and the infection in his eye had grown worse. For some years past he had been reconciled to Mrs Salusbury, indeed, had grown fond, yet he could not help regarding her as a rival now that the attentions of her daughter were so diverted from himself. Mrs Thrale knew the best of him did not want to be a trouble, but his was a need not sufficiently seen to in childhood.

Nor were there others in the household who could distract him. Baretti had been charged with keeping the younger children out of the way of their dying grandmother, and Henry Thrale, the only man who held sway over Johnson, had absconded to Southwark, detesting sickness in women. Save for a brief visit from Frances Reynolds and a tedious one from a rustic pair of Streatham neighbours, company no longer came to the house. Johnson continued to instruct Queeney in Latin, but the pain of his eye shortened his temper and he grew weary of begging her pardon.

He took to following Mrs Thrale from room to room, endeavouring to engage her in conversation. If she did not answer him immediately or her gaze wandered from his face, he showed his displeasure by stamping his foot. When she hid in her chamber and did not answer his peevish knocking, he paced the passage outside, muttering aloud between bouts of coughing.

One warm afternoon when she was resting in the drawing room – she was yet again expecting a child and her back ached – her mother dozing on the couch and Queeney reading at the table, Johnson entered on tiptoe, finger to his lips, and made an elaborate dumbshow of searching for a book left in the recess of the window. Unaware of the sleeping dog, he trod full upon it, at which Belle let out a hideous howl, causing Mrs Salusbury to start up in terror. Exasperated beyond endurance, Mrs Thrale cried out, 'This will not do, Sir,' and burst into noisy tears.

She sought him out some hours later and made her peace with him. He was seated at his desk separating orange peel into heaps. She had thought he would upbraid her, but he was pathetically pleased to be forgiven and covered her hand with kisses. She was not sure she liked him abject, for his roughness of manner and strong convictions were the qualities she found exciting.

The servant bringing up a bowl of warm water, she bathed Johnson's eye most tenderly. 'It is not', she said, 'that I hold you in less regard than formerly, merely that I am preoccupied with my mother and Lucy. My mother I know I shall lose . . . I pray that Lucy will be saved.'

At this his tears ran so freely there was no need of salt. When he was able to speak, he said he had written her a letter which he wished her to read when she was alone. It was not for careless eyes and was in French.

'Why French?' she asked.

'The sentiments in it', he said, 'are best conveyed in another language.'

She waited until Mrs Salusbury fell asleep before reading it. It was true she was not alone, Queeney sitting on the opposite side of the bed holding her grandmother's hand, but she felt that neither the young girl nor the old woman could be categorised as careless.

Johnson's words were not easy to make sense of, his sight having become so impaired that his handwriting was jagged. He began with accusations of neglect disguised beneath protestations of his own unworthiness and recognition of her sweetness of soul. As he did not want to be a nuisance, could she not invent a routine for him that would avoid putting the harmony of the house in peril? Seeing that he was expected *to spend several hours a day in profound solitude, should he prescribe himself to confined limits in the house*? Had he not, some time in the past, *provided her with the means by which she could enforce such a restriction*? It would be more befitting a *mistress* if she herself took the initiative and spared him the necessity of constraining himself. He would keep to his chamber . . . she had only to turn the key in the lock twice a day. Her inconsistency of nature had led her to forget her promises of help and forced him into repeated solicitations for her attention, provoking in him an abnegation of pride which he found horrifying. He concluded with the hope that she would continue to keep him *in that slavery you know so well how to make happy.*

Having read the letter through, Mrs Thrale felt first bemusement, then anger – she crumpled the paper in her fist – then sadness, at which emotion she smoothed out the page as though calming a bird with a damaged wing. Despite its bold phrases and dictatorial tone, it was the letter of a man struck down . . . though, on reflection, perhaps that of a spoilt child was nearer the mark.

She rose at once, determined to put his mind at rest, and no sooner had put foot to stair than he appeared on the landing ahead. It was now dusk and the servants had not yet lit the lamps; he was holding a candle in one hand and his shadow leapt the wall.

Queeney, curious as to her mother's abrupt departure from Mrs Salusbury's bedside, followed her. She was astonished to see Mr Johnson and Mamma struggling together on the landing. They seemed to be wrestling for possession of a length of chain attached to some metal object that knocked repeatedly against the wainscotting of the window.

Mr Johnson shouted out, 'You will use it,' and Mamma shouted back, 'I will not,' and at that moment from the nursery above came the sound of desperate crying; it was Lucy, a martyr to the infection in her ear. Mamma dropped the chain and fled higher.

Queeney stared up at Mr Johnson. He was holding the candle flame too close to his head and a small curdle of smoke issued from the top-piece of his wig. Dashing his fist against his forehead he turned and stumbled off to his room, the chain and its attachment, like a dead dog on a leash, bouncing behind him.

The next morning when Queeney asked what had disturbed Mr Johnson, Mamma said he was unhappy for Mrs Salusbury. 'The thought of death frightens him,' she explained. 'His own as well as hers. I am trying to persuade him to accompany James Boswell to Scotland.'

Though Queeney had not met Mr Boswell she knew he was a lawyer who was in awe of Mr Johnson, hung on his every word and desired he should go with him on a tour of his native Hebrides. Mr Garrick likened him to the buffoon Pantalone, and Mr Goldsmith said he was of no account, but Papa held he should not be so easily dismissed.

Later that day Mrs Thrale replied to Johnson and left the letter on her work table while she attended to Mrs Salusbury. As it was not folded, Queeney read it; she found it overdone. Mamma asked what more care could she give her dear Mr Johnson that she did not already give, what tenderness that he had not already experienced? Diversion would be his best medicine and Boswell his best physician. Farewell and be good, the letter ended, and *do not quarrel with your governess for not using the rod enough*. Queeney reasoned this last sentence was meant to be humorous, for it was only children that got whipped.

All the same, she thought it an odd exercise, writing to someone who lived under the same roof.

To Miss Laetitia Hawkins,
2 Sion Row,
Twickenham

December 6th, 1807

Dear Miss Hawkins,
You persist, and with each enquiry I am drawn back
to years best forgotten. I regret I can tell you little
regarding the failure of the Thrale Brewery; I was
but eight years old at the time and my dear father
did not think it necessary to acquaint me with the
facts. Sufficient to say, that, owing to my mother's
desire for expansion, both at Streatham Park and the
Brewery, my father was forced to borrow money at
exorbitant rates of interest, a debt he did not shake
off for a further nine years – which burden
undoubtedly led to a decline in his health. At the
time of the crisis, my mother, though it is to be
presumed that she acted without malice, was
peculiarly supportive of Perkins, chief clerk to the
Brewery, who, seeking financial advantage,
threatened to resign, thus causing my dear father
further aggravation.

    I cannot, at this distance, remember the name of
Miss Porter's cat, the death of whom was
commemorated by a candlelit ceremony conducted
beneath the mulberry tree. Dr Johnson did indeed

have a pet hen. It was called Socrates, on account of
its persistent squawking.

My grandmother died in her bed at Streatham, a
day or so after my father had carried her in his arms
to see the finishing of the library.

The argument you mention, the one between Mr
Goldsmith and Dr Johnson on the subject of the
regrettable peeling of oil paint – it was the colour
crimson that was at fault – from the canvases of Sir
Joshua Reynolds, took place in Bolt Court. I have
every reason to remember the occasion as only that
morning my father had given me an amber necklace,
which treasured possession I wear to this day.

I remain,
Yours sincerely,

H. M. Thrale

I do not recall Dr Johnson speaking of Francis
Barber in other than the warmest of terms. Nor did
he treat him as a low servant. Once, in my presence,
Mrs Desmoulins referred to him as a *blackamoor*, at
which Dr J, exceedingly vexed, told her to mind her
tongue.

YESTERDAY *n.f. (from* ᵹᵻᵲᴛᴀɴᴆᴁᵹ, *Saxon)*

The day laſt paſt; the next day before today

To-morrow, and to-morrow, and to-morrow,
Creeps in this petty pace from day to day,
To the laſt ſyllable of recorded time;
And all our yeſterdays have lighted fools
The way to duſty death.

Shakeſpeare's *Macbeth*

A fter visiting the nursery to kiss little Ralph goodbye – his head was very large and his mouth drooled in spite of his not yet teething – Mrs Thrale went down into the hall and stood inside the porch to watch her husband direct the loading of the carriage. Through the pale mist came the bleating of sheep and the trill of birdsong.

'There is something wrong with his understanding,' she said, to no one in particular. She was referring to the child whose fat cheek she had just pecked and in whose eyes she had seen no sparkle of wit. It crossed her mind that his shrill cries were not unlike the twitterings of young thrushes . . . and who could distinguish the tweetings of hunger from those of vacuity?

She reasoned her fancies sprang from the strain of settling the children before embarking on her travels. Yesterday
she had taken Sophy to lodge with her sister Susannah at
Mrs Cumyns's boarding school in Kensington. The death of
Mrs Salusbury, followed so swiftly by that of dearest Lucy,
had chilled her heart; she felt herself less capable of affection
than before and would not miss either girl too much, Sophy
being petulant and Susannah not immediately likeable.

Harry was her main concern, for though he was content
enough to attend St Thomas's School by day, he refused to
board nights and had threatened, should he not be fetched
home to sleep, to run away to sea. He had inherited his
father's inordinate appetite and she feared that in her
absence he would take liberties in ordering his own dinners,
thus overloading his belly. He had such winning ways she
did not trust the servants to disobey him, though New
Nurse, who had fast become Old Nurse, swore she would
thwart him.

The carriage ready, Mr Johnson had to be sent for twice.
The footman reported that he was dressed, but was having
difficulty in deciding which books he should leave behind.
When at last he did appear he descended the steps with
speed, his face expressing great good humour. Since his
jaunt to Scotland with Boswell, and the completion of his
journal of the Hebridean tour – only that week he had dispatched the first sheets back to the printers – he was in
favour of motion and was looking forward to introducing
his dear master and mistress to his home town of Lichfield.
Yet, even as the occupants of the coach shifted to make
space for him, he abruptly turned and made off in the
direction of the library door at the side of the house. He
was dressed in his Sunday coat, but his shirt tail hung out

at the back. This comical oversight prompted Henry Thrale to repeat for the benefit of Mr Baretti one of Garrick's many anecdotes concerning Johnson's dismal efforts, in the early days of his marriage, to run a school in Staffordshire.

'There were but three pupils . . . Davy the oldest. Late at night . . . young gentlemen had the habit of peeping through keyhole of Johnson's bedchamber. One occasion . . . spied Sam at table . . . heard Tetty's pleas that he should come to bed. Aware of something dangling alongside his chair . . . Sam mistakes it for his shirt . . . tucks the cloth into his breeches and strides about, reciting aloud what he has just written . . . Tetty, shivering, tries to retrieve departing bedclothes . . .'

'I see him, I see him,' cried Baretti, slapping his thigh in delight.

'Her complaints grow louder . . . Sam, misinterpreting feverish cries . . . discards shirt in flurry of expectation . . . shouts out, "I'm coming, my Tetsie, I'm coming."'

At this conclusion, Baretti laughed so loudly that Mrs Thrale thrust her handkerchief into his mouth. She was not a moment too soon, for just then Johnson reappeared at a run, puffed past the carriage, climbed the steps to the porch and knocked with his fist three times upon the stone head of the griffin beside the door.

Mrs Thrale thought again of the child in the nursery; no matter how vigorously one tapped there would never be a response.

On the journey to London, Henry Thrale and Johnson dozed on and off, neither being given to liveliness much before noon. Queeney coughed and wriggled a great deal. As they approached the river, she suddenly asked her father why Mr Garrick had peeped through keyholes and if it was not rude of him. Fortunately, Johnson was asleep and Thrale too drowsy to reply, although Baretti uttered a bellow of mirth wild enough to wake the dead. But for his presence Mrs Thrale would have slapped Queeney.

Baretti was volatile and had odd ideas on the nurturing of children. He was forever hiding the ivory whistle she used to summon the younger ones for punishment; nor had she forgotten his snapping the nursery rod in two after she had whipped Harry for scribbling across Mr Johnson's globe. Sometimes she reflected on how long it might be before the Italian, in one of his tempers, would resort to the fruit knife that had so nearly sent him to the gallows.

Baretti said his goodbyes when the carriage reached Joshua Reynolds's studio in Leicester Fields. He was to sit for his likeness, one of a series of portraits of Streatham habitués commissioned by Thrale, of which those of Garrick and dear, lost Goldsmith were already completed and could be seen displayed on the walls of his library.

Johnson, shirt still dangling below the tails of his coat, insisted on alighting and accompanying Baretti to the top step, where, as Thrale observed, he shook his friend's hand as though they would not meet again this side of the grave. Miss Reynolds appeared briefly in the doorway; seeing the carriage, she darted out of sight, but not before Mrs Thrale had taken notice of her dishevelled appearance; it was probable she and her brother had been indulging in yet another of their disagreements.

Intrigued by the strange roarings and shriekings coming from the garden across the square, Queeney scrambled down into the street. She grew excited and would have run off to investigate if her mother hadn't caught hold of her skirt.

Returning, and learning the reason for the child's animation, Johnson told her that John Hunter lived across the way
and promised he would take her one day to visit him. The
beast noises coming from the garden, he explained, were
those of a tiger and a collection of gibbons, the latter being
a species of monkey, grey in colour, almost hairless and pos-
sessing hind legs capable of leaping great distances. Had she
been here the week before she would have heard the barking
of numerous dogs, some of whose stomachs had been cut
open and filled with warm milk before being hanged.

'Why?' questioned Queeney, wide-eyed.

'It was an experiment to ascertain the absorption of fat
through the abdominal lymphatics into the thoracic duct.'

'Why?' Queeney repeated.

'In the pursuit of knowledge, Sweeting,' Johnson said.
'The day after, by Dr Levet's account, Mr Hunter dissected
an old man and observed that the veins of his intestines
were filled with white fluid instead of red blood.'

'Did Mr Hunter hang the old man?' Queeney asked.

'Come,' ordered Mrs Thrale, frowning at Johnson and
pulling Queeney into the carriage.

Seated and addressing Mrs Thrale, Johnson acknowledged he was not acquainted with the anatomist, but had
attended two of his lectures in the company of Levet and
found both instructive. One had dealt with states of mind,
in which it was proposed, and who could gainsay it, that
the mind was often in opposition to itself, and that one
state of mind, if strong, would always get the better of
another state which is weak.

'How true,' murmured Mrs Thrale, thinking of
Johnson's own mind, and in particular of its perilous state
when overcome by melancholy.

'The second lecture', Johnson told her, 'had to do with sexual selection. A man, according to Hunter, has an appetite to enjoy all women; but if the mind has formed itself to any particular woman, the appetite or enjoyment can be suspended until—' here, he caught Mrs Thrale's reproving glance and broke off in mid-sentence. Moments later, as the coach turned out of the square, he remarked, 'The skin is affected by feelings of shame . . .'

'As in blushing,' supplied Mrs Thrale.

'Quite so. The secretion or even the non-secretion of the testicles takes place under certain states of the mind—'

'Enough, Sir,' barked Henry Thrale, and instantly obtained silence.

They drove to St Albans, where they halted to enjoy an excellent dinner with Ralph Smith, a first cousin of Thrale. Mrs Smith went through the usual stages, disbelief followed by growing regard, experienced by those encountering Johnson for the first time. As she afterwards confided to Mrs Thrale, what with that ill-fitting wig, those tremulous hootings, that untucked shirt – not to mention the convulsive jerkings of lower limbs – she feared they had brought an idiot to sit with them at table. It was with difficulty the party got away to continue on their journey to Lichfield.

The coach approaching Offley, Mrs Thrale grew warm with memories of times gone by. It was hereabouts she had spent girlhood summers in the house of her father's brother, Sir Thomas Salusbury. As the carriage rolled down the country lanes and slowed to cross a timber bridge above a stream, she recalled going fishing with her father, perched on a grassy bank holding a willow twig from which dangled a length of cord with a hook tied to its end.

'Cast, cast,' her father had bidden, only her throw was too feeble and the cord sailed backwards and fell across a tussock of weed. 'Damn you, damn you to hell,' shouted her father, shaking his fist at the horizon. She had taken to her heels in tears, thinking it was she who made him angry, until her mother had explained it was Sir Thomas, out hunting and hill-topping in a postchaise, whom he cursed.

'Stop . . . stop the coach,' Mrs Thrale ordered.

'Are you ill, Hester?' called her husband, as she stepped out into the evening air. She didn't reply, at which he followed her, though merely to piss into the hedgerow.

Mrs Thrale, staring upwards at the racing clouds, divined in their flight across the heavens a likeness to the fleeting years. She had been fortunate, she thought, for in their swift passing there had been nothing to cause her lasting despair, not even the harvesting of her children – for death was a natural event and in accordance with God's will.

She was cheerful when she returned to the carriage, so much so that she was moved to kiss the sniffling Queeney on both cheeks. Johnson was ready to explode; any unwarranted delay on their journey to Lichfield caused him agitation.

They spent the night at Dunstable, in an inn close by the parish church. The accommodation was far from pleasing, the rooms unclean and the food served up on scratched plate. The service, too, was tardy, owing to the landlord being deficient of a leg, which loss, so he would have them believe, he had suffered when the ship on which he had served his country had run aground near Providence, Rhode Island, and been attacked by patriots.

Queeney's cold now gathering strength – she coughed and sneezed in rotation – Mrs Thrale was anxious to put her to bed. She had not brought female servants and was obliged to attend to the child herself. This was not as irksome as it might have been, for Johnson was wearying them all with his knowledge of the town, informing them that its name was derived from the wool market or 'staple' established in the region of the chalk downs by Augustine monks in the twelfth century. Neither skirmishes in North America nor weaving in Bedfordshire arousing her interest, she retired, leaving the talkative Johnson in the company of a comatose Henry Thrale.

The following morning it was past ten o'clock before the party left Dunstable. Johnson, who the night before had insisted on a departure not later than six o'clock, failed to rise for a further four hours. Nor did he apologise, though Mrs Thrale could tell by the way he left his breakfast roll untouched that he felt discomforted.

It was moonlit midnight when their coach clattered into the yard of the Swan Inn, Lichfield.

When Queeney awoke, Mrs Thrale brought her a dish of warm bread and milk. Owing to a prodigious sneeze, the milk slopped on to the quilt. Anxious to appear well – her mother was a great advocate of dosing and purging – the child subdued her cough and professed to feeling quite herself again. In spite of this, Mrs Thrale swore she detected an obstruction in her breathing and warned that an application of goose fat to the chest might be necessary.

Dressed, and about to descend the stairs, Mrs Thrale was surprised to spy Mr Johnson pacing the hall below. Seeing her, he bounded upwards and, fiercely studying her garments, cried out, 'No, no, it will not do.' On her enquiring what was wrong, he informed her that the morning gown she was wearing was of too dark a colour, and that she must change into something more gay and splendid. For one so poorly sighted, and one, moreover, so slovenly in his own dress, it was astonishing how critical he could be of the apparel of others.

Cross, but bearing in mind that he wished her to make an impression on his Lichfield acquaintances, Mrs Thrale did as he bid and presently returned in a hooped gown of blue silk edged with swan feathers. Her husband murmured that it was inappropriate, the weather being unsettled and the inhabitants of Lichfield more than likely rustic in attire.

'I cannot please everyone,' she said, exasperated, to which Thrale replied, 'It is fortunate I am a good-natured man.'

No sooner were the words out of his mouth than Mrs Thrale turned pale, the phrase having been used for the title of a play by poor Goldsmith, who had died, submerged in debt and in great torment of mind, earlier that year. Hand to her heart, she looked anxiously at Johnson. Conscious of her concern, he said gruffly, 'I loved Goldy, but though I can *say* I miss him, I cannot swear to *feeling* it.'

Much relieved at his attitude, for had he descended into a gloom their visit to Lichfield would have been past mending, the Thrales followed him out of the inn.

They had scarcely set foot in the street before Johnson was waylaid by numerous passers-by, all of whom claimed to have known him intimately in his youth. Some had splashed with him in Stowe Pool or else daydreamed beside him on the school bench; others had stood guard while he raided the orchard in George Lane, run whooping at his elbow as the cattle swayed home from the darkening meadows. He was clearly gratified at the respect shown to him, though in an aside he confessed he did not know from Adam many who so vigorously shook his hand.

To reward Queeney, who, in order to deflect Mamma's medical attentions, was conducting herself with great fortitude, Johnson first took them to Mr Green's Museum behind the cathedral. Here they viewed a curious collection of natural and artificial rarities, chief among them the skeleton of an Oronuto savage from Ethiopia, his bones sprouting porcupine quills. This wondrous monstrosity, it was asserted, was the only one of its kind in the world.

Mr Green was absent when they arrived. Word being sent, he came on the trot and greeted Johnson with great civility, indeed, fussed over his visitors to such an extent that after barely a quarter of an hour Henry Thrale declared himself fatigued and was escorted to Mr Green's inner sanctum, where he lay down on an ancient couch believed to have belonged to the Emperor Nero.

Queeney was enchanted with a statue of the dog Cerberus, minus two of its heads, seated beside an enthroned Hades, and insisted on fondling its chipped ears. According to her, the remaining head bore a resemblance to Belle, being equally bad-tempered about the snout. She told Mr Johnson it was a pity her cabinet was not large enough to hold a similar object, Brighthelmstone shells and Mr Pope's snippet being but poor substitutes for such rarities. He agreed and promised to search for something equally exotic, if smaller in size, when next in Oxford. Mrs Thrale pinched Queeney for being so outspoken and hurried her away from the statue, for its accompanying written information dwelt in some detail on the lord of the underworld's rape of Persephone.

Johnson, although not in Mr Green's hearing, grew

heated at the labelling of the Oronuto savage as a monstrosity, wondrous or not. He argued that if the poor wretch had indeed had the misfortune to grow quills instead of hair, then it would have been better to have buried him six foot under rather than expose his remains to the gaze of an ignorant populace. Nor was he convinced of the authenticity of the exhibit, having seen the very same phenomenon on show at Mr Leary's establishment in Hampstead. 'It is a copy,' he shouted, rattling the skeleton with his stick, 'and one inferior in every degree.'

He grew so red in the face that Mrs Thrale felt alarm, the more so because she understood the reason for his outburst; hadn't Johnson himself, from an early age, been an object of curiosity? Tears filling her eyes at the thought of his boyhood misery, she pretended an interest in the intestine of a sturgeon. Queeney, watching as always, noticed the way she clenched on her lip to avoid yawning.

Next they visited the cathedral, where Henry Thrale, complaining of a stiffness in the joints, said he preferred to stroll about the Close and view the Bishop's Palace. Queeney begged to accompany him, but Mamma wouldn't hear of it.

'You must see inside the Minster', she said, 'and gaze upon the spot where Mr Johnson, when a child, nearly perished from a collapse of the roof. Imagine the scene . . . the din of masonry, the screams . . . the volume of dust billowing outwards . . . and small Samuel, hands like talons, scrambling upwards to leap from a window.'

Hearing this, Johnson shook his head in mock despair. 'As is the way of women, Sweeting, and of Mamma in particular, her account is beset with inaccuracies. The falling of a roof, or rather the dropping of a few pieces of mortar and stone, took place at St Mary's church in the Market Square—'

'This church, that church,' cried Mrs Thrale, 'what does it signify?'

'—after which mild disturbance my father took me by the hand and walked me through the door.'

'It is the nub of the story that matters,' persisted Mrs Thrale, an assertion which Johnson was strenuously about to dispute when he was approached by the Subchanter of the cathedral, a sober gentleman who miraculously made no reference to a schoolyard encounter and merely evinced a knowledge of his reputation.

Queeney, trailing in their wake, presently lagged so far behind that she found herself alone. At once she turned tail and sped out of the doors in search of her father. At her headlong arrival in the Close crows lifted from the trees and soared croaking into the heavens. The clapping of wings was so clamorous that she stopped on the path and stuffed her fingers in her ears; in her head stones spilled from the skies. Just then she spied Papa, approaching from the west corner of the Bishop's Palace. He was smiling. She ran to him; Papa had a beautiful smile, one that always took away her fright. He told her that he had met a comical old man, a beater of silver who vowed he was yet another friend of Mr Johnson when young.

'Did you believe him?' asked Queeney. 'Did he tell you that he had swum with him in the pool, or had shared the same Grammar in school?'

'Neither learning nor water was mentioned,' said Papa, 'only that Sam was a prodigious climber of trees.'

The sun sailing free of the clouds, he led her to a convenient seat, where they lolled companionably together in its golden rays and amused themselves with the recitation of nursery rhymes. Though she considered herself far too old for such childish entertainment, Queeney submitted to it for Papa's sake. It was not a chore, for he made her giggle when he stuck his thumb in his mouth and played at being Little Jack Horner.

An hour later Mrs Thrale and Mr Johnson emerged from the cathedral. Engaged in bidding farewell to the Subchanter, they dallied so long on the steps that Thrale, patience fast fading, shouted out brusquely, 'Come, Hester, the morning is almost gone.'

Mr Johnson, with considerably more alacrity than Mrs Thrale, hurried towards him. Puffing, he asked if curiosity would persuade him to view the house in which he had first drawn breath, to which Thrale replied kindly enough, 'Love, not mere curiosity, will dance me there, Sam. Be so good as to lead the way.'

They were walking the short distance to the Market Square when Queeney uttered a yelp of pain. Her mother, scurrying behind, had trodden on her heel. 'Keep up,' urged Mrs Thrale, and forged on.

The street now becoming more crowded, Johnson looked round to make sure his companions were close. Seeing the hopping Queeney, he retraced his steps and asked what was wrong. Tearfully she told him Mamma had struck her shoe against her heel, and indeed there was a small stain of crimson on her stocking.

'Does it hurt?' he asked.

'Yes it does,' she wailed, 'the more so because Mamma did not say she was sorry.' She stared resentfully ahead at the figure of Papa weaving his way between the market stalls, chased by the bobbing feathers of Mamma's bonnet.

Mr Johnson said, 'Would the hurt go away if Mamma expressed sorrow?'

'No,' she admitted, 'but at least Mamma would know what she had done.'

'What advantage is there if injury has to be spelt out?' he demanded.

'It is not you who have been trodden on,' she retorted.

'That is true,' he allowed, 'which is why we must keep it from Mamma, for should she learn of the wound she will most certainly insist on returning to the inn to attend to it. Such a fuss will hinder the excursion to my birthplace.'

'It is not a wound,' Queeney admitted, 'merely a scraping.'

'Quite so . . . and Mamma does not always have a gentle touch, particularly when anxious.'

Observing him, Queeney was aware of the trembling of his large lips, of the expression of dismay in his oyster eyes. He was not, after all, as arrogant as he would have one believe.

She said, 'Heaven forbid I should be a hindrance,' and, limping, followed him across the square. He and Mamma have much in common, she thought, for both are selfish.

The house in which Johnson had been born faced St Mary's church and the Market Hall. It had been built by his father, the bookseller, and Johnson still held the lease. Miss Porter, daughter of Tetty by a previous marriage, had lived here until the death of his mother; inheriting money from an uncle, she had then moved to a residence of her own. It was presently occupied by an impoverished schoolmaster who, given notice of the arrival of his landlord, had seen fit to absent himself for the day.

Mrs Thrale was surprised at the size of the building; she

had understood Johnson came from humble beginnings. Unwisely, she said as much, at which he snapped, 'In regard to myself, Madam, the word humble, implying acceptance of one's station, is not one I would choose. Straitened circumstances is the phrase best illustrative of my father's later years.'

At that moment, fortunately for Mrs Thrale, he noticed that a section of the railing encircling the cellar steps had rusted away. His vexation diverted, he stood there, muttering and gesticulating, as though such a loss of ironwork would cause the house to totter on its foundations. It was Thrale who took him by the arm and marched him to the door.

As he conducted his friends from room to room, Johnson regaled them with childhood reminiscences. For instance, on a certain step on the stairs his brother Nathaniel – little Natty – in pursuit of a mouse had tumbled over and bumped to the bottom, where he lay bleeding from a cut above the eyebrow. The blow was superficial, but he had feigned insensibility. On aping a return to consciousness his piteous moans and tragic glances had rivalled those of a Davy Garrick. This recollection was firm in Johnson's memory on account of his mother blaming him for Natty's mishap and shutting him in the coal-hole for several hours by way of punishment. He emerged, so he said, as dusky of hue as Frank Barber, and not only on the outside; in suffering such an injustice his heart had turned black.

In the cellar kitchen he pointed a finger at the self-same stool on which he had sat reading *Hamlet, Prince of Denmark*, and, coming to the scene in which the shade of the dead King appeared, had found it so scary that he had

flung the book aside and rushed up into the street to be rid
of ghosts. 'Nightly in the adjacent room', he continued,
'my father closed his account books and leaving behind an
outer door rotting on its hinges, climbed the stairs to bolt
the front entrance against thieves.'

The recalling of these last two incidents, the one, as he
acknowledged, induced by an excess of imagination, the
other from an absence of it, caused him to shake with
laughter.

'I do not think a heart can turn black,' Queeney said,
'not unless the blood is disordered.'

Catching Henry Thrale regarding him with something
like alarm – he was a man made uncomfortable by extremes
of feeling – Johnson strove valiantly to control himself.
Dashing the water from his eyes, he spluttered, 'There is
something in the cadence of the words, *Adieu, adieu,
Remember me*, that to this day strikes a chill to my soul.'

Mrs Thrale, understanding the ambiguity of his mood,
smiled reassuringly. Merriment often seized him inappro-
priately, due to a surplus of emotion.

She was glad his sight was deficient, for the place was in
a sorry state, woodwork dull, ceilings stained with damp
and not a rug on the floor free from the attentions of moth.
As if he read her thoughts, Johnson said, 'It does not appear
that the schoolmaster is a man much given to the pursuit of
cobwebs.' Leaping into the air he struck out with his stick,
and added, 'But then, no more am I,' which was indeed the
truth.

'I have heard', said Mrs Thrale, clawing at her cheek to
remove a gossamer strand, 'that spiders make very good
mothers,' a remark which tickled Queeney and provoked
giggles.

In spite of herself, Mrs Thrale began to feel uneasy as she traipsed about the house, a sensation which threatened to overwhelm her upon entering the room in which Johnson's mother had given him life. He had confided in her so many details of his beginnings that here the ghosts of yesterday came crowding in, for the bed was still there, the same on which he and little Natty had lain while their mother read to them of Hell-fire.

Above the bedhead a square of wall was scorched, as though a candle flame had flared too close. Attempts had been made to rub it clean, and merely enlarged the discoloration. Gaze fixed upon the mark, it seemed to her that it took on the form of a child's face, mouth open in a wail of silent terror. Outside, rain fell, blurring the outline of the church in which Johnson had been christened; in the tiny spatterings against the window glass she heard the crackle of flames.

Turning faint, she sank on to a chair, one of whose castors was missing, causing it to lurch sideways. Johnson protested this was not the time for her to grow lethargic – she had not yet seen the upstairs rooms once inhabited by Dr Swinfen, player of the violin and father of Mrs Desmoulins.

Anxious to disguise her feelings, Mrs Thrale told him she was taking in the sounds of the market place, as he must have done as a child.

'What sounds?' he probed.

'The bellowing of an animal in pain,' she improvised, for just then Queeney succumbed to a fit of coughing. 'Similar to the tortured bear in the Market Square.'

'What bear?' he demanded.

'The one Mrs Desmoulins spoke of,' she said, 'the time

Dr Delap fled down the stairs and we fetched you home from Johnson's Court.'

'You talk in riddles,' he thundered. 'There were never bears in Lichfield Market, tormented or otherwise, only bulls.'

They left the house soon after, being expected, so he told them, at Miss Porter's a little before noon. Mrs Thrale demurred at going on foot in the rain, but Johnson said she would look foolish travelling so short a distance in a carriage. She protested he must at least allow her to return to the Swan Inn to put on overshoes. He said she couldn't; growing irritable, he flapped his hand at her as though shooing away a fly. She thought he was possibly agitated at the prospect of introducing her to Miss Porter and held her tongue.

The number of pedestrians thronging the narrow thoroughfare forced the party into a straggling procession. Mrs Thrale was much inconvenienced by the width of her hooped gown. When the cathedral bells rang out to mark the hour, crows pecking at the garbage-strewn cobblestones surged upwards and flew so close to her bonnet that she shrieked. Repeatedly she had to look over her shoulder to make sure Queeney was safely keeping to the wall; the child had refused to walk ahead and was limping to draw attention to herself.

They found Miss Porter sitting at cards with three elderly ladies, sisters to one another, and a gentleman with a patch over his eye. The ladies openly studied Mrs Thrale from head to foot; indeed, one was ignorant enough to rise from the table and encircle her.

Smiling graciously, Mrs Thrale strove to be pleasant. She was curious to discover in the daughter something of the departed wife, the better to understand the attraction

Sam had once felt. Save for Garrick, she knew no one who had been well acquainted with Tetty; there was Mrs Desmoulins, it was true, her companion for many years, but she, still smarting under the delusion that the Thrales had robbed her of Johnson, could scarcely be persuaded to be civil, let alone forthcoming.

Queeney was astonished at the antics of Miss Porter. From what Mr Johnson had led her to believe, there was fondness between them, yet here she was, for the benefit of her Lichfield cronies, back turned to him, rolling her eyes and grimacing to indicate how odd she thought him – Harry couldn't have behaved worse. Fortunately Mr Johnson was too busy bowing and kissing hands to notice.

The introductions over with, he gave his attention solely to his stepdaughter and the one-eyed gentleman, who, it transpired, he had known in his youth and who had travelled from Birmingham to renew their acquaintance. New people he never loved to be in company with, except young and fair ladies, in which category the sisters could not by any stretch of the imagination be said to belong.

The conversation that ensued had to do with changes in the town since Johnson's last visit, Miss Porter's aches and pains and the continuing scandal surrounding the widow Mearns, who was widely suspected, though it could not be proved, of poisoning her husband by means of honey cakes.

Mr Johnson became animated; he said the first classical description of honey death was to be found in Xenophon's *Anabasis*, Book IV, Chapter VIII. On the march to Trebizond the soldiers found a large number of beehives . . . all who had eaten a little of the plundered syrup resembled drunken men; those who had eaten a lot were like madmen and died mouthing obscenities.

'How unsettling,' said Miss Porter, handing round the biscuit barrel.

Queeney found some of the talk difficult to follow, as did Papa, who was considerably foxed by the broad vowels of the company. Mamma was smiling away and nodding, but she was surely putting up a pretence. They were familiar with Johnson's speech, the way he pronounced 'once' as 'woonce' and 'there' to rhyme with 'fear', but the gentleman with the eye-patch had a language of his own. When offered a third glass of wine, he said something like, 'I dare'st not, for I may then becoom joongle-brained and later an admiral of the High Seas.'

Papa said, 'I do not follow. Are you an admiral, Sir?'

'Nay,' came the reply, 'do I look it?' at which one of the old ladies said, 'He means, Sir, that if he drinks overmuch he will likely vomit into your lap.' Papa thought this funny and laughed out loud. Mr Johnson looked gratified; he hadn't heard the exchange, but was delighted that Papa was enjoying himself.

The rain having stopped and, as she comically expressed it, the sun come out to play, Miss Porter suggested Queeney might like to see the little garden behind the house. 'Mrs Scase will go with you,' she said. Queeney would rather have gone on her own, although Mrs Scase did not seem as decrepit as her sisters; the hair drifting from her cap was red in parts and she walked without tottering.

The way into the garden was through a kitchen upon whose shelves, amid a clutter of pots and pans, was propped a glass case containing a fish, its shiny scales and bulging eye shimmering in a beam of sunlight. Mrs Scase said, 'At last we have found something here that makes you smile,' and led her outside, where she was encouraged to sit on a bench made from a length of gnarled wood laid across two barrels, the one smaller than the other. Queeney perched herself on the higher end, legs dangling.

It was an unusual form of seating, but then, neither was the garden of the usual kind, being without flowers and its beds entirely filled with giant cabbages, their leaves much disfigured from some seasonal blight. Beside a drooping pot plant on the path lay a dead bird eaten about the breast.

Mrs Scase was also not usual, in that she treated Queeney as an equal, seeking her opinion, without condescension, of the town, the people she had met and of Mr Johnson. While waiting for a reply the old woman leant forward and looked at her lips rather than into her eyes, as though she needed to be sure where the words came from. Queeney told her that she found the town pleasant enough and as yet had not truly met anyone. As for Mr Johnson, why, he was so much a portion of her life that opinions had long since been replaced by feelings, at which Mrs Scase slapped her knee and cried out, 'Well done, little Miss.'

Mrs Scase knew all about Mr Johnson, or rather about the boy he had once been. An aunt, she said, long dead, was cousin to a woman who boasted of being on calling terms with Mr Johnson's mother. Much of what she related was not new to Queeney, but Mrs Scase had a singular way of painting pictures in the head. The scars on his neck and the side of his face, she explained, came from a tubular disease, an infection, according to Dr Swinfen, caught from the babe's wet nurse, whose milk was tainted and whose own infant had been similarly afflicted. As she talked she stabbed the air with one plump finger by way of emphasis; at her side the blighted cabbages whimpered in the breeze.

Mrs Johnson, in spite of pride in her exalted Ford relations – they were a cut above those of the bookseller, Michael Johnson – put it about that it was an inherited condition, to lessen the guilt she felt at having farmed him out so perilously. The marks on the child's face stuck out more when his skin was new and if that wasn't enough he was partially deaf, all but blind in one eye and deficient of vision in the other. His Aunt Ford, seeing him for the first time, said she would not have picked up such a poor creature in the street.

'It is a wonder he did not die,' Queeney murmured, looking at the bird putrefying on the path. In the sunlight its black feathers shone blue. She thought of Lucy, who had merely suffered from a running of the ears, and of the dead Penelope in the cradle, who had expired from nothing at all.

'His mother took him to London to be touched by the Queen,' Mrs Scase told her, and Queeney said she knew that and had often fingered the medal Mr Johnson wore round his neck.

'Mrs Johnson thought the touching had saved him, but Dr Swinfen, being cautious, insisted an issue should be cut in the boy's arm to let out the infection, a wound which remained open until he was six years old.'

Poor little arm, thought Queeney, ashamed of the fuss she had made of her scraped heel.

'He was clever even then,' said Mrs Scase, 'forever learning things off by rote and scribbling verses and the like. Not that it raised much gaiety in him, for his home circumstances were blighted by reason of his father suffering under a sensation of gloomy despair, which mood was habitual to him. Nor was his mother, by all accounts, of much relief, for she had not the nous to understand either the child or the husband.'

How common that is, mused Queeney, gazing at the mottled cabbages.

'As a child he was remarkable for a violence of temper, no doubt due to his brain being too large.'

'He has a temper now,' Queeney said, 'though afterwards he often says how sorry he is.'

'There was one time in particular,' continued Mrs Scase, 'when he was but three years old. My aunt's cousin's neighbour was a witness to it, having set off to sell a piglet. The child attended a dame's school not a hundred yards from Breadmarket Street, taken and fetched each noon by a servant girl. One May morning, placing the pot to boil, she burnt her finger on the coals and spent too long jumping up and down to cool it. Samuel set off home alone, closely followed by the dame, who was anxious for his safety . . . she was a widow woman who had lost five children of her own to the small-pox and ever after laboured under an impediment of speech. At the junction of the road, unable to see clearly, Samuel got down on all fours and, feeling his way by means of the kennel running along the middle of the street, began to crawl towards his father's bookshop. The blue jacket he wore was stained black above the elbow . . . from the blood seeping out of the cut in his arm. "S-S-Sam," called the dame. "S-s-stop." A speckled hen, escaped from a market pen, strutted ahead of him, head jerking from left to right . . . my aunt's cousin's neighbour remembered the hen to her dying day—'

'Some hens are more memorable than others,' said Queeney. 'Mr Johnson had a pet one called Socrates.'

'The dame, fearful he would be run over by carts, ran to

haul him upright, at which he kicked out at her in a fury. When his mother took him to task for treating the dame so shamefully, do you know what the little creature replied?'

Queeney shook her head.

'That it was difficult for someone sick not to behave like a scoundrel. There were tears in his eyes, even before his whipping.'

'And the hen?' enquired Queeney. 'What of the hen?'

'Nothing is known,' said Mrs Scase, 'though I expect someone boiled it for dinner,' and she licked her lips as though tasting chicken meat. This amused Queeney; joining in the mime she jumped up and flapped her elbows. Her sudden movement unbalanced the seating – the plank of wood slid sideways, depositing Mrs Scase beneath the cabbage leaves.

The resulting cries of distress brought her sisters hobbling into the garden. It had not been much of a fall, but Mrs Scase made the most of it and moaned pitifully as she was helped upright. She was a well-nourished woman and by the time her sisters had got her indoors both trembled from their exertions. Miss Porter was talking to Mr Johnson and barely looked up, and Papa and the old gentleman with the eye-patch now dozed, so it was left to Mamma to fuss over Mrs Scase.

'Is it your ankle?' she cried, endeavouring to sound concerned.

'I have damaged my fundament,' Mrs Scase wailed, at which the old gentleman chortled. It was possible he was dreaming, for his eyes remained closed.

Mamma tried to break into Miss Porter's monologue. 'It would perhaps be advisable', she said, 'to send for a surgeon to check there are no bones broken.' Miss Porter replied,

'To the best of my knowledge there are no bones in the fundament,' and continued to address Mr Johnson. She was telling him about the cathedral and how the Brethren of the Corporation were threatening to censure the Dean for allowing the roof to fall into disrepair. Mr Johnson looked grave and made tut-tutting noises. All at once he rose from his chair and announced that they were to dine with Peter Garrick at four o'clock and must now take their leave. Mamma prodded Papa quite roughly on the shoulder; waking, he helped himself to the remaining crumbs in the biscuit barrel.

Miss Porter accompanied them to the door. Halfway there Mr Johnson turned round, murmuring that he had neglected to say goodbye to the sisters. Queeney, looking back as he opened the parlour door, clearly saw Mrs Scase sitting bolt upright, head swinging like a bull about to charge, feet scraping the carpet. It was a passable imitation, albeit exaggerated, of the mannerisms exhibited by the visitor who had supposedly departed. Caught in the act, Mrs Scase covered her face with her hands.

She need not have worried; Mr Johnson, having taken one foot over the threshold, came under his sometime compulsion of having to spin in a circle before continuing and observed nothing. Kissing the hand of each disconcerted sister, he bowed his way out.

Once in the street he expressed his disapproval of Miss Porter. Mrs Thrale, eager to learn the cause, hastened to keep pace with him. She had hoped it might be a personal objection and was disappointed, for his vexation was apparently due to her criticism of the Dean. 'If indeed lead is being removed from the roof,' he said, 'I do not doubt that it is a transaction undertaken for the benefit of the dispossessed.'

Mrs Thrale made no reply to this, having often remarked that Johnson had more regard for the poor than any man alive. Once, while walking with him past the cheap cookshops lining a particular alleyway in Covent Garden – they were to take tea with Davy Garrick – she had referred to the area as Porridge Island, at which he had snapped that she should not make light of what was serious to many. She had retorted that he misunderstood her intention and, stung by his tone, wondered aloud if it was not an affectation on his part, seeing his own circumstances were now so improved, that he should identify to such an extent with those less fortunate than himself. At this distance she could not remember his response, beyond his cheeks had glowed purple.

'I admired Miss Porter,' she told him, not altogether insincerely, 'though perhaps the more so when she checked my suggestion that a surgeon should be called.'

'She has little of Tetty in her,' said Johnson, 'if that is your meaning.'

Arriving at Dam Street, he pointed out the infant school he had attended. He added nothing more, save for remarking that it was here he had learnt his letters. Upon reaching the steps of a house some doors further, he stopped, and indicating the porch with his stick urged his companions to bow their heads and give thanks to God for a certain deaf mute named Dyott. A monument, he said, should be erected to the man, for in the Civil War it was he who had caused the death of Lord Brooke, leader of the Parliamentary forces, a stray bullet from his musket entering Brooke's visor and displacing his brain as he stood on that very step.

Queeney paid particular attention to the porch, even

going so far as to rub a licked finger across the woodwork, as though hoping to bring it away bloodstained. Mrs Thrale rebuked her sharply, but Johnson said he had performed the selfsame gesture as a boy and that imagination must never be crushed.

Mrs Thrale could not let that pass. 'By degrees the reign of fancy is confirmed,' she quoted. 'Then fictions begin to operate as realities. They grow first imperious, and in time despotic. False opinions fasten on the mind, and life passes in dreams of rapture or anguish.'

'You have it in the wrong order, Madam,' he said, but could not help looking pleased that she remembered what he had once written.

On their return to the inn Mrs Thrale hurried upstairs to change her gown, its feathers bedraggled from the rain.

'Queeney,' she sighed, peering into the looking glass on the dressing table, 'it is a misfortune to belong to the weaker sex. We do not see either Papa or Mr Johnson hastening to repair his clothes or attend to his complexion.'

'Why is Miss Porter so old?' asked Queeney. 'Mrs Strickland has a daughter from a previous marriage and she is not yet seventeen.'

Mr Johnson's wife, Tetty, Mrs Thrale explained, was twenty years older than he and no longer young when they married, to which Queeney, studying her mother's reflection, said, 'It is kind of him to like old women, is it not, for most grow cruel with the years?'

In the glass Mrs Thrale's eyes became sad. The child told herself she did not care; her heel had begun to throb.

Johnson changed his wig for his visit to the Close. At Streatham it was customary of an evening, on Thrale's instructions, for a footman to waylay him as he left his room and replace his everyday wig, much charred about the top-piece, with one more fit for dining in company. The night well advanced and Johnson at last persuaded to retire, the same footman was waiting to whisk it off his head lest he should hold the candle too close during his small hours' reading. For the rest, he had on his brown suit with the horse-hair buttons and his shoes with the silver buckles.

Mrs Thrale wore grey and dared anyone to utter a word of dissent. Her husband, mindful of her temper, had her carried to Peter Garrick's in a chair, Queeney perched on her lap. Though the rain had stopped, a fierce wind tossed the chest-nut trees in the stable yard. Thrale himself complained of feeling unwell, an indisposition Johnson held would be easily rectified by a brisk walk to the Close.

The market now over and the square deserted save for scavengers, Thrale biliously opined that Lichfield lacked industry. Johnson retorted that while Birmingham worked with its hands, Lichfield folk used their brains. Henry Thrale was amused at this, seeing their champion had found it necessary to desert his native town so early in life.

In Johnson's honour, Peter Garrick had assembled a lively collection of learned old friends, among them Erasmus Darwin, scientist and inventor, and Dr James, for whose *Medical Dictionary* Johnson had written the preface. There was an atmosphere of accord in the house which Mrs Thrale found relaxing. She was fond of her host, who had many times sat at her table in Southwark. He was not, it was true, as diverting as his brother, but that was all to the good; Davy could often be tiring, particularly after

triumphing in some production at Drury Lane. The second
Mrs Garrick was also likeable, being somewhat simple in
the correct sense of the word.

It was she who brought up the subject of Johnson's recent
journey to Scotland. She said she had met Mr Boswell two
years previously and found him curiously affecting. He had
told her, in detail, of his first case as an advocate in the
Edinburgh courts, when he was required to defend a man
accused of stealing a sheep. By his diligent efforts he secured
an acquittal, thus saving his client from the hangman's
noose. Eight years on the very same man committed a similar offence and was this time found guilty. 'Mr Boswell',
Mrs Garrick said, 'spent hours in the condemned man's
cell, trying to give comfort to its occupant. He devised a
plan to cut down the poor wretch immediately after the
drop and arranged for a physician to be on hand to revive
him. Alas, it was to no avail. He was much disturbed by
the event, for he said the dead man's eyes remained open
in death and that in them he fancied he saw his own
reflection.'

There was a moment's silence around the table, broken
by Thrale proclaiming that stealers of sheep must be punished, else there would be no mutton left in the land. A
female cousin of Dr James chirruped with laughter and
went so far as to tap the table with her spoon.

'Mr Boswell has no side,' Mrs Garrick said, and added
somewhat quaintly, 'All his sentiments come from a heart
open to the heavens.'

At this, first Garrick, then Thrale, then Dr James
opposed her; tripping over themselves to drag Boswell
earthwards, they stressed his vanity, his absence of intellect, his desire to shine. Mrs Thrale was surprised they left

out his drunkenness, but then, save for Johnson, there was
not one among them who was not a sot. Johnson took no
part in the discussion. It was never his habit to butt in
unless addressed directly. Mrs Thrale, knowing how he
valued Boswell's friendship, and having had recent reason to
be grateful for the attachment, turned to him and asked, 'It
is true, is it not, that you found him an entertaining companion and would gladly travel with him again?'

'Indeed I would,' he replied. 'As Mrs Garrick rightly
observes he is a man who calls forth love, and that in spite
of faults, of which he has many.'

'I thought you had little time for Scotchmen,' Garrick
said slyly.

Johnson took this in good part, merely remarking that he
found Boswell the most unscottified of his countrymen.
Garrick then pressed him as to whether it was true that
Boswell was keeping a journal of their conversations
together, and indeed of Johnson's discourse in general, and if
so, did he not find it intrusive?

'Why, no, Sir. Why should I? It will not be accurate, for
man's compulsion is to replicate himself. Think of painting – one has only to examine a portrait to see in the sitter
a resemblance to the artist. And did not Mrs Garrick say
that Bozzy saw his own image in the eyes of a dead man?
Besides, he does not expect me to read what he has written.'

'What if others read it', persisted Garrick, 'after you are
gone? What will you think then?'

'Think then, Sir! Think then . . .' spluttered Johnson.
'Why, Sir, I will think nothing, for if the "gone" you refer to
is the grave I dare say I shall have nothing to think with.'

Mrs Thrale, noting how manfully he was trying to
subdue his temper, hastily changed the subject, enquiring of

Dr James his considered opinion of the health-giving properties of sea-bathing. She herself, she said, found the reverse
to be the case, her outer self being much in conflict with the
briny following a childhood encounter with a jellyfish. 'I
have only to put a toe in the water', she told him, 'for a
swelling to start up.' She was exaggerating, but felt a diversion was necessary.

Fifteen lengthy minutes later, a considerate Mrs Garrick
guided the yawning Queeney up the stairs to her bedchamber, where she gave into her hands an illustrated book
of fables. 'Thank you,' said Queeney and allowed her head
to be patted.

Left to herself, she got up and examined the contents
of Mrs Garrick's dressing table. There was a small pot of
rouge, a bowl with a lid in the shape of a cat and a bottle
of fragrant oil. Inside the bowl lay an amber necklace,
similar to the one she had once owned. Returning to the
bed she lay down and picked up the book; soon, a page or
two turned, she drifted into sleep.

The guests leaving the table and the wine liberally
poured, Thrale began to make sheep's eyes at the cousin of
Dr James. The lady, all of forty years old and as yet unmar-
ried, responded beyond the call of etiquette. She had a dab
of rouge on either cheek and her gown of sprigged muslin
would not have gone amiss on a woman half her age. Mrs
Thrale, mortified, thought of mutton rather than lamb and
smiled a great deal. Presently, Mrs Garrick sat with her and
after much inconsequential chat to do with Lichfield, the
weather and the service at the Swan Inn openly asked what
she had made of Miss Porter.

'She is strong', Mrs Thrale said, 'and somewhat mischiev-
ous. The company she keeps is not up to her standard.'

Mrs Garrick agreed as to Miss Porter's vigour of mind. According to gossip, she had shown no animosity towards her mother's curious choice of husband, unlike her two brothers, who had been against the union from the start. 'The eldest boy never forgave her. He went away to sea and never saw her again.'

'A second marriage', murmured Mrs Thrale, 'must always be injurious to the children of the first, owing to loyalties.'

'It is rumoured that Mr Johnson's affections were first directed to Miss Porter and only later fixed on the mother.'

'I did not know that,' Mrs Thrale said. She did, but was in no mood to set Mrs Garrick straight. The misunderstanding had centred around a love poem written by Sam many years before, in aid of his friend, Edmund Hector, who had been sweet on a girl in the neighbourhood of Birmingham.

'The younger boy,' continued the loquacious Mrs Garrick, 'so I have heard, called once at the house in Gough Square and ran away before Tetty could be fetched downstairs . . . too upset to look on his dear mother's face.'

Thrale's hand now creeping across the knee of Dr James's painted cousin, Mrs Thrale ground out, 'We must accustom ourselves to knowing that men are fickle and have an appetite for all women. For myself, I do not mind, for I do not love any man.' She uttered these last words with such vehemence that she flushed red. 'Where is Queeney?' she asked, rising to her feet in consternation.

Mrs Garrick took her upstairs. At their entrance the little girl clenched her fists to her chest, but did not wake. 'Such a pretty child,' whispered Mrs Garrick, primping her hair in the looking glass. 'What a comfort it must be to have a daughter.'

'Yes,' said Mrs Thrale. 'Though not as often as one might suppose.'

This silenced Mrs Garrick, if not for long. She commenced to babble her opinion of Mr Johnson, declaring she had never seen him looking so well, and how it was doubtless due to the care he received at Streatham. He dressed better, his temper was less uncertain and he had altogether mellowed . . . it was obvious to all that Mrs Thrale's influence was paramount, as was his fondness for her.

'The affection is mutual,' Mrs Thrale said, 'though he is not always easy to live with.'

Mrs Garrick expressed it a wonder he had not married again. 'My husband once told me that a very fine lady had once told him that Mr Johnson was a very seducing man when he chose to be so.'

Mrs Thrale remained mute; there was something upsetting her, and it had little to do with the humiliating conduct of her husband.

'—though I understand he did consider marriage, and that in spite of his protestations of grief, a bare twelvemonth after his bereavement.'

Mrs Thrale stared at her. She said, 'To whom?' so loudly that Queeney stirred in her sleep. Modifying her tone, she repeated the question.

'Why,' came the reply, 'none other than Anna Williams.'

'Mrs Williams!'

'The very same.'

'Never. Not so.'

'I have it on good authority', whispered Mrs Garrick, 'that at one time there was more, much more, than a friendly attachment between the two.'

'What authority?' demanded Mrs Thrale.

'Why, that of Mrs Desmoulins.'

'Fiddlesticks,' cried Mrs Thrale. 'It is a travesty of the truth. Mrs Desmoulins has been besotted with Samuel for twenty years . . . her word cannot be trusted.' Agitated, and muttering excuses to do with the lateness of the hour and the advisability of getting Queeney back to the inn, she shook the child awake and pulled her from the bed. 'She is exhausted', she said shrilly, 'and is suffering from a chill. See how she clutches her chest.'

Hurrying her bleary-eyed daughter down the stairs she called to Peter Garrick to summon the sedan chair. 'Hester,' her husband remonstrated, 'she will rest here more comfortably. I, for one, was much bitten in the night.'

'I am surprised you noticed,' she retorted, 'seeing you lay as one dead.'

Johnson did not look up when she left, nor did he trouble to break off his conversation with Mr Darwin.

The moon obscured by cloud, Mrs Thrale kept tight hold of Queeney in case the pole-carriers stumbled as they jolted through the dark streets. She herself would not have minded an upset, particularly one that would have bumped the thoughts from her head.

When she arrived at the inn and laid the little girl down, she saw in the candle glow the glint of tears on her cheeks. She asked what was wrong, but Queeney merely whimpered; drifting into sleep, the child's fists uncurled and let spill Papa's amber necklace upon the bolster.

Mrs Thrale tossed and turned in her bed; she could not shift the crotchety Mrs Williams from her mind. Johnson had twice brought the faded woman to dine at Southwark, professing it a kindness to include her. Both times Mrs Williams had worn scarlet. On Mrs Thrale politely admiring her choice of gown, she had said Mr Johnson liked her to dress brightly. On each occasion, her sightless eyes turned to his face, she had chided him for wolfing his food, and he, with surprising meekness, had replied, 'Yes, yes, you do right to check me,' and made an effort to chew less ferociously. Was that not the response of a man much under the thumb of a wife?

Telling herself she was being fanciful, Mrs Thrale pulled the bedclothes over her head and threw them off again at the sound of a commotion beneath the window. Rising, she peered down into the road. The sky had now cleared, and below, in the brightness of the moon, she saw Peter Garrick swaying on the cobblestones and Johnson, humped over, Thrale slung across his back like a bag of coals. After a prolonged thumping at the inn door, the landlord descended and let in the inebriates. The cacophony continued, Garrick's voice being uppermost, and beneath it that of Johnson, urging hush. Mrs Thrale drew the bolt on her door, then released it; she did not want Henry accusing her of pique.

An hour or so later there was a further uproar on the landing, after which the door opened with some force and Johnson staggered in, supporting Thrale under the armpits. Propelling him forwards he came to the bed and tossed his burden down. He muttered something when he left, but it was in Latin and Mrs Thrale, cowering beneath the quilt, could not make out the words.

The weight of her husband's shoulder pinning her to the mattress, she punched him. The blow was ill judged; waking, Thrale rolled on top of her. His thrustings afforded him little relief and much exertion. He uttered not a word and neither did she, and when the unsatisfactory business was over she toppled him roughly from her. Just then the moon shone full through the window and in its cold light she was bewildered to see a froth of petticoats above his naked buttocks.

Queeney slept fitfully and woke at first light from a dream in which she had been captured by a highwayman and robbed of all her jewels. The highwayman wore a handkerchief over his nose and mouth, and when she pulled it away it was Papa's face underneath.

She got up and dressed herself, then practised walking up and down the room. Her left shoe was not comfortable, but she adjusted her stocking so that the stain of yesterday's blood was visible. From her window she watched a barefooted boy creeping towards the goose pen in the yard.

She went downstairs and let herself out into the grey dawn. The boy would have run away at her approach had she not called out that she would not tell on him. He had been sent for, he stuttered, by the landlord. A lady who was lodging in the inn wanted a letter delivered most urgently to a house in the Close. Queeney said, 'Give it to me. I am just on my way there,' at which he dug obediently into his pocket. One of the eggs he was hiding in his ragged shirt fell to the ground and splattered its yolk across his feet.

Queeney went back into the inn and was about to return to her room when she was arrested by the picture hanging on the stair wall beneath the antlers of a stag. The painting was of an old man dressed in a black linsey gown and a snuff-coloured velvet coat with gold buttons. One hand was thrust into the bosom of his shirt, the other held out a letter with the subscription: 'To Mr Farthingale'. She had looked at the picture before, but until now the letter had escaped her attention.

She was turning the bend of the stairs when she spied Mr Johnson tiptoeing from her mother's room. He did not see her and continued in the direction of his own chamber, trailing a petticoat behind him.

At mid-day, horses having been hired, Johnson and the Thrales, accompanied by Peter Garrick, prepared to ride into the countryside. Thrale was pale as a ghost, Garrick stupid and Johnson lethargic.

Very early that morning Mrs Thrale had dispatched a note to Mrs Garrick, apologising for the abruptness of her departure the night before and quoting, by way of excuse, the dear lady's own innocent and well-meaning reference to daughters being of comfort. *The subject is a painful one*, she wrote, *for though I have three living girls, my sweet, lost Lucy was dearer to me than all the rest.*

Now exhausted, she had intended to let the others gad off without her, but the transformation wrought in Queeney at the sight of the white pony waiting in the yard altered her mind. Such a shine on her face, such a pleasing curve to her pink mouth, lightened her heart. At breakfast the child had gazed at her coldly and when spoken to had twice pretended deafness.

In spite of the lack of sleep suffered by all, it was not long before the beauty of the day affected the mood of each and every one. The stormy weather having dissipated and the sun now serenely beaming in a blue heaven, it was hard to remain dull. Johnson went so far as to assert that sunlight was possessed of chemical properties, as yet undiscovered, similar to alcohol and conducive to a heightening of the spirits. 'How else', he said, pointing at Thrale just then galloping ahead, voice raised in song, 'are we to explain Henry's renewed energy? Four hours ago he had not the use of his legs.'

'Nor of any other part,' murmured Mrs Thrale, recalling her rude awakening.

Trotting beside Stowe Pool, she was startled by a kingsfisher thrashing among the rushes. 'There, there,' she cried, spreading her arms in imitation of its awkward wings. 'That is nothing like,' said Queeney, although her tone was free of scorn.

Mr Johnson held the landscape much changed and for the worse. His father's parchment mill had been allowed to fall into decay. Even the ruins of it had vanished, obliterated under nettles and bindweed. The weeping willows, whose branches had once swayed above the waters of the pool, had been hacked down. 'In my yesterdays,' he told them, reining in his horse and indicating the lower reaches, 'it was here my father taught me to swim. In a mild voice he instructed me to breathe out, breathe in . . . to wield the legs in the actions of a frog.'

'Frogs have legs,' said Queeney. 'They are not like fish.'

'Nor are we,' Johnson said, 'which is why they are worthy of copy.'

Continuing along a rutted path between fields of rough pasture, they passed into the shade of an ancient oak. Johnson dismounted and bade the others do likewise. He wished them to look back at Lichfield, at the spires of the cathedral and the tower of St Mary's church. 'It is often advantageous', he said, 'to view things from a distance. Close up, we are apt to see a part rather than the whole.'

Mrs Thrale stayed on her horse; the ground was waterlogged and she feared for her shoes. Upon Queeney jumping down, mud rose up and spattered her dress.

Johnson, staring into the hazy distance, intoned, 'He left a name, at which the world grew pale, To point a moral, or adorn a tale.'

'If I am not mistaken,' said Mrs Thrale, 'you are speaking of Charles XII.'

'In this instance,' he said, 'I am remembering my poor father.'

His adult companions kept a respectful silence and looked sombrely towards the town. It was rare for Johnson to refer to his father, and rarer still for his memory to be recalled in such an exalted manner.

Addressing Mr Johnson, Queeney asked if he knew a man called Farthingale. He repeated the name several times and then shook his head. He asked why it mattered to her, and she explained it was on account of the picture in the Swan Inn and the letter in the old man's hand. 'I had not noticed the letter before,' she said, at which Mr Johnson remarked that a similar thing had happened to him in regard to the painting, in that he had not been conscious of the old man's gold buttons until he had observed that one was missing.

'Missing?' said Thrale.

'What old man?' asked Mrs Thrale, baffled.

'The third one down,' Johnson said.

Mrs Thrale could make neither head nor tail of the conversation and said no more.

Presently Queeney wandered off in search of wild flowers. Peter Garrick stretched his arms above his head and proclaimed it a capital morning. He acknowledged his wife was displeased with him owing to the bedraggled state of her petticoat, but she was not a woman long to hold a grudge.

'Perhaps I should make peace on your behalf,' said Thrale. 'I seem to recall it was I who wore it through the streets.'

'You did indeed, and to great effect,' Johnson told him. 'In Bird Street, Sir, you were accosted by a ruffian who called you a pretty wench and offered you sixpence for a trembler against the wall.'

'The moon was hidden,' Garrick said, 'which accounts for the proposition. You would have obliged, but I dragged you away lest he should squander his money.'

'A fool and his money are more easily parted than a man from his petticoat,' remarked Johnson. 'When I made haste to retrieve it earlier this morning, you fought for possession.'

Amid laughter, Thrale asked him if he considered a pretty woman to be superior to one of a studious disposition, to which he answered in the affirmative. 'Sir,' he said, 'a pretty woman may be foolish; a pretty woman may be wicked; a pretty woman may not like me, but beauty of itself is very estimable.' At this Mrs Thrale spurred her horse forward and waited further off. She did not think herself pretty, nor ever had.

After some minutes Johnson came to her. He said, 'We are having merry times, are we not, Hester?' She refused to answer him and busied herself flapping away gnats. He laid a hand on her arm. 'Come, come,' he said, 'do not spoil the morning. We are all men in our own natures frail, and capable of frailty.' 'Frail indeed,' she snapped, at which, chuckling, he murmured, 'Dear, peevish little creature,' and patted her hand as though humouring a child.

They rode in a wide circle back to Lichfield. Queeney had threaded meadowsweet into her pony's mane. Now and then she leant forward and pressed her lips to its neck.

By degrees, conversation faltered and finally died. Entangled in separate dreams, the party swayed through the balmy morning to the hum of bees.

To Miss Laetitia Hawkins,
2 Sion Row,
Twickenham

December 14th, 1807

Dear Miss Hawkins,
You will forgive my somewhat abbreviated answers
to your many questions, but, as you rightly
conjecture, I am much preoccupied with
preparations for my forthcoming marriage to
Admiral Keith.

My mother was indeed a great traveller; her
numerous letters give proof of a singular curiosity
and an aptitude for enjoyment, which virtues she
retains to this day. I recall a letter she wrote from
Milan stating her intention of returning to Verona
and thence over the Tyrol into Germany, for the sole
romantic purpose, as she put it, of washing her
mouth in the Danube. Her letters to me often ended
with the injunction that I must aim for happiness,
movement and gaiety. Alas, I do not feel I have
inherited her longing for fresh pastures, nor her
capacity for happiness. It is hard to travel and be gay
when one is burdened with the baggage of the past.

Of Dr Goldsmith I remember little, apart from
the game of Jack and Jill and the tightness of his
breeches – that and a remark attributed to him
regarding Dr Johnson's ferocity of argument – 'If he

(Johnson) misses with his pistol, he hits you with the
butt end.' This was told me by my father. Dr
Johnson was distressed at Goldsmith's death; I
remember he wept at the mention of his name when
we stopped at Lichfield on our way to Wales in the
summer of '74 – but then, as was the fashion of the
time, Dr Johnson was not alone in finding it easy to
shed tears.

On that same excursion we did indeed become
acquainted with Miss Porter. She was somewhat
coarse, but worthy. She referred to Dr Johnson's
mother, whom she had nursed when dying, as
Grannie. I remember a fish in her kitchen and a
dead bird in the garden. There was also a puff-
headed mushroom under some cabbages, which
burst apart when an old woman fell on it. These
bleak memories are possibly to the fore on account
of my mother having left behind at Streatham my
infant brother, Ralph, whose head was swollen and
wanting a brain. My mother loved but two of her
many children, the one being Lucy, the other Harry.

To the best of my memory, the story of the
drowned man, as told by Dr Johnson, was as
follows. A man called Saltmarsh, by trade a brick
builder, was walking one Sunday through Hyde Park
in the direction of Kensington. He had with him his
Newfoundland dog. Idly, he threw a stone into the
Serpentine, at which the Newfoundland leapt in and
re-emerged carrying a man's hat – a gentleman's hat.
Laying it down at his master's feet the dog dived into
the water again and this time brought out a wig. A
third time he returned, and now he pulled to the

surface a man, or rather held the shoulder of a man gripped between his teeth. The dog was not strong enough to carry the man out of the lake, but he dragged him into the shallower water. His master was then able to wade in and bring the body on land. The dead man wore a coat with silver buttons and there was nothing in the pockets save for two sixpences and a gold box of French design in which reposed a lock of golden hair – not his, for he was almost bald and swarthy with it. No sooner had the body been laid down than the dog began to drag at the coat, and though it was driven away several times, it at last worried the sodden material so persistently that a piece tore free and hung from its jaws, one silver button catching the sunlight. Then the animal ran off, and reaching a patch of earth, scraped out a hole, dropped down the rag, covered it over and lay across it, like a hen on an egg. On enquiries being made, it was found that the drowned soul was a Mr Farthingale, who had done some injury to a young lady of a lower class than himself, and whose conscience was afterwards so troubled that he threw himself into the lake. At the close of the story, Dr Johnson observed, 'Without buttons, we are all undone,' which remark caused some of the company to guffaw and others to weep.

Dr Johnson's watch, which on numerous occasions he left under his pillow at Streatham and often required my father, at some inconvenience, straight away to send after him, cost seventeen guineas and was encased in tortoiseshell. It was engraved with an inscription in Greek, the words later scratched out owing to Dr Johnson thinking them ostentatious. On his death I believe your own dear father, Sir John, removed it from the bedside table, no doubt for safety, along with certain papers. Dr Johnson's executors insisted on its return, after which I understand it was given to Francis Barber.

I have no explanation for my mother's fallout with Mrs Garrick, who you say was offended by some rudeness done her without subsequent apology, nor do I recall mention of a missing necklace.

In haste, I remain,
Believe me, affectionately yours,

H. M. Thrale

REVOLUTION *n.f.* *(revolution,* French, *revolutus,*
Lat.*)*

1 Courſe of any thing which returns to the
point at which it began to move
2 Space meaſured by ſome revolution

At certain revolutions are they bought,
and feel by turns the bitter change.

Milton

The fortunes of the Thrale Brewery much improved
due to the exertions of its chief clerk, Perkins, Henry
Thrale fastened on the notion of going to France. The
party would consist of his wife, Baretti, Johnson, Queeney
and two female servants. Accordingly, the child's eleventh
birthday and Johnson's sixty-sixth were celebrated on
September 15th, three days early, at the house of Sir John
Hawkins. Frank Barber was not included, an omission
which offended Johnson. Dr Levet received an invitation
but failed to arrive on account of his dropping into a pothole on his way home from Houndsditch, a mishap spelt
out in a letter from Mrs Desmoulins awaiting them at
Dover. She wrote that Levet had lain on his back for some

hours, but, judging from the raucous singing that accompanied his eventual descent of the cellar steps, had returned none the worse for wear. The veracity of this report caused Johnson some concern; Mrs Desmoulins cared little for Dr Levet, though more so than Mrs Williams.

It was generally agreed that the festivities in Twickenham were not so conducive to merriment as those annually conducted in the summer house at Streatham Park. Hawkins was less than generous with the wine and Thrale woke in the night complaining of hunger. Mrs Thrale flew out of sorts owing to Queeney, on some provocation never adequately explained, tugging at the hair of Laetitia, daughter of Sir John, and reducing her to tears. The next morning it was a disgruntled group that left for the coast in two coaches.

An enthusiastic Baretti had put himself in charge of all travel arrangements; for months he had been writing to his contacts in Paris in order that his friends should be well received. Mrs Thrale, worn down by the birth of yet another sickly daughter and the death of Ralph, allowed herself to be swept along by events. She inclined towards Johnson's view that anything was better than vacuity.

The party dallied so long in Canterbury, admiring the beauties of the cathedral, that they arrived too late to catch the tide at Dover. Baretti, who had gone on ahead to oversee the crossing, was considerably put out and fell into a sulk. He became more agreeable after Thrale expressed himself mightily pleased to have time to explore the fort and the castle. Johnson, flinging stones down into Julius Caesar's Well, said that the reverberations emphasised the truth that the echoes of men's actions, good as well as bad, were always susceptible to revival. He was thinking, though he did not voice it, of Levet's stumble in the dark and of his muddied calls for help.

In the evening, walking along the shore, they witnessed a blood-red sun sliding into the waves. One moment its rays splashed the cliffs with crimson, the next the world turned black. Mrs Thrale cried out it was a wonder the sun's drowning was not accompanied by a gigantic hissing, as when a kettle on the coals jerked water from its spout. It was a domestic observation, yet apt.

The journey through France passed enjoyably enough, though Johnson became weary of the continual oohs and aahs of appreciation loosed by his companions at this or that aspect of the landscape. There was, he felt, little to distinguish one clump of trees, one stretch of pasture, from another, and nothing to say of either save that they could be seen. For himself, he would have preferred a vista of book-shelves.

He grew more cheerful when, crossing the Seine for the third time and approaching Vernon, he glimpsed his first vineyard. It was a delightful novelty to step from the chaise, take but a short clamber down the bank at the side of the road and fill one's hat with grapes. It was the next day, when approaching St Denys, that things turned sour. It happened thus. Mrs Thrale, in the butterfly way of women, was twittering on about the sunlight darting silver arrows from the leaves of a field of asparagus, when she suddenly brought up the name of James Macpherson, author of *Fingal: An Ancient Poem*. The night before, she said, she had dreamt that Macpherson had approached her with *fire in his eyes*. The implication was obvious, for she began to simper and fan herself as though grown hot. It was true the weather was warm, but the window of the carriage was let down and a breeze ruffled the pages of the book on Johnson's knee.

He said with admirable restraint, 'I have never met Macpherson, yet know him to be a scoundrel. His attack upon me regarding a passage in my *Journey to the Western Isles*, in which I state my opinion that the poems of Ossian are impostures of the crudest sort, was not the response of a scholar.'

She: 'Or of a gentleman—'

He: 'I care not whether my opponent is a knight of the realm or a herder of swine, only that his intellect be sound.'

She: 'I believe he accused you of falling into the same error some twenty years since.'

He, with less restraint: 'To which error, Madam, do you refer?'

'Why, that of—' she began, and broke off abruptly, eyes widening in alarm as a distant clamour disturbed the air.

He said again, 'What error, Madam?' though he was only too aware she alluded to the regrettable mistake he had made in writing a complimentary preface to a pamphlet published by the schoolmaster William Laud, alleging that Milton in his composing of *Paradise Lost* had been guilty of plagiarism. It was unforgivable of her to bring up the subject, and cowardly to feign deafness when challenged, for he had surely expressed himself loudly enough to be heard above the screams and whinnyings that now irritated the ear.

Just then the horses were reined in with such abruptness that the carriage shuddered on its wheels and tossed the servant girl, Mags Hewson, on to his lap; in other circumstances the encounter would have been welcome.

'Which error, Madam?' he repeated, thrusting the girl

from him, but Hester was opening the door and dropping into the road without the aid of the step. He leapt after her, demanding an answer; she ran ahead, skirts stirring up dust, towards a horse rolling belly up, hooves pawing a sky thick with circling gulls. Beyond stood a stationary carriage, much tilted.

Sitting down some yards distant, he busied himself snatching red petals, without malice, from the heads of common leadwort growing amid the grass. He refrained from indulging in the futile business of she loves me, she loves me not, and instead engaged in an argument with Macpherson. The man had not a leg to stand on: his supposed sending of a letter offering to produce the original manuscripts of the Ossian poems was an outright lie. No such letter had ever existed. The impudent rogue had even gone so far as to threaten him with violence if he failed to publish a retraction. Boswell had advised him to purchase a stout new stick to replace the old one mislaid on his visit to Flora Macdonald – in case Macpherson should seek him out.

At the recollection, he could not help laughing out loud at the idea he would have needed anything more than his fists to see off such a nincompoop. It had come to nothing, of course; the fellow was a bladder of air. As for poor William Laud, without the provision of a preface he would have been imprisoned for debt. One would need a heart cast in iron to turn one's face from the suffering of others.

Glancing up, he saw the horse was now on its feet, albeit unsteady, and that Hester was running round in circles, squealing like a stuck pig. A moment later he was astonished to observe Baretti staggering up from the side of the road supporting a ghostly Henry Thrale, covered from head to foot in some white substance. On the grass verge, rocking back and forth, crouched Queeney, bonnet askew.

It was a full two hours before the journey continued, during which time a dozen or more peasants wearing hats quaintly woven of straw appeared from nowhere and attended to the torn traces and the buckled shafts. The postilion believed his leg to be broke, until, revived with a flagon of wine, he ran about with hardly a limp. Henry Thrale's complexion, to be sure, was bloodless, but that was on account of his roll in the dust.

Once on their way again Johnson tried to engage Hester in conversation, but she, tight-lipped, merely clasped Queeney closer in her arms and refused to answer directly. Once, she uttered the mysterious phrase, 'Such indifference,' and another time, 'It is scarcely credible . . .'

It was not a comfortable ride. The sun was now at its height and a quantity of flies, drawn by the smears of grape juice in his hat, buzzed relentlessly about his head. It was only later, when they reached St Germain, that Hester deigned to speak to him, and then with such coldness that he would have wished her to have kept silent. It discomforted him to be spoken to so angrily in the presence of Queeney and Baretti.

His casualness towards the fate of the occupants of the first carriage, namely Baretti, Thrale and Queeney, was, in her opinion, unworthy of a true friend, indeed, of a member of the human species. 'I would not have believed you capable of such callousness,' she said. 'You . . . who take pride in doing good, who would give the clothes off your back to the lowest wretch in the gutter—'

'I take no pride—' he began.

'To appear so unconcerned', she continued, pearls of

sweat clinging to the pale and delicious hairs trembling above the scar on her lip, 'towards the plight of those you have been pleased to call your family—'

'If you had not insulted me by ignoring my question,' he protested, 'I might have been more conscious of the gravity of the incident. As it was, I was preoccupied.'

'Incident . . . incident,' she shouted, though her voice was so high in pitch it approached a scream, 'why, three of those closest to you nearly met with their deaths.'

She was wrong; there was but one close to him, and she unhurt.

'The word incident', said he, 'does not detract from the seriousness of the situation. My *Dictionary* defines it as fortuitous, casual, an accidental happening—'

'I am not concerned with definitions,' she spat, 'only with your lack of imagination.'

'Imagination,' he spluttered, 'what part has imagination in this?'

At which she gazed at him as if seeing him for the first time and then asked, why, as a child, had he fled out into the Market Square after dwelling upon the apparition of Hamlet's father? Before he could reply, she added scornfully, 'Though on that we have only your word. Indeed, for all any of us know, it could have been the fable of Cinderella you read, and it was the turning of mice into footmen that caused you fright.'

Shocked, he turned to Baretti for support, but he, false friend, took her part and thunderously proclaimed that lives had been saved by the greatest providence ever exerted in favour of three human creatures.

Such nonsense rendered him speechless, but Baretti was not yet done. Did Johnson not understand, he raged, nostrils flaring, dark eyes flashing contempt, that with the traces snapped, the carriage careering with dangerous rapidity downhill, one animal overrun, the other galloping them to destruction, Henry Thrale, fearful for the safety of his daughter, had jumped out with the intention of averting disaster? By misfortune, his courageous leap had landed him on so steep an incline that he had been bounced sideways and deposited in a chalk pit. 'The action your Master took,' he concluded, 'one embarked upon with the sole aim of helping others, was the likeliest thing in the world to produce broken limbs and death.'

Their combined hostility so unnerved him that he was reduced to muttering that it was not unconcern for Henry that had made him appear disaffected, rather anger at Mrs Thrale for starting up a controversy and then shying away from its denouement. He spoke in a contrite tone of voice, though inwardly he bridled at the Italian's impudent bandying of the word Master, an appellation which, used by anyone but himself, reeked of servitude. Baretti's stance struck him as curious in the extreme; it was not often he saw eye to eye with Hester. Why, when Queeney, in spite of calm seas, had grown nauseous on the crossing to Calais, he had loudly attributed it to a proximity to her mother.

The next day, when they reached Paris and things turned out better than had been feared, Mrs Thrale made her peace with him. 'Sam,' she bleated, 'you will forgive me, will you not, for speaking in the heat of the moment?'

'Madam,' he replied, 'it is I who should ask pardon.'

'When we heard you laughing,' she said, 'even Queeney spoke out against you.'

'Laughing?' he echoed. 'Who said I laughed?'

'There was no need for the saying of it,' she replied, 'for

the sound travelled quite clearly from where you sat beside the precipice.'

He had no remembrance of giving way to amusement, and might have argued the point had not sense prevailed; women had ever been against logic.

'The tormenting of flies so addled me,' he told her, 'along with thoughts of the rascally Macpherson, that I was scarce myself.' At which Hester was gracious enough to acknowledge that he, being a man who lived in the head rather than the body, had behaved no worse than could be expected.

He was grateful for her forgiveness and made amends by acceding to her wishes in regard to mixing with people he found uncongenial and visiting places which held no interest for him, such as dining with Madame de Brocages and running from church to church. The former outing was memorable for the close stool in the dinner room, a pewter pot in which to spit and a large and ancient cobweb trembling above the table. Mrs Thrale said the food was poor, the dish of hare being not merely tainted but putrefied, the beans old and the sugar plums uneatable. He had taken the spitting pot for an ornament and noticed nothing out of the ordinary save for the presence in the hallway of a number of footmen playing cards.

Their circle of acquaintances grew as the weeks advanced, the Abbé François and the Benedictine Father Wilkes being worthy of mention. There were also two Italian counts, one of whom, Manucci, introduced by Baretti, paid particular attention to Mrs Thrale.

When they were not dining in or out, the company spent far too short a time inspecting the King's Library and that of the Sorbonne, and far too long going to operas,

fairs and pleasure gardens. The amount of attention wasted
on egg races, rope-walkers and shopping would have tried
the patience of the saints, most of whom appeared to have
been interred in Paris.

Thrale suggested to Hester that she leave the 'studious
Mr Johnson' to his own devices, but it had little effect.
Wherever she went he felt obliged to follow, on account of
his allegedly churlish behaviour on the road to St Denys.

On one of their many excursions to places of worship
they suffered a second falling out concerning his insistence
that they should leave before the elevation of the Host.
Had they stayed they must have got to their knees, a the-
atrical gesture which Mrs Thrale professed herself perfectly
willing to undertake and one for which he, rather than
comply, would have gone to the scaffold.

Johnson's reasons for flight had not been as pure in
motive as he would have her believe. They had sat close
by the choir stall, so close that his hearing was
undimmed; it was not the first time he had been disturbed by the effects of music on the emotions. The
workings of the mind, he conjectured, were as aimless as
the motes of dust drifting within the rays of sunlight illuminating the nave. As the angelic voices soared
heavenwards, his thoughts had dwelt upon the mother
who had failed to understand him, the wife he had neglected, the temperament that had condemned him to
idleness. Dashing the sudden tears from his eyes, he had
blundered his way from the church.

Hester had delayed following him due to her straying
into a side chapel and coming upon the statue of an angel
bearing a child in its arms, at the sight of which she had
tripped, so she said, and hurt her foot. He had rebuked her

for keeping him waiting, and she, eyes glittering, had termed him an *impossible man*. There was also some reference to Count Manucci and the recalling of an exquisite delicacy of manner.

Later that afternoon, when Queeney had gone with her father and Baretti to the theatre, she had softened towards him and described the terror she had experienced upon seeing the statue. At once he warned her not to give way to such fancies, and urged her to talk out her fears.

'The child in its arms', she told him, voice unsteady, 'bore a distinct likeness to Harry. As I approached, I almost fell . . . and yet there was nothing in the way to cause me to stumble. And it was then that I was seized with such a heavy sense of dread that I all but fainted.'

'No doubt from the pain in your foot,' he reasoned, but she cried out, 'No . . . no . . . it was the thought . . . the premonition that some ill had befallen Harry. Why, when an old man passed by and I enquired to whom the chapel was dedicated, he replied that it was to the guardian angel of children.'

'Well, then,' he said, 'that is all to the good, is it not?'

'You have often spoken of bad omens,' she protested. 'Think of the time the clock stopped in Perkins's office, two days before the discovery of Henry's near bankruptcy . . . think of when Frances Reynolds threatened to break Sir Joshua's head with the bust of Pope—'

'They could scarcely be called omens,' he interrupted, 'the one being an example of mechanical failure, the other of a woman's temper. Besides, there are good omens as well as bad ones, and I would suppose a guardian angel to be among the former. Harry is a strong and healthy boy and you must rid your mind of such morbid thoughts.' It had taken more of the same to restore her, but before nightfall she smiled again.

Afterwards, to show her renewed fondness for him she chose to take breakfast each morning – mercifully at a late hour – in his chamber on the second floor of the house in the rue Jacob. She said it was the change of air that caused her to lie abed so long, and how companionable it was that both could now be classed as *Sleepy Heads*.

Together, they often leant on the windowsill to watch the spectacle in the narrow street below. So near was the house opposite that they could plainly see a man with a tuft of hair under his nose and a nightcap on his head, sitting up in bed. At first they had pretended not to notice him, but he had taken to waving to them in a cheery manner and had once, in full view, even made use of his close stool, at which Hester had burst out laughing; both had agreed that the French were remarkably free of reticence in regard to bodily functions, and possibly with good sense.

Standing so close to her, elbow to elbow, he was enchanted by the dazzle of light on her bare arms, the primrose hue of her small mouth; as her breath, with its odour of warm chocolate, blew against his cheek he was convinced that he knew happiness.

One morning, watching her capering free of slippers about the room, he was moved to sink to his knees and seize her tiny foot in his hands, the better to examine it. It resembled, he thought, in its warmth and softness, a pink and newborn creature whose fur had not yet grown. She misunderstood his gesture, or else his lips tickled her, for she shook him off so violently that both lost their balance, he falling on to his back and she on all-fours – at which moment Queeney entered the room complaining of a sourness to her breakfast milk.

On October 18th Mrs Thrale rose from her bed and immediately encountered vexations. Entering her daughter's room to make sure she was being dressed as instructed, she grew aggravated and alarmed at the child's constant squirming and scratching as she suffered the maid to brush her hair.

Until that morning their stay in France, save for the horrid accident on the way to Paris, had been remarkably free of upsets and petty quarrels. It was true that Johnson had caused them to spend many hours in dusty libraries, but he had declared himself more than satisfied both with his visit to the Sèvres porcelain works and his introduction to Mrs Femore, Abbess of the Austin Nuns of the English Convent in the rue St Victoire, she who had known Mr Pope and not liked him, though for what reason she would not say. He had been even more intrigued by the mechanical table they had seen at Choisie, which could rise up out of the floor and sink again. Count Manucci had told them it was for the use of the King when he wanted to dine in private with his mistresses, but Sam had argued that nothing so ingenious could have been invented merely to further the seduction of women. 'A draught of wine', he had said, 'and a finger up the petticoats would have sufficed,' an indelicate summation which had astonished his audience, for he was a man known to despise talk of a bawdy nature.

'Worms,' deduced Mrs Thrale, studying the wriggling Queeney, and at once ordered that she be purged, followed by the swallowing of patent pills. Scarce five minutes later the sly girl ran to Mr Baretti and told him of her ordeal, at which the Italian, wigless and wrapped in a morning gown of lurid colours, stormed into the Thrales' marital chamber and accused Hester of endangering the child's health by the administration of a physic he considered dangerous. 'Those damned tin pills are as likely to kill as to cure,' he thundered. 'The scales settle equally between life and death.'

At such moments of conflict Mrs Thrale detested Baretti, yet, in the arrogance of his manner and the quickness of his temper, she could not but affectionately recall her dead father. 'I am in full charge of my own offspring,' she countered, pointing a scornful finger at Henry, who lay in his bed as though ready for the graveyard, 'and am prepared to take the consequences.'

In the middle of this exchange, Johnson, attired in a nightgown much soiled from the spilling of some brown liquid down its front, appeared in the doorway demanding to know why she had not yet come to his chamber to break her fast. A week before, anxious to show her gratitude for a kindness he had done her, she had twice drunk chocolate with him, a ritual she fancied he now took to be fixed in stone. Pushing him from the room, she shut the door in his face.

It was upsetting that such a disagreement should arise before undertaking the coach ride to the château of Fontainebleau. King Louis and his court having retired there for six weeks of hunting, the estimable Count Manucci had obtained a pass for his new friends that would admit them to the royal apartments, a circumstance – so Mrs Thrale excitedly babbled – beyond her wildest dreams. Now, with Baretti in a huff and Queeney disordered, she did not imagine the journey could be accomplished without storms, and was pleasantly surprised. No sooner had they rattled into the rue de Richelieu than Baretti laid a wager with the occupants of the carriage as to how many hours they would spend on the road. She herself staked fifteen livres, Johnson a louis and Thrale treble the two amounts, which put the Italian in a good humour as he appeared mightily confident of winning.

They arrived in the hamlet of Fontainebleau in late afternoon, having travelled through countryside reminiscent of the approach to Tunbridge Wells – though more rocky – and took up rooms in an inn procured through the offices of dear Manucci. Had this wretched accommodation not been recommended by the charming young nobleman, Mrs Thrale might have fallen into a sulk. As it was, she ignored the unclean linen on the beds and the scamperings of mice beneath the floorboards and dined in high spirits. Henry, possibly due to an absence of other members of the female sex, paid her much attention, and Baretti, who had won his wager – there were those among them who suspected he had made the journey before – was sweet as honey.

It was he who turned the evening sour, though it was surely unintentional. Observing a fly drowning in his wine, he elaborated on the suicidal behaviour of scorpions, which, so he said, placed in a circle of coals in the squares of Italy, ran round and round in extreme pain, until, rather than suffer longer, like true Stoics they coiled up and darted stings into their own heads.

Johnson held this was nonsense, maintaining that the turning of a tail to the head was merely a convulsion brought about by heat. 'No creature', he said, 'has so miserable an existence that it seeks its own destruction, for what may follow is not to be contemplated.' At this, Mrs

Thrale tried to divert the conversation, for talk of death would likely cause Johnson to dwell on his own extinction. 'I believe', she began, 'that the gardens of Fontainebleau are famed for their beauty—'

'I take it', said Baretti, 'that you are in disagreement with Roman law and do not consider suicide to be a legitimate choice of rational men?'

'No man takes his own life in a rational state of mind,' shouted Johnson. 'The fear of death is so natural to a rational man, Sir, that the whole of life is but keeping away the thought of it.' Here Baretti opened his mouth to argue further, at which his opponent bellowed, 'No, Sir, let it alone. It matters not how a man dies, but how he lives.'

Later that night when Hester had gone to her bed, Henry Thrale, sitting in candlelight with Baretti and the morose Johnson, confessed that he was feeling unwell. Baretti held it was not to be wondered at . . . had not the physician attending him at St Germain expressed astonishment that he still breathed?

Thrale shook his head, and after much prevarication acknowledged that his disorder was possibly due to an old infection, one no doubt venereal, seeing a swelling of the right testicle could not wholly be explained by his unfortunate ejection into the chalk pit outside St Denys. Johnson questioned him as to other symptoms, and after some thought made reference to a publication whose pages he had riffled through in a bookseller's shop next door to the saddler's in the rue Jacob.

'In regard to a diagnosis?' asked Thrale.

'Not so,' Johnson said. 'It had more to do with the avoidance of ill effects, its subject being onanism and its subtitle, "A Treatise Upon the Dangerous Effect of Excessive

Venery". I did not agree with its premise, as it appears to me that onanism has much to recommend it, in that it does away with the mingling of harmful fluids.'

'It does away with many things,' argued Baretti. 'Not least a woman's heat.'

'Such heat, Sir,' rebuked Johnson, 'is the root of the problem. It would be wiser to practise onanism rather than engage in other than lawful congress.'

'Practise . . . practise,' cried Thrale. 'I have been adept at the habit since my seventh year . . . and scarcely need practice. Besides, I was tossed enough on my way through France,' a remark which provoked such an outbreak of merriment that Johnson burst the buttons on his waistcoat.

The next morning he found himself wedged between Thrale and Baretti amid a murmuring line of onlookers intent on observing a man and woman eating in the gilded chamber beneath. He was shocked at himself for watching so common a ritual with such a degree of reverence.

A procession of footmen entered from the left bearing silver platters and waited their turn while a major-domo lifted the covers and sniffed at the contents. Waved on, four other footmen approached the table and set about the serving. The first course consisted of five dishes, of which the Queen tasted nothing but a quantity of pie under a crust; her companion partook heartily of whatever was put before him, save for a mess of pottage which he poked with his knife and appeared reluctant to shovel into his mouth.

A buzz of excitement raged through the gallery at this exception, for though the actors on stage spoke not a word it was as if the spectators were privy to some play in which poisoning was suspected. A stink of fish, riddled with garlic, seeped upwards. Even Henry Thrale was driven to pinch his nostrils together.

Johnson was dazzled by the reflections of silver plate in the multiplicity of mirrors lining the walls. He could see that the King was stout, but could not discern his features. Marie Antoinette, as far as he could tell, was pretty, in that she was slender enough not to spill from the confines of her chair. A stream of sunlight from the end window caught her elaborate hairpiece and spun it gold. But a few yards to the left of her chair, at the front of a gawping crowd, he spied Queeney and Mrs Thrale.

Peering down at Hester, it occurred to him that it was impossible to have both affection and veneration for one and the same person, and that if it came to a choice the former sentiment must inevitably triumph, not least in regard to his dear mistress. There was, he pondered, much in her character to inspire love and little deserving of respect. Even as he scrutinised her, she said something to Queeney that caused the child to wilt. He could not make out her expression, but the girl's shoulders slumped.

Turning, he was confronted by an image of himself in the vast mirror on the gallery wall and did not recognise his features. It was as though the shaving glasses at Streatham Park and Johnson's Court, deceived by familiarity, had presented a false portrait, for here the mouth that he had privately considered generous appeared licentious in its fullness, and his large eyes, at home seemingly so expressive of candour, were lit with a sly regard, as of a man fixed on himself.

He would have nudged Baretti for a denial of such an interpretation had he and the Italian still ploughed the same furrow, but following Thrale's brush with death, Baretti had been less than respectful: only the previous night, when buttons had gone missing, he had stayed sluggishly in his chair and neglected to join in the search.

Just then Henry Thrale took Johnson by the elbow and urged him to come outside. 'I may fall asleep if I stay much longer,' he grumbled. 'That the King feeds himself with his left hand as we do does not greatly add to my knowledge of his character, nor does it add to the gaiety of my stomach to see Marie Antoinette refuse so many dishes.'

Together they descended the stairs to the lower floors. They had intended to go into the back courtyard and the grounds beyond, but instead found themselves lost in a maze of passageways and steps. Once, during their many twists and turns, they came face to face with two ancient liveried footmen, both of whom proved too intoxicated to be of help.

After further minutes of aimless wandering Henry thrust open the door to a storeroom, whose casements overlooked a yard in which a number of horses could be seen at exercise. There being no other means of exit, he promptly heaved open the nearest window and clambered out.

Johnson was about to follow when he noticed a bulky shape lying in the far corner, partially hidden under a damask cloth. Intrigued, he approached and tugging aside the covering saw it was the sculpture of a naked man, arms spread wide, the wrists manacled and lengths of marble chain trailing the dusty floor. He imagined it must be a likeness of Prometheus, though the rock was absent.

For some time, looking upon that face, mouth carved in a rictus of agony, his mind remained vacant; he saw rather than recorded. Then, like bubbles in a glass, his thoughts rose upwards, and with their surfacing the sculptured features began to dissolve and reconstruct themselves . . . and now he stared down at a different countenance, one known to him from long ago. Gradually he grew conscious of a dreadful emptiness, as though his inner being had been sucked from his body and what remained was hollow darkness. But for the thumping of his heart, loud as drum beats, he might have imagined himself dead. With a gigantic effort of will he switched his gaze to the chain in the dust and, link by marble link, dragged himself back to life. At last, shuddering, he flung the cloth over those blind, accusing eyes, and quite forgetting the open window, stumbled from the room.

Once again he wandered the numerous passages, until, climbing some stairs and putting his shoulder to a door mercifully unlocked, he emerged into the dappled sunlight of a deserted avenue lined with stately trees, leaves ablaze in autumnal glory.

I, too, he thought, am about to encounter the fire before the fall, and still in the grip of terror and remorse he set off at speed towards the horizon. Above his jogging head, like sails in a blue sea, white clouds flapped the heavens.

The spectacle of the royal dinner concluded, Mrs Thrale, accompanied by Baretti and Queeney, spent an hour or more searching for her husband and Johnson. It was upsetting that she could not find them immediately, for she had momentous news to impart – no less a person than Marie Antoinette had commented on the prettiness of Queeney and asked who she was. This thrilling information had been passed on by darling Count Manucci, who had given assurances that he had answered such an enquiry with the right amount of reserve and discretion. No, he had not supplied the address of their lodgings in the rue Jacob, but he had let it be known that the Thrales were visiting France in the company of the eminent Samuel Johnson.

Mrs Thrale was not surprised that her daughter had been noticed; she had observed the extraordinary crookedness of posture exhibited by the inhabitants of Paris, and the predominance of trusses and the like displayed for sale in shop windows. Deformities of the spine in such numbers, she reasoned, were to be explained by the French habit of putting children into stays as soon as they could stand upright. The resulting inhibition of limbs and retardation of growth had produced a population unable to walk in an easy manner. That here, as at home, Samuel was stared at in the street was due more to his remarkable freedom of movement than to the dramatics of his rolling gait and his sometime revolvings.

Queeney herself was far from overwhelmed at being the subject of royal attention, but then her looks had never been matched by a warmth of temperament. From infancy she had shown coldness, though it was true she had shed tears when Papa had flown into the chalk pit. 'It is an honour to be singled out by the Queen of France,' Mrs Thrale remonstrated. 'It would do you no harm to appear gratified,' to which the child tartly retorted that her mother was showing enough gratification for both of them.

They found Henry tramping the straw of the royal stables. When told of the attention Queeney's presence had aroused, he said it was no more than he would have expected and that he had no idea where Johnson might be, save that, like a man long incarcerated underground, he had sought the air.

Some quarter of an hour later it was Queeney, striding sullenly ahead of an exasperated Mrs Thrale, who spied him in the distance seated on a bench beside a luminous stretch of ornamental lake. Mrs Thrale told her to run on ahead and fetch him. 'I am not a dog,' the girl murmured and deliberately slackened her pace.

It took some time for her to reach the bench. Mrs Thrale watched intently and was astonished to see Johnson remaining in his seat and Queeney returning alone. She was limping again, an affectation assumed following a lesson with her Parisian dancing master, during which she swore she had suffered a stubbed toe, an injury requiring the temporary postponement of further instruction. Mrs Thrale suspected the toe to be an excuse, the girl having run about quite agilely the following day when taken for an airing in the gardens of the Tuileries.

Queeney coming within earshot, she called out, 'What is wrong? Why is Mr Johnson not with you?'

'He insists he is not fit company', Queeney said, 'and is saying his prayers.'

Much perturbed, Mrs Thrale hurried down the path. Johnson sat bent forward, leaning on his stick, eyes lowered. 'Samuel,' she shouted, 'we are ready to leave—'

'Go about your business . . . I am best left to myself,' he replied, in such tones of muffled despair that she stood momentarily aghast.

Familiar as she was with his moods it was not always possible to find the correct approach. Sometimes he was so angry and out of sorts that it did no good to reason with him; at others it was talk he needed and a sympathetic ear. Glancing at his face, it was pitiful to see the misery etched upon it . . . and yet, the dying day was so lovely in its aspect – the purple shadows on the grass, the silver sheen upon the water, the flash of wings as birds swooped from the fiery canopy of the trees – that she could not feel his sadness, and with an honesty of spirit was compelled to tell him so. Seating herself beside him she placed one small hand on his stout knee, where it perched like the lid on a teapot. 'Look up,' she bade him. 'Look up at the sky.'

For some time he could not bring himself to obey her; patiently, she waited. Presently, voice hoarse as though from speechifying or weeping, he said, 'I am not such a good traveller as I thought myself to be.'

She knew this to be true, for she and Baretti had remarked on his lack of ease away from London, and in particular his refusal to speak French, which kept him out of the conversation when in the company of strangers; he would either talk Latin or not talk at all.

'The French are a silly people,' he said. 'They have no common life. Nothing but the two ends, beggary and nobility. Nor do they have any common sense, common manners, common learning . . . with them it is either gross ignorance or *les belles lettres*—'

'We shall all be glad to be in England again,' she lied; she herself found Paris more stimulating than either Streatham Park or the Brewery in Deadman's Place. Still, she was touched by his obvious homesickness and tapped his knee affectionately.

He looked up then, but she could tell he did not take in the radiance of the fading day; she had been in the right of it when sometime past she had accused him of being a man who lived in the head rather than the body.

Suddenly, he said, 'I have had cause to remember my brother, Nathaniel—'

'Little Natty,' she prompted.

'Little Natty,' he repeated, and lapsed into silence again.

She watched the scarlet streaks flooding the darkening sky and thought of other things: of the Queen's gown made of gauze adorned with flowers and of the pearl bracelets on her wrists; of the French way of cruelly whipping their horses over the face; of the infants in the Foundling Hospital pining away to perfect skeletons and expiring in neat cribs with each a bottle hung to its neck containing a milk mess, which if they could suck on they might live, and if not, would die; of the anniversary of her wedding day some two days past and of Henry presenting her with flowers and stammering she had been a good wife to him. That she had never been in love was not a great deprivation, for what one had never known was scarcely to be fretted over.

'I have had reason to think of the manner of his death,' said Johnson.

For a moment she could not recall who it was that occupied his mind, and then, remembering his dead sibling, asked what it was that had revived the memory.

What Samuel told her was incoherent, and besides, she who had suffered the loss of so many children could not be expected to waste much thought on a man who had been dead for nigh on forty years.

'He died but a few hours, a day at the most, after Davy Garrick and I left Lichfield for London.'

'He was ill when you set off,' she probed.

'No. Not so—'

'A sudden illness, then—'

'I had not seen his face, not even in dreams, until today—'

'It is strange', she said, 'how an image can suddenly come into the mind. Some years ago, I remember I was—'

'He was lying in the dust—'

'The dust . . .' she repeated, distracted by the sight of Queeney whirling round and round on the path.

'In fetters in the dust.'

At once, she gave him her full attention. When Samuel dwelt on restraints it was a sure sign he was beginning to allow a morbid melancholy to overpower his senses.

'It was in my gift to have helped him', he said, 'and I did nothing.'

'He died in prison?' she asked, trying to make sense of it.

'Neither in a prison nor a madhouse', he said, 'and for that is now in a worse place than either,' after which curious utterance he beat his fist against his breast with such force that she started up in alarm and attempted to tug him to his feet.

'Sorrow', she cried, quoting one of his own metaphors, 'is the putrefaction of stagnant life and is remedied by exercise and motion.' He laughed at this, but there was no humour in the sound. She shouted to Queeney to seek out Papa and Baretti; her voice was so charged with urgency that the girl sped off immediately.

'In the dust,' Johnson repeated. 'In the everlasting dust—'

'Samuel,' she said, 'there is little in my own life to keep me in that state of mind called happiness, but such is my trust in God that I do not question His will and am convinced there is a purpose to it all.' At that moment, fearful for his sanity, she believed in her fairy tale. 'You yourself', she continued, 'have written that the antidotes with which philosophy has medicated the cup of life, though they cannot give it salubrity or sweetness, have at least allayed its bitterness and tempered its malignity. The balm which she drops on the wounds of the mind abates their pain—'

'—though it cannot heal them,' interrupted Johnson, and reminded her that those were Seneca's thoughts, not his. 'I am missing a button,' he suddenly confided. 'Mags Hewson found but two to sew on my coat,' and got to his feet.

Giddy with relief, Mrs Thrale linked her arm in his and guided him towards the distant windows glowing with first candlelight.

As they walked, he endeavoured to conduct a conversation, but the sense of it was hard to follow, punctuated as it was by prayer. 'The ducks on the lake', he said, 'are very fine specimens . . . giver and preserver of life, by whose power I was created, and by whose providence I am sustained, look down on me with tenderness and mercy . . . but not so fine as those at Streatham Park—'

'They are indeed fine', Hester gabbled, 'and of a rare breed—'

'Grant that I may not have been created to be finally destroyed; that I may not be preserved to add wickedness to wickedness . . . I have a mind to buy a new wig before I leave Paris—'

She said, 'There is a wig-maker further along the rue Jacob. Count Manucci told Henry he has a good reputation—'

'Repent me of my sins, and so order my life to come, that when I shall be called hence, like the wife whom thou hast taken from me . . .' Here Johnson stopped in his tracks and gazed about him with a face so expressive of despair that Mrs Thrale fought back tears; to succumb to the emotion of the moment would have been of little benefit to her dear friend.

'When I think of my dead father,' she said, 'which I often do, I take care to think of the times when we were in accord. I remember him taking me fishing—'

'Tetty had golden hair,' he interrupted, 'bright as though the sun shone on it—'

'Like Marie Antoinette,' she said.

'I was not a good husband,' he groaned and lumbered ahead of her down the path.

'Wait,' she called, and watched as a single streak of gold leaked from the sinking sun and stained the sky.

'Gold as corn,' Johnson called back, and allowed her to catch up with him. 'On our wedding day,' he said, 'I taught her a lesson and rode on ahead . . . Almighty God, forgive me my transgressions—'

That night Mrs Thrale told Henry of the anguish she had experienced. 'He was not himself,' she wailed, 'and I am still in the dark as to what caused the disturbance.'

Henry said there had been intimations earlier, when he and Johnson, lost in the cellars of the Palace, had witnessed an act of buggery in the archway of a wine vault. He himself had not been affected unduly, but Samuel had trembled with disgust at the sight of the coarse hairs sprouting from the buttocks of the perpetrator, and had afterwards hidden himself in a storeroom.

Mrs Thrale climbed into bed and turned her face to the wall. Though her eyes were closed she could see her anniversary flowers dead on their stems.

The Thrales left Paris on November 1st and arrived in the town of Lille a week later. The closer they got to the coast the higher Johnson's spirits rose. He became remarkably even of temper, so much so that Baretti, try as he might, was unable to provoke him into argument. When the Italian, in the course of an intemperate evening in an inn at Douay, impudently asked if it was not a disadvantage to remain sober, Samuel replied mildly that though the habit of drinking eventually led to a dysfunction of the intellectual mind, it was of considerable benefit – in that it released the appearance of thought – to those persons who had little in their heads and much to say.

Foolishly, Mrs Thrale had turned on Baretti and told him that Johnson's sobriety had arisen from the best of motives, a wish to set an example to a wife grown dependent on brandy and opium. No sooner were the words out of her mouth than she regretted them, yet such was Johnson's tranquillity of mood that save for a lowering of the brows he gave no evidence of displeasure. Then, on the afternoon of their departure for Dunkerque, an incident took place which convinced all who witnessed it that Samuel had lost his mind.

In the morning they had driven about Lille in a fiacre, the streets of the town being too dirty to traverse on foot. They stopped to visit a very showy church adorned with pictures of souls in Purgatory and statues of saints hung about with little silver ears and eyes. On enquiring as to what these trinkets signified, the party was informed that various miracles had been granted to supplicants requesting restoration of sight and hearing.

Mrs Thrale, anxiously viewing the scenes of Purgatory, whispered to Baretti how fortunate it was that Johnson's eyesight was poor, at which he reminded her of their visit to the Bibliothèque du Roi, and how when inspecting the incunabula it was only Sam who had been able to deduce from the appearance of the letters in several volumes whether they were printed from wooden or metal types. His deficiency of vision, Baretti observed, was generally most in evidence when he had no interest in the subject before him. True or not, on this occasion it was the moneyboxes fixed beneath each depiction of Hell that appeared to vex Johnson, an irritation he showed by striking out at them with his stick.

Next, at Thrale's insistence, they visited a magazine of corn, a vast building with nothing in it save a heap of rice in one corner. Henry said the French had little knowledge of agriculture and failed to make proper use of their land. Mrs Thrale thought the lack of industry had something to do with their frequent holy days which were scrupulously kept, though they appeared to have scant respect for the sabbath. Monsieur Le Liever, Queeney's dancing master, had cried off on All Saints' Day but had been only too willing to attend her on Sunday mornings, a request dear Queeney had declined on the grounds that it was against her Christian principles.

On leaving the corn magazine Mrs Thrale instructed the driver of the fiacre to take them back to their lodgings; Queeney had earlier complained of a pain in the belly and she was anxious to dose her with ipecacuanha.

They had gone a little way along a narrow street when their vehicle halted beside a house under scaffolding. Henry, stepping down to investigate the cause of the delay, found himself in the rear of a crowd silently peering at some object close by the front door. He was attempting to push himself closer when a low muttering began, after which, as though seized by a common anger, fierce shouting broke out accompanied by the shaking of fists. He was still trying to force his way forward when the crowd surged back a pace and stared upwards, and now hats were thrown into the air and cheers rang out.

Mrs Thrale and Baretti, peering into the street, were astonished to see Johnson hauling himself up the front of the house by means of the scaffolding. Above him, at an open window beneath the eaves, could be seen a solitary figure, who stood with arms held out as though ready to catch bounty from the heavens.

Even as she watched, the tail of Samuel's coat caught on a projection of rotten wood and he was jerked sideways. The spectators let out a hiss of alarm. Queeney started to laugh hysterically. Mrs Thrale turned to admonish her; she moved too abruptly and the child lost her balance and cracked her head against the seating.

And now Johnson had drawn level with the attic window; he swung himself inwards, collided with its framed occupant, clutched him in a necessary embrace and tumbled from view.

Mrs Thrale saw Henry reach the steps of the house. He was taller than those around him, and as he stood there, head bent, he brought his arms up, either in shock or to hold back the crowd pressing at his heels.

On his return he stepped into the fiacre without uttering a word. All his movements – the way he shook his head from side to side, the way his clenched fists drummed on his knees – expressed disquiet; as for his face, never before had Mrs Thrale seen such horror in his pale blue eyes.

Baretti demanded, 'What is the commotion about? Where is Samuel? What is happening?'

'A child,' came the faltering reply. 'A fallen child.'

'Fallen,' echoed Mrs Thrale.

'Dropped,' Thrale said. 'Either by accident or from intent.'

'A dead child,' screamed Mrs Thrale.

'A dead one now,' said he. 'I saw its auburn curls.'

Mrs Thrale began to weep. She knew it was foolish to shed tears over an unknown infant, but oh, the sadness of it – to spill like a fledgling from the nest.

Presently the door of the house opened and Johnson came running down the steps. Approaching the carriage, he shouted, 'Money, give me what money you have.' Taking off his hat, he held it out like a begging bowl and urged them to hurry. The occupants of the fiacre obeyed him without question, and when the hat was heavy with coins he sped off, the torn pocket of his coat flapping at his side, and disappeared once more into the house.

The story Johnson told them later that day was a curious one. The object Thrale had seen was not the body of a child, but that of a small sack filled with river mud and bound about with rags. Some years before, the man at the attic window had been employed as a nightwatch in the court-yard of the Bastille; he had a wife and a little daughter. He was, by his own admission, a prodigious drinker, and for this reason was shortly dismissed from his work. One stifling Sunday in summer his wife had given him the child to hold while she went to beg food from a neighbour. The bells were pealing for mid-day mass, and he stood at the open window rocking the babe in his arms and dreaming upon a time when he would be able to provide for his family. I will provide, he thought, and on the thought opened his arms to embrace the future. Soon after, his wife drowned herself in the Seine.

Ever since, he had wandered from town to town, always living in attics, always standing at an open window to drop his burden, always waiting with arms held out lest by some miracle time reversed itself and God gave back his daughter.

'But I saw the child,' protested Henry. 'I saw the auburn curls above its rags.'

'He snipped off her curls before they buried her,' said Johnson, 'and stuck them into a turnip head.'

Mrs Thrale felt a warm indignation. Though the original incident was dreadful, she could scarcely be expected to feel pity for a madman who dropped sacks of mud from windows and caused bystanders to grow faint.

'The money,' she said, 'I had thought it was to pay for a decent burial, and now I suppose it will be spent on drink.'

'Would that drink could drown such misery,' Johnson retorted. 'Besides, I will repay every penny,' which put Mrs Thrale in the wrong and made her appear uncharitable.

Henry Thrale held tight to Queeney's hand. His grip was fierce, but she endured it; she sensed Papa wanted to keep her safe.

To Miss Laetitia Hawkins,
2 Sion Row,
Twickenham

March 8th, 1809

Dear Miss Hawkins,
You will forgive my tardiness in replying to your
numerous letters, but I have been staying in
Dumbartonshire with my husband Admiral Keith
and have only recently returned. I am somewhat
surprised that you are still engaged on your
reminiscences of Dr Johnson and friends. Such
drawn-out labour must be wearisome indeed.

I am afraid I can give no very satisfactory
estimation of the character of Mr Langton, for he
was so very tall and I so short that we did not often
look one another 'in the eye'. That he and Mr
Topham Beauclerk were both good friends of the
Doctor I know to be true, though there was one
occasion – I think at Bolt Court – when Mr
Langton, bemoaning the serious illness of his
mother, was savagely rebuked by Dr Johnson for not
going at once to wait on her. My mother considered
it hypocritical of him to speak so harshly as he
himself did not see his mother for nigh on twenty
years, not even when Miss Porter wrote to say that
she was dying. Nor did he go to her funeral.

Mr Beauclerk was interested in the Sciences, as was

Dr Johnson; the latter tried to persuade my father to set up a laboratory for chemical experiments, but, following a near explosion in the school-room at Streatham Park, the idea was abandoned.

Dr Johnson was a prodigious swimmer. I often bathed with him in the sea at Brighton. Indeed, he was so strong in the action and such was the quantity of water he disturbed, that it was advisable to keep one's distance for fear of being submerged.

Mr Perkins, the chief clerk, was killed at Brighton races by Lord Bolingbroke's horse, Highflyer. Agitated by some insect at the moment Perkins was passing, the animal lashed out and kicked the unfortunate clerk in the head. His widow, whom I remember for her habit of humming under her breath, lived at one time near my mother, though I do not know if she and the 'bee' kept up their acquaintance.

I do not care to comment on my mother's relationship with Dr Johnson; sufficient to say she needed an audience and he a home.

As to my own relationship with him, I cannot in all honesty say that I loved him – he was too large, too variable in mood, too insistent on the attention of my mother. His was a melancholy disposition, an affliction shared by his younger brother, who, it is believed, perished by his own hand. Still, I was fond sometimes, for he exhibited a remarkable understanding of children and their needs, a quality singularly lacking in my mother.

His preoccupation with orange peel was due to persistent indigestion, a malady brought on by his irregular eating habits; he either fasted or gorged himself. I believe he ground the peel and dissolved it in a spoonful of hot port wine. Though he drank heavily in his younger days he was abstemious after, or nearly so.

I remain,
Sincerely yours,

H. M. Keith

I remember little of my visit to Paris in '75, save for suffering the unwelcome attentions of a dancing master who treated me with untoward familiarity, an outrage my mother refused to acknowledge. That, and the amount of letters Dr Johnson wrote – two to Mrs Desmoulins and one each to Mr Boswell, Dr Levet and Francis Barber. I recollect the letters because he told me that Mr Boswell was languishing under the onset of melancholy, and that before leaving England Mrs Williams had fallen out with Mrs Desmoulins, and Dr Levet with both of them – on account of the last disturbing the household following an encounter with a pothole. 'I must endeavour', Dr Johnson said, 'to heal differences and allay fear.'

I remarked that to quarrel was a 'bad thing', to which, rocking back and forth at the table, he replied, 'Not so, Miss, for the less we quarrel the more we hate.'

As a child I scarcely understood the perception of this observation, but in adult years have found it to be true.

No, I do not remember your presence at
Streatham Park that Christmas, and for good
reason – my mother's tenth offspring, named after
an earlier infant, having died some two weeks before
the festivities.

DISASTER *n.f. (disastre, French)*

1 Misfortune; grief, mishap; misery; calamity

This day black omens threat the brightest fair
That e'er deserved a watchful spirit's care,
Some dire disaster, *or by force or flight;*
But what, or where, the fates have wrapt in night.

Pope

On March 20th – it was a Wednesday – Mrs Thrale went to fetch her daughter Susannah from Mrs Cumyns's boarding school in Kensington. She took Queeney with her and on the way they quarrelled; it was a trivial matter of the child's amber necklace hanging in a lop-sided manner about her neck. Mrs Thrale reached forward to pull it straight, whereupon Queeney impudently struck her hand away.

On the return journey, in spite of young Susan whining a good deal and Queeney remaining sullen, Mrs Thrale managed to control her temper. Heart quickening in antici-pation, she thought of dear Count Manucci, who had travelled to England earlier in the week and was expected at Southwark in the morning.

Arriving at the Brewery, she had scarcely stepped down from the carriage before Harry ran up and said he had seen an advertisement for Arthur Murphy's play, *The Way to Keep Him*, and that he *must* be taken to see it that very night. On being told he could not go, he seized her dress and twirled her round with such vigour that she all but lost her balance. Pestered thus, she gave in, and made arrangements for one of the clerks to accompany him to Drury Lane that evening.

Henry took issue with her for having agreed to such an outing. Guests were expected for dinner and he was anxious to show off his son. Mrs Thrale would have answered in kind but for further thoughts of the Count.

The dinner party consisted of Sir John Hawkins and his daughter Laetitia, Baretti, Lady Lade, sister to Henry, and Perkins and his wife. At first the talk was exclusively concerned with the visit the Thrales intended to make to Italy later in the year. The excursion to France having proved such a success, and Johnson more than willing to be included, Henry Thrale was content to leave all the arrangements for such a trip in the hands of Baretti. The Italian, puffed up with excitement at the prospect of showing his country to his friends, monopolised the conversation to such an extent that Mrs Thrale grew weary. Finding his tone proprietary and overbearing, she said loudly, 'We have had enough of Italy, and of Italian opinions.'

The table fell silent, until, eyeing a dish in the middle of the table with a seated cherub on the lid, Mrs Perkins remarked that the china embellishment must surely be cast in the image of Susannah. 'Such a little angel,' she cooed, looking from the dish to the child. A general murmur of agreement arose, to which Mrs Thrale responded as a mother should. First she smiled in appreciation, then she jumped up and kissed the *little angel* on both cheeks, a showy demonstration which was copied by each of the guests in turn. Susannah, flustered, covered her face with her hands.

Seated again and still smiling, Mrs Thrale suddenly stiffened in her chair. Without warning, a picture of the statue in the church at Lille, of the angel bearing a boy in its arms, swam before her eyes. She immediately left the table and went to enquire if Harry had yet come home. Returning, she made the excuse that she thought she had heard the cries of an infant.

'There are no infants in the house,' Queeney said. 'They are all dead.'

'A mother's ears', retorted Mrs Thrale, 'are so governed by the heart that echoes are ever present.'

At this Baretti gave a snort of derision, so loud and unrestrained that Mrs Perkins began to hum, a habit she resorted to when in the grip of embarrassment.

Within half an hour Mrs Thrale again quit the table; this time Henry greeted her return with a frown. It was a mild enough rebuke, yet she burst into tears. Comforted by Lady Lade, she confided that she was sure something monstrous had befallen Harry.

'The clerk has abandoned him,' she wailed. 'At this moment he is wandering about Covent Garden . . . prey to every ruffian in sight.'

In vain did Mr Perkins seek to reassure her that the clerk in question was a responsible fellow, that he would entrust his own children to his care without a qualm. Mrs Thrale would have none of it. Harry was now being carried off into some dark alleyway to be beaten and stripped of his clothing. The servant having recently served the damson pudding, she looked down at the crimson mess on her plate and shrieked so loudly that Queeney spilt her lemonade on to Laetitia Hawkins's lap, and now she too began to cry.

At midnight Harry came home, sound of limb and half mad with delight at the events of the evening. Mrs Barraclough had performed well, if inaudibly, until, the occupants of the pit creating a rumpus, she had opened her mouth wide and bellowed like a bull. The second act had been interrupted by a fight breaking out between two players in minor roles. The catcalls growing in volume, Arthur Murphy had clambered on to the stage and ordered the curtains to be lowered, whereupon both actors had set about him with their fists. Little had been seen of the resulting disturbance save for a savage billowing of the cloths accompanied by the sound of muffled shouts and curses.

According to Harry, this had greatly added to the enjoyment of the evening, though Mr Crick, the clerk, had been all for leaving at once. Mr Crick had said he would never again take on the task of escorting him anywhere, let alone Drury Lane, but when Mr Murphy came up and expressed himself delighted to make his acquaintance, he turned pink and lost his bluster. Mr Murphy had a cut lip and the beginnings of a purple shadow under his left eye.

This reminded Sir John of how the actor Charles Macklin had murdered Thomas Hallam in the Green Room of Drury Lane. 'It was over a wig', he said, 'borrowed without permission. When Macklin demanded an explanation Hallam called him a clodhopper and a buffoon and threw the wig in his face. Enraged, Macklin lunged at him with his stick and pierced him through the eye. He lived but three hours.'

Not to be outdone, Thrale recalled that Quin had killed no less than two of his fellow thespians, though not at the same time – one in a duel at Hampstead and a second by bribing a fly-man to drop a weight on his adversary in the middle of *Coriolanus.*

'Peckham,' corrected Mr Perkins. 'The duel took place in the meadows of Peckham.'

'Poor Quin,' said Mrs Thrale. 'He lost his teeth while denouncing Desdemona.'

'Poor fly-man,' argued Perkins, 'for it was he, I recall, who went to the scaffold. Neither Quin nor Macklin suffered punishment.'

'In mitigation,' Sir John said, 'it has to be taken into account that all actors are volatile. It is a disposition natural to the profession.'

The resulting discussion raged for some time. Mrs Thrale drank freely and went so far as to apologise to Baretti for having been short with him earlier. Now that Harry was safe most things could be forgiven.

The next morning Queeney woke with a pain in her head. She kept it from her mother lest she was left at home when the others went into the City to visit the Tower. Mrs Thrale remarked on her flushed cheeks at breakfast, but was too agitated at the arrival of Count Manucci to pay exact attention. She was wearing a gown made from material bought in Paris; whenever the Count looked at her she laughed, high and shrill, like Susannah did when tickled.

While Thrale and Baretti were showing the visitor the complexities of the Brewhouse, Harry ran in with the news that one of the ships in the river was on fire. It had been bound for Boston with a cargo of Papa's beer. Mr Baretti hastened off to see for himself and returned elated. The flames had not yet been doused, he said, and there was a pall of smoke billowing across the gardens. Just then the chief clerk came up and assured Thrale that matters were under control. 'You can see our porter is good, Mr Perkins,' shouted Harry, 'for it burns special well.'

By the time they left Southwark for London Queeney felt herself better, if drowsy. Sometimes, when spoken to, the words seemed to come from a distance, as though there was cloth in her ears. All the same, she watched her mother closely, observing in her movements a giddy extravagance of gesture and in her voice an unnatural note of deference. She did not doubt this play-acting was for the benefit of Count Manucci, who, equally false, hovered about her like a fly above a jampot.

As they passed through the western gate of the Tower, Harry began to recite passages of history he had learnt by heart. 'The White Tower', he babbled, 'was built by William the Conqueror . . . and then Henry II turned it into a fortress.'

'Henry III,' interrupted Queeney, at which her mother tapped her hard on the shoulder.

Undeterred, Harry told of kings and queens being imprisoned in the dungeons and of how the young sons of Edward V had been murdered while they slept. 'They were but a year or two older than myself,' he said cheerfully.

'They never put royalty in the dungeons,' contradicted Queeney, stepping out of reach of her mother, 'and the princes were the sons of Edward IV.'

Descending the steps to the Menagerie, Count Manucci went ahead of Mrs Thrale and led her by the hand, at which she oohed and aahed in an absurd manner, as though adrift on a mountainside and in mortal danger of slipping. When she reached the bottom she thanked him with such simpering regard that Queeney felt quite queasy; her head began to throb again. She thought of Mr Johnson's dictum that it was advisable to acknowledge at an early age that life was a masquerade, and that to mistake an impression for reality was to court madness. It did not help much, and some minutes later it appeared to her that the ground beneath her feet was not fixed.

She remembered little of what she saw that afternoon, save for the lions padding back and forth and the flame of the lanthorn flickering in the opaque eyes of the brown bear sat in a pool of its own piss. That, and the blackened appearance of Harry as he whooped up and down before a cage of wolves, face, hands, white stockings, blue coat smeared with gunpowder.

Something miraculous happened as the carriage crossed Blackfriars Bridge. She was peering out at the Thames when suddenly the smoke-laden clouds shifted, and for an instant the rays of the sun shimmered in a glittering stairway from water to sky. She had only to put one foot on to the lowest step—

Mrs Thrale screamed when the door opened and Queeney lurched forward. Had Manucci not interposed his body between the child and the drop, the outcome would have been tragic indeed. The door secured and Queeney restrained in her mother's arms, the carriage rolled on to Southwark, where, following the administration of an emetic, Mrs Thrale put the girl to bed and sent Old Nurse to fetch Mr Lawrence, the family doctor. He, God forgive him, never arrived.

She spent that night in Queeney's room, rising frequently to see whether the child still breathed. At four in the morning, the tears coursing down her cheeks, she knelt at the bedside and addressing God begged that her firstborn should not die in punishment for her own iniquities. 'Take me,' she cried. 'Spare Queeney and take me.'

Pacing beside the chamber window – a half-moon battled through tumbling cloud – she talked to the absent Johnson; he alone was capable of understanding her fears. She confessed she had not always treated her daughter in a fair and gentle manner, not least when dealing with the child's strong affection for Henry, but this was on account of the adoration she had felt for her own papa, the dead John Salusbury. She had not wanted Queeney to suffer the same disappointment. To love a daddy to excess was to render inadequate him who must one day take a father's place.

At the fifth hour – Mrs Thrale counted the chimes of the clock sounding from the wall of the mill house – Queeney raised herself from the pillow and complained of hunger. On devouring a slice of cold mutton, she vomited and fell back insensible.

Baretti had not accompanied the Thrales back to Southwark, being expected for supper that evening at the house of General Paoli. The next day he called on Sir Joshua Reynolds, and it was there, some time in the afternoon, that Manucci's servant sought him out and requested that he return immediately to the Brewery.

He was let into the house by a weeping maidservant and shown into the nursery, where he saw Thrale, hands in the pockets of his waistcoat, seated on a child's chair, so stiffly erect and with such a ghastly smile on his face that all who looked upon him shrank back in horror. Close by stood a spotted rocking horse with a missing tail. Count Manucci and Old Nurse, both pale as ashes and panting for breath, were attending to Mrs Thrale, who, when she was not sinking to the floor in one swoon after another, threw herself about like a madwoman.

Presently Thrale put his hand on the nose of the horse and began to rock it up and down. It made a creaking sound, like the squeal of a child at play.

The news reached Johnson some three days later in Lichfield, when he and James Boswell were taking breakfast with Miss Porter. It being March, the monthly anniversary of Tetty's death, he was already gloomy. When he had read the letter – it was from Perkins – he sat for some time in silence, crumbling his breakfast roll. At last, sighing heavily, he said, 'One of the most dreadful things that has happened in my time,' and called for pen and ink to compose a reply. He wept as he wrote.

The phrase 'in my time' was so portentous that Boswell thought something of a public or general catastrophe had taken place, such as the assassination of the King or a disaster comparable to the Fire of London.

Mrs Thrale, on receipt of Johnson's condolences, sat dry-eyed and not simply because she had no more tears to shed . . . *in a distress which can be so little relieved, nothing remains for a friend but to come and partake of it. Poor dear sweet little boy . . . When you have obtained by prayer such tranquillity as nature will admit, force your attention, as you can, upon your accustomed duties and accustomed entertainments. You can do no more for our dear boy, but you*

must not therefore think less on those whom your attention
may make fitter for the place to which he has gone.

Attention ... attention, thought Mrs Thrale, he is thinking merely of himself, and stuffed the letter into a drawer.

Johnson came back to Bolt Court on the Sunday. He was in
a distressed state of mind. Mrs Williams wept with him
and Mrs Desmoulins did her best to appear in accord. He
told them that he had left Lichfield soon after learning the
awful news and that, stopping for one night only at Dr
Taylor's in Ashbourne, had travelled on to Southwark,
where he had found Mrs Thrale in her carriage at the very
gates of the Brewery, about to depart for Bath with
Queeney and Baretti. Dr Jebb had advised that a change of
air was imperative if the girl was to remain well; the two
younger children had already been taken back to Mrs
Cumyns's school by Lady Lade. Waving the carriage away
with many a sad look, he had gone at once to comfort
Henry. A servant had stopped him on the stairs and said
that his master wished to be left alone.

'Such discourtesy,' cried Mrs Desmoulins.

'Discourtesy!' Johnson shouted. 'The poor man is distraught. If it had been I who had suffered such a blow, I too
would wish to be solitary.'

Mrs Desmoulins checked her tongue. Upon Tetty's
death, Sam had demanded company day and night.

From Perkins Johnson had learnt of the events leading
up to the fatal afternoon. There had been an expedition to
the Tower. Young Harry had been in perfect health and
clambered so energetically about the cannons and the
mortar employed to defeat the Spanish Armada that he had
come to resemble Frank Barber. When Count Manucci had

complimented him on his knowledge of history and urged that he should be a soldier like himself, Harry had retorted, 'I would not fight for the Duke of Tuscany because he was a Papist.' Later, according to Baretti, he had taken pains to show the Count the instruments of torture used by the Spanish.

'Such a precocious child,' murmured Mrs Williams.

'His mother boxed his ears for it,' said Mrs Desmoulins.

It was Queeney who had shown signs of sickness. There had been an incident in the Menagerie when she had pushed her hand through the railings and rattled the chain of the bear. 'Poor thing,' said she, though only Count Manucci heard her, 'you too are caught by the neck.' Then, on the return journey across Blackfriars Bridge, she had attempted to throw herself out of the carriage, on the delusion that she saw a pathway to Heaven. Harry's sudden collapse a day later had come as a complete surprise. There had been no evidence of illness until a mere half-hour before his demise.

'Not so,' corrected Mrs Desmoulins, who had been visited by Old Nurse and had all the sorry details at her command. 'In the morning, the day after the visit to the Tower, he rose quite well, went to the baker's for his roll and ate it in the company of the clerks in Brewhouse Yard. After this, he bought two penny cakes for Susannah and Sophy and tickled them so much that they ran about shrieking. Mrs Thrale spoke to him harshly for it—'

'She was worn out', countered Mrs Williams, 'from sitting up all night with Queeney. A half-hour on, he was playing in the nursery, banging his drum and generally behaving in a boisterous way, when he suddenly began to cry. Alarmed – he was not a crying boy unless hurt – Old

Nurse hurried into the breakfast room to acquaint Mrs Thrale. She rebuked him for the noise he was making and held up his sister as an example, for Queeney, much recovered, was insisting on pouring out tea for her papa and Mr Baretti—'

'Mrs Thrale was busy fussing over that Italian count—' interrupted Mrs Desmoulins.

Voice high and cracked, Mrs Williams said, 'It was then that he vomited and Mrs Thrale, coming to see the change in him, sent the servant off to fetch whatever physician could be found. Then she ordered a tub to be filled with hot water, and laid him in it, and gave him an emetic in wine, all the time crying out most pitifully. At last Dr Jebb arrived and gave him more hot wine, then Usquebaugh, then Daffy's Elixir. Harry was now in his bed sitting upright and talking quite briskly, so much so that Mr Baretti said he should be whipped for giving his mother such a fright. But then Mr Jebb said he must go with the utmost speed to ask Dr Heberden's help in the matter, which put all into a fright again—'

'Some two hours later', said Mrs Desmoulins, and now her voice too began to waver, 'there was a terrible shriek from those around the bedside. Harry had been thrusting his fingers down his throat, trying to make himself vomit; then he stopped and turning to Old Nurse said very distinctly – "*Don't scream so . . . I know I must die.*" '

'Enough,' said Johnson, greatly affected. 'I have heard enough and can bear no more.'

He stood for a while at the window, looking out into the Court. Behind him Mrs Williams continued to sniff. Outside, clad in his white wolf coat, Mr Kranach walked round and round, finger stabbing the winter air as though conducting an invisible quartet. Life goes on, Johnson thought, and pondered whether this was a *good thing*.

Neither Mrs Williams nor Johnson being cheerful company, Mrs Desmoulins descended below stairs to the kitchen. Frank Barber had gone out to meet one of his sooty friends and only Levet was at the fireside.

'You,' said she. 'Idle as usual.'

'You,' said he, 'ill-natured as always,' and getting up left through the scullery door.

Sitting in his vacated chair she stared into the flames. How easily, she mused, one's sight registers alteration and how quickly the impression fades. She was thinking in particular of Samuel, of how when she beheld him after an absence she perceived him as old and tired, only to find in a blink of an eye that he had become the man she had known so many years ago.

'God willing,' she said aloud, 'it is the same for him,' and knew it could not be, for her gaze was dimmed by love and his clear of such mist.

It had not always been so. Time was, when she had been companion to Tetty in Hampstead, in those lodgings in Church Row to which he came infrequently, he had looked upon her differently. Tell him I am unwell, Tetty had urged, when word was sent that he would come. Tell him I need you to lie beside me. It was not Tetty's fault; she was above twenty years older than he who would so urgently require her wifely embraces.

She had done as she was bidden, leaving Tetty giddy from laudanum, the expression on her face disordered, her nightcap askew. Then, all a tremble, she had filled his warming pan and thrust it between the sheets, and gone to crouch on the stairs for his knock at the door. How the small hour chimes of the church clock had quickened the beat of her heart! What shameful fantasies had swarmed within her head! When she twiddled her hand about in the candlelight, a rabbit nibbled the shadowy wall. Sometimes, Lord help her, she had opened the wig cupboard on the bend of the stair and touched the powder dust to bring him closer.

Hearing his thump upon the door was both dreadful and full of joy; seeing him stomping in, boots splashed with mud, wig sparkling under raindrops, large eyes so full of desire, caused her words to quiver. 'Your wife is not well. It is best that I sleep in her bed tonight.'

'It is not best that she keeps me from her bed,' he retorted, 'and I doubt if illness has much to do with it.'

Later, when Samuel was in his nightshirt – he knew she was hovering on the landing – he called her into his chamber and persuaded her to lie down beside him. First, they indulged in pillow talk. She had pleaded with him to lower his voice, to curtail his feverish thrashings about the mattress; when he fondled her he was apt to shout in triumph at the discovery of a protuberance or a suspicion of moisture. But then, at the very moment when, in spite of God's teachings, she would have welcomed a final assault, he had thrust her from him and bid her quit the room.

A moral man, she had then thought, and revered him for it, but now – now that it was all too late – she was not so sure. Perhaps a cowardly man was nearer the truth. It was curious, was it not, that great men who compiled dictionaries, whose intellect enabled them to expound upon the state of nations, had not the words or the understanding to define the small business of love?

Rising from the table, Mrs Desmoulins poked at the fire.

The way the cinders fell and died on the hearth, leaving the young sea coals to flare up anew, confirmed her worst fears. She was, she reasoned, a woman snuffed out by the abominable Mrs Thrale.

It afforded her some satisfaction to discover Levet's shoes stood beside the scuttle. He, at least, would be tramping ice-footed through the mire of the world.

Mr Baretti's relationship with Mrs Thrale had never been easy. They were too alike in temperament, both being fiery, and had fallen out many times in the past, yet such was his tenacity and her shrewdness – she had a high opinion of his qualities as a teacher – a patching of sorts had always been possible. Then, a mere week after she had fled to Bath to take the waters, a more serious rift occurred. It arose from a rumour, believed to have been spread among the servants by Baretti, concerning a letter she had received from Dr Jebb. According to the Italian, Jebb had requested most urgently that she stop giving tin pills to her daughter, for the remedy might prove more fatal than the affliction. Mrs Thrale had denied receiving any such letter and charged him with scandalmongering.

At the time, in spite of her liking for Mr Baretti, Queeney had sided with her mother who for a whole seven days had behaved towards her with unaccustomed sweetness. By day Mamma had taken to scarcely ever raising her voice in temper, and at night had got into the habit of lying beside her as she drifted into sleep; she said nothing, merely held her close, one hand clapping against her back in imitation of a heartbeat. It is true her dosing and purging had intensified, but this was understandable in the circumstances and but a small price to pay for such a display of motherly love. Then, Mr Baretti having soured her mood, she reverted to her old self and once again became crotchety.

Mrs Thrale spent the remainder of the year moving from Bath to Brighthelmstone and back again in the company of what she referred to as the ruins of her family. Sometimes Johnson joined them, though apart from sea bathing in Brighthelmstone he found both resorts dull.

In the New Year they returned to Streatham Park. Mrs Thrale had made a new acquaintance, that of Dr Burney, a man renowned for the teaching of music and one whose instruction she had long sought for Queeney. On meeting this eminent personage, Baretti spoke boastfully of his own knowledge of the art and generally behaved in a boorish manner. Mrs Thrale was annoyed; she feared he would prevent Dr Burney coming to the house on future occasions.

There were other worries on her mind, the most serious being Thrale's state of health. Shortly after their return from France the previous year he had complained of a testicle swollen to an enormous size. She had thought only of a cancer and had pleaded with him to get the best help he could find. Far from calling on Jebb or Cruikshank, he had insisted on consulting a quack named Osborne, whose services were sometimes advertised in the paper and who claimed to have studied under Monsieur Daran, a physician famed as a practitioner in the venereal afflictions. And all the while Henry had gone on protesting it was neither a cancer nor an infection, but a swelling caused by his leap from the chaise between Rouen and Paris. During this fretful time Johnson was of considerable support, urging prayer, and more importantly, a trust in physic. He corresponded with Dr Heberden, who recommended the rubbing of Mercury ointment into the skin around the affected area, and the taking of a nightly dose of Balsam Copabia, which stopped the running but not the inflammation. Thrale complained bitterly of a soreness of the mouth and a loosening of his teeth. Sometimes of a morning tufts of his hair lay shed upon the pillow, a circumstance he insisted was natural seeing he was now in the fifth decade of his life.

'If he should die,' wailed Mrs Thrale, 'we are all lost,' an observation overheard by Baretti, who retorted, 'If he does, then it will not be long before Mr Johnson stands in his place.' This remark so disconcerted Johnson that he raised his stick as though to strike the Italian to the ground. Shortly after, due no doubt to the stream of prayers issuing heavenwards, the swelling abated.

Now, it returned. She had no sooner settled back at Streatham Park than she was required to get to her knees night and morning to hold poultices to the injured part. At such illuminating moments Mrs Thrale could not help but recall the words of her father, who had prophesied that if she married such a scoundrel as Henry he would give her the pox. Nor did she receive much thanks for her administrations, Thrale being sunk into self-pity and constantly berating her for being either too rough or insufficiently firm in her applications. He still protested that his sickness was brought about by his tumble into the chalk pit, and stoically refused to give up wine and the excessive eating of meat as advised by Osborne. Samuel, though in accord with the strictures regarding bloody beef and fatty cuts of pig, went along with the notion that Henry's swelling was merely a consequence of a jolting of parts. Poor fool that I am, thought Mrs Thrale, it is best that I believe it.

What with the nursing Henry needed and Johnson falling under an attack of gout, for which he demanded sympathy and wearisome talk as to the causes of the complaint, she felt much put upon. It was not to be wondered at that matters at last came to a head between herself and Baretti.

The night before, he had bullied her into tears over the cancellation of the trip to Italy. Henry was at the table, but it was only she who was upbraided for what Baretti called the wilful breaking of a sacred promise. It was a well-known fact, Baretti argued, that an alteration of scene was of benefit to those suffering from bereavement and, in any case, was it not better to be miserable in Italy where the sun shone, than in England where rain never ceased to fall? He had made so many plans. His relatives had expected them; his friends had incurred expenses through the arranging of excursions and accommodation. Were they to be left under the misapprehension that he had invented such a visit, that he was a man given to untruths and fantasies? Henry, befuddled with drink, had said he would recompense him for the trouble he had gone to, but Baretti's eyes had fairly blazed with anger.

Then, the following morning, he overreached himself in the presence of Miss Reynolds and Mr Langton. Dr Burney, who in spite of his earlier encounter with the Italian had accepted an invitation to dine that evening, was fortunately closeted with Johnson, who sat at his desk composing one of his many charitable letters. Queeney observed the confrontation.

Old Nurse, the tears coursing down her cheeks, came into the drawing room clutching a toy soldier which had belonged to Harry. She wanted to know what she should do with it.

'Burn it,' Mamma cried, and snatching it from her flung it on to the fire. After a while there was a spitting sound as the paint began to bubble from the wood. Papa, pale as snow, stared into the flames.

It was then that Mr Baretti said, 'Would that the consuming of an object could eradicate a mother's guilt,' at which Mamma flew into a fury and accused him of stepping beyond his position.

'My position, Madam,' he shouted back, 'is that of a man who wishes to save this family from further grief.'

'What do you know of grief,' Mamma retorted, 'or guilt for that matter, you who stood trial for murder . . . ?'

'My murder', he retorted, 'was committed to prevent my own life from coming under the threat of extinction—'

'Come, come,' interrupted Papa, rising to his feet in agitation, 'this goes too far.'

'Did Dr Jebb not write', demanded Mr Baretti, stabbing a quivering finger in the direction of Mamma, 'that if you continued your meddlings with patent medicines you would tear Queeney's bowels to pieces?'

'You forget yourself, Sir,' she screamed.

'—And that if you persisted you would soon send the daughter to join the son.'

At this dreadful reminder Papa left the room rather in the manner of Belle, head lowered and a growl coming from his throat. Mamma sank into a chair and Mr Langton strode to the window, where he stood staring up at the mild sky. As for Miss Reynolds, she hid her face in her hands, either from shock or to hide a smile. It is not easy, thought Queeney, to feel something that does not directly affect oneself.

Some moments after, waving a piece of paper, Mr

Johnson bustled in. He announced he had finished his petition on behalf of the unfortunate Dr Dodd, now approaching sentence of death for forgery, and was anxious to read aloud what he had written.

'*My Lord Mansfield,*' he began, '*but a few days – and the lot of the most unhappy of created beings will be decided for ever! I know the weight of your Lordship's opinion. It is that which will undoubtedly decide whether I am to die an igno-minious death, or drag out the rest of my life in dishonourable banishment. O my Lord! Do not refuse to hear what I in my humility dare to—*'

Glancing up from the page, he saw that Mamma was gazing about her distractedly. 'It is somewhat flowery, I agree,' he said, frowning, 'but it is written as if from the pen of the wretched Dodd.'

'What do I care for Dodd?' wailed Mamma.

'What do you care for anyone?' sneered Mr Baretti.

'What is wrong?' asked Mr Johnson, perplexed and none too pleased at the reception given to his morning's labour.

'There has been a disagreement,' Miss Reynolds squealed, a description Queeney considered less than adequate.

'Concerning what?'

'Concerning me, Sir,' cried Mr Baretti defiantly and, quitting the room, slammed the door so violently behind him that smoke billowed out from the hearth.

Queeney followed. Her belly ached; she had been purged before breakfast. Had she stayed and run to comfort Mamma, as she wished, she might have faced rejection. Her mother was again expecting a child and was therefore unpredictable.

Johnson called out, 'Sweeting,' for he had noticed the

girl's bereft expression, but she did not hear him. Nor could he get a word out of Mrs Thrale as to the reason for Baretti's anger; she sat bolt upright, a vacant look in her blue eyes, as of one whose gaze, too long fixed on the fires of Hell, was now burnt clean.

Observing her, he became anxious on his own account, for it was he who had introduced Dr Burney to the household and such an atmosphere of disorder would surely reflect badly on himself. The Doctor had come expecting intellectual harmony, not the settling of scores. Urging Miss Reynolds to attend to Mrs Thrale, Johnson went out on to the terrace with Langton and sought an explanation.

Langton's version of events was puzzling. According to him, Baretti had accused Mrs Thrale of being the cause of young Harry's death, from the too frequent administration of tin pills.

'Tin pills!' said Johnson. 'Harry never suffered from worms in his life.'

'I merely repeat what I heard,' said Langton.

'A monstrous calumny', exploded Johnson, 'and not the first to be spread abroad. Why, on the night in question, it was said that a clerk of the Brewery, after a visit to Drury Lane, had taken the boy to an alehouse and returned him home out of his senses.'

'And was there truth in it?' asked Langton.

'Certainly not,' Johnson exclaimed. 'The clerk is a family man and one in whom Perkins had the utmost confidence.' Agitated, he caught hold of a branch of lilac just then coming into bud beside the wall, and twisted it about so violently that it snapped off. His look of horror as he contemplated the broken wood in his grasp, and the groan that escaped his lips, followed by the words, 'How simple it is to check growth,' unnerved Langton, who blurted out, 'My gardener is a great believer in the practice of pruning at this time of the year . . . now that there is no longer a danger of frost.' He attempted to seize hold of the branch, for now Johnson had taken to whipping himself savagely about the legs, and failed. Anxious to distract him, Langton enquired if he believed the Reverend Dr Dodd would escape the hangman's noose. 'Your letter', he flattered, 'will surely count for something.'

'Not so, Sir,' Johnson said. 'He is to be made an example of and there's an end to it.' Nor, said he, would the subscription raised by James Boswell and others, to secure a quick transportation of the body to the surgery of John Hunter, prove efficacious.

Langton disputed the point; he said that resuscitation had been successful some years before in the case of a felon – the name escaped him – hanged for sheep stealing.

'The name is not on your lips', Johnson countered, 'because the sheep stealer was of no account, and for that reason the highway was empty of spectators when his friends bore him away. Time is of the essence if life is to be restored. When they cut Dodd down, the length of the route to Tyburn will be packed end to end with those who pretend an interest in him, thereby blocking his chance of a return.'

Studying the mutilated lilac branch, and finding it past mending, he tossed it over the wall. 'Baretti', he observed suddenly, craning forward to watch where it fell, 'would do well to remember that second chances are hard to come by. Purging would perhaps do him good.'

'Purging?' echoed Langton.

'We must consider the meaning of the word in the

original sense – to expel impurities from the human body. The mind is subject to the same imperfections. For instance, ambition is a noble passion, and one requiring a certain degree of resentment towards those whose ambitions have already been fulfilled. But, as in the case of Baretti, when a man carries his ambition too far, we pity him . . . for he is no longer in control of his passions.'

'Baretti is certainly colicky,' said Langton.

'Whereas you, my dear Lanky, have no such impurity—'

'I am, I confess, singularly lacking in ambition,' agreed Langton cheerfully, at which Johnson, spluttering with laughter, commented that such a lack was no doubt a consequence of inherited wealth. Still guffawing, he descended the steps into the garden and set off in the direction of the summerhouse, a rustic structure a generous Henry Thrale had built for his use some years before.

A genius, thought Langton, is one whose nervous power and sensitivity are largely in excess – and let him go. In London Samuel could not bear his friends out of his sight, but this, the Literary Club reasoned, was because Mrs Thrale was not of the company. The Sam of Streatham Park was a different being from the Samuel of Bolt Court and the taverns of Fleet Street. The latter was a personage who welcomed intellectual stimulation in the company of men who recognised his genius, and who, on rare occasions, could best him in combat; the former, one content to wallow in the capricious sunlight of a woman's affections.

As Johnson receded unsteadily into the distance he still appeared shaken by mirth. At intervals the snort of swans alighting on the lake echoed his whoops of merriment.

For the remainder of the day Baretti kept to the school-room. Nor did he join the guests at dinner, and instead requested food be brought to his chamber, for which relief Mrs Thrale gave heartfelt thanks. It enabled her to pay proper attention to the discussion of a new work to be undertaken by Johnson, for which a committee of the most reputable booksellers in London were proposing to pay him two hundred pounds. The publication would consist of accounts of the lives of the English poets and criticism of their verse; Sam was honeyed enough to declare, in the presence of Dr Burney, who had been per-suaded to stop the night, that he would appreciate her help. His exact words were, 'Your judgement, my dear, is of value, for you are not burdened by excessive scholarship and your perception is fresh.'

Mrs Thrale immediately insisted on the inclusion of Milton and Gray, the one in parts a favourite of them both, the other, in her opinion, a poet vastly overrated, 'The Prospect of Eton College', in particular, suggesting nothing which every beholder was not capable of thinking or feeling for themselves. 'Gray's supplication to Father Thames', she elaborated, 'to divulge who drove the hoop or tossed the ball is useless and puerile.'

'Well said, Madam,' cried Johnson and patted her fondly on the head. Some weeks before, troubled with an infesta-tion of the scalp, she had left off wearing her wig. Both he and Henry had applauded the change in her appearance and gone so far as to claim they saw moonbeams dancing in her hair.

She spent a disturbed night attending to her husband, for he spat out a tooth in the small hours. There and then she resolved as soon as possible to return with him to

Brighthelmstone – sea bathing would possibly bring about a cure for his ills. She came down to breakfast nervous of encountering Baretti, having decided he must be left behind. He appeared half an hour later, and wished her good morning in so loud and defiant a tone of voice she was convinced he was about to insult her again. Sitting down, he asked if she did not think it was a pleasant day. Had she noticed the young leaves beginning to sprout on the chestnut trees in the avenue?

'I have not yet been out, Sir,' she said, and head lowered mashed away at the shell of her breakfast egg.

'The whole garden', said he, 'is coming into life, as it should be at this time of the year, unless stricken by blight.'

He was smiling, but she detected a sinister undertone to his remark, and stared at him coldly; in her mind she recalled Hamlet's judgement on the murderous Claudius – *one may smile, and smile, and be a villain.* Baretti looked startled and for a moment she imagined she saw hurt in his eyes; the next he put down his cup with a clatter and rising from the table went out into the hall. There – for Mrs Thrale sent Queeney to spy on him – he picked up his hat and his stick and left the house. Miss Reynolds, hard on Queeney's heels, reported seeing him striding away along the drive without a backward glance.

That mid-day Queeney walked to the ornamental gates of the Park and looked out into the lane, in case her teacher should come back. From the elm trees came the call of wood pigeons, and in their melancholy purring she heard Mr Baretti crooning to her in the school-room, the day the small Penelope got born, and died.

Weeks later, Mamma said Mr Boswell had told Mr Johnson that Baretti had informed him that he had been treated with such contempt in the presence of strangers – it was believed he meant Dr Burney – that he had had no other course than to leave Streatham Park for ever. Hatred one can bear, he had confided to Boswell, for it comes from the heart . . . contempt from the head.

When he sent for his clothes and his books, Mamma murmured, 'Good riddance,' though not entirely with conviction.

Johnson, for the third time in as many minutes, asked Mrs Desmoulins whether Frank Barber had polished his shoes. 'If you are enquiring', she replied tartly, 'whether Frank has been told to clean them, the answer is yes. Has he done so? . . . No. They remain on the scullery table much bespattered with mud.'

'Take no heed,' cried Mrs Williams, 'she is out to vex you. I felt them myself an hour ago and they were smooth to the touch.'

Mrs Desmoulins swept out of the parlour and tripped across the cat, who fled yowling; she was annoyed with herself for having been caught out. Samuel had been invited to a party at Dr Burney's. Of late, he had taken to showing more concern for his appearance, at least when Mrs Thrale was to be present; when he went to the Literary Club he was not so fussy, but then, no one there looked lower than his mouth. By all accounts, Mrs Thrale was now firm friends with Dr Burney, who was teaching music to the indulged Queeney; a week before the spoilt girl had been bought a harpsichord.

Mrs Desmoulins went to her room and waited in the dark until she heard the thud of the front door. Then she scurried on to the landing and looked down into the Court to watch Sam depart. It was a bitterly cold night and as he walked his shoes crunched on cobblestones sharp with frost. How lightly he turned his back on his home! With what little feeling he strode away from those who held him dear!

Dr Burney lived in St Martin's Street in a household of motherless daughters. The accommodation was not large and Burney had wisely decided the party could not be on the scale usual at Streatham Park. His principal guest, apart from Johnson, was to be his patron, the wealthy and high-born Fulke Greville, whose emaciated wife was the celebrated author of *Prayers for Indifference* and something of a bluestocking. Both Grevilles had long wished to meet Johnson. Seward, the anecdotist, an old friend of the Thrales, had also been asked. All the same, Dr Burney had not felt quite easy at the prospect of Greville encountering the tradesman Thrale and the sometimes irascible Johnson, and had taken the precaution of hiring an Italian contralto named Piozzi to entertain them should conversation begin to flag or else grow too heated.

The evening began well enough, though it was difficult to keep the drawing room warm due to the different times at which the guests arrived and the necessary opening of the front door. When at last everyone was assembled, Fanny, second daughter of Dr Burney, sensibly had an old carpet rolled up and placed at the foot of the door to combat draughts. Hot punch was served and a quantity of sweet-meats passed round on platters, one of which Henry Thrale mistakenly took to be for his sole use and whose entire contents he rapidly devoured.

The first harpsichord interruption was listened to quietly enough, save for an outbreak of coughing from Johnson. When it was over there was a mild clapping of hands, above which Mrs Thrale could be heard boasting of her recent visit to Court and of how the King had said she did not come often enough up to town. Mrs Greville held up her eye-glass and studied her quite openly.

Fanny Burney took an instant liking to Queeney, who, though only fourteen years of age to her twenty-five, appeared quite able to converse on equal terms. Fanny went so far as to confide that she was an inveterate scribbler, particularly of plays, to which Queeney replied that she herself lacked imagination and was thankful for it, but admired the quality in others.

Mrs Thrale, made uncomfortable by the stiff atmosphere – Mr Greville was too grand to start up a conversation and Samuel never one to initiate talk unless challenged – began to laugh a great deal without obvious cause. Mrs Greville went on studying her, which made matters worse, for she was as tall as Bennet Langton and twice as thin, and Mrs Thrale could not help noticing the skeleton outline of ribs beneath the expensive silk of her gown.

It was not, as she later told Henry, that she had found Dr Burney's guest a figure of fun, merely that it had struck her as comical that it was herself, rather than Mrs Greville, who had become an object of scrutiny. Hence, she protested, she had been unable to stop tittering.

Dr Burney, alarmed, signalled to Piozzi to start singing. This time Johnson's coughing got so out of hand that Mr Seward felt obliged to beat him repeatedly between the shoulder blades, provoking Mrs Thrale to laugh louder than ever. Worse, to divert the company, she suddenly began to mimic the singer, gobbling like a fish and gazing pop-eyed at the ceiling.

Outraged, Dr Burney shouted, 'Madam, this is not

polite behaviour,' at which Johnson, scowling at Mr Greville, who had planted himself in front of the hearth, cutting off all heat except to his own backside, leapt to his feet and bellowed, 'Sir, if it were not for depriving the ladies of the fire, I should like to stand at the hearth myself.'

Mr Piozzi, seemingly deaf to the uproar, continued to render 'Sally in Our Alley', a popular refrain from *The Beggar's Opera*, and when finished turned to bow to his unruly audience. Mrs Thrale clapped louder than anyone else; Johnson thought she did so from guilt at being the instigator of the disturbance. Not so Queeney. Mrs Thrale's expression had turned tender, lips parted as though to utter endearments. Piozzi was small in height, fair of complexion, and his eyes, light in colour, looked only at Mamma.

Soon, thought Queeney, she will want him to instruct me in singing.

To Madame d'Arblay,
54 rue Basse,
Passe,
France

August 4th, 1810

My dear Fanny,
I read your letter with amusement and not a little
relief, for now that Miss Hawkins has turned her
energies towards yourself I have every hope that she
will leave me alone. She is, as you have already found
to your cost, remarkably persistent.

Over the years her letters to me have rained down
like autumn leaves, and neither evading her many
questions, not a few of them of an impertinent
nature, nor ignoring her correspondence has
procured the desired result, namely that she let
matters rest.

The letters still come, and I fear her enquiries as
to the general order of things at Streatham Park stem
more from a wish to settle old scores than from a
genuine and creative impulse to add to the gaiety of
nations. Mrs Piozzi's published anecdotes
concerning Dr Johnson and his circle cannot but
have served to stoke the fire of Miss Hawkins's anger,
for Sir John was not treated kindly, and though it is
generally agreed that my mother is a mistress of
inaccuracy, her comments on his meanness

undoubtedly touch the spot. There was the
unfortunate matter of the missing watch and the
removal of certain private papers belonging to Dr
Johnson.

I beg you, my dear Fanny, to be cautious in your
dealings with Miss Hawkins. You, who, when I was
too young to know discretion, became the
confidante of my childish fears, know full well that
which I would prefer to remain hidden, not least the
events of a morning in Paris when Dr Johnson and
my mother rolled about the floor, and an earlier
occasion in Lichfield when I spied him dragging my
mother's petticoat from her chamber.

At the time, you were steadfast in support of my
mother, and for my own peace of mind urged that
my *imaginings* should not be allowed to run away
with me. I had, as you remember, boldly declared
that I was lacking in imagination, and it was not
until later, when my mother embarked on her final
degrading and selfish course of action, that you took
my side and confessed to a regrettable blindness.

In your letter you kindly ask after the well-being
of my sister, Mrs Mostyn. Recently I had the
pleasure of a visit from her. She is so changed, so
plump, such a picture of robust health that you
would not know her. She and I spent many a night
talking until the sun came up, an indulgence my
husband, Admiral Keith, took in good part. There is
more virtue in my sister than could be expected
from the strange education she got. We have agreed
that we were both exposed to injuries from a quarter
where it was least to be expected in the common

course. She is convinced that our mother's original
and persevering dislike of her children arose from a
hatred of our father, and certainly her general
conduct to the whole family – when she received
news that my sister Harriet was dying of the
whooping cough she stayed on in Bath until the
child expired – savours of that nature.

Forgive me, dear Madame d'Arblay, for dwelling
on myself and not enquiring before now as to the
health of your husband, the General, and your dear
son, Alex. Had I been born into a family
unacquainted with Dr Johnson, whose reputation as
a man of letters appears to burn ever brighter, I
would not be forever facing myself. The attention
given to the numerous emendations to Mr Boswell's
Life, and the spate of reminiscences and
contradictions trailing in its wake, constantly
resurrect memories I would wish lost in the mists of
time. For one so cold of temperament, an affliction
my mother laments I inherit from my dead father, it
is surprising how my emotions see-saw. I understood
as a child that age brings forgetfulness, and am
considerably inconvenienced to find that the
multiplication of years renders the past more real
than the present.

You mention your affection for Dr Johnson, and
seem puzzled as to my own lack of engagement. It is
not that I had no fondness for him, rather that I was
wary of allowing my fondness to grow, a state of
affairs much helped by his disgusting manners at
table and the often strong odour about his person.
That being said, I do know he was a man of rare

sense and that his belief in God was genuine and free of cant. When I was but ten years old I asked him why, if God was so infinitely good, did He find it necessary to condemn human souls to the fires of Purgatory – I was thinking of the probable fate of my mother – to which he replied that God was infinitely good on the whole, but that for the good of the whole, some individuals had to suffer. Though now the logic of such a statement is open to question, at the time I took it to be a reasonable explanation and did not so often cry myself to sleep.

I dreamt of him when my sister was staying with me, doubtless because he shambled through our talk of days long gone. I was in France again, in the dining hall of the royal apartments at Fontainebleau; Dr Johnson stood in the gallery above. I was twisting about between my fingers a button he had lost from his coat the night before, and my mother, aggravated by my fidgeting, stabbed me so savagely in the back with her fist that my grasp loosened and the button fell to the floor; above the buzz of the spectators watching the King and Queen at table, I heard Dr Johnson cry out, 'My wife's hair was golden.' I looked down to follow the spiralling of the button across the flagstones, and of a sudden it changed into the bouncing head of Marie Antoinette, mouth curved in a smile, the sunlight leaping through the gossamer web of her wig. At this horrid moment my sister shook me awake, for I was crying out in my sleep.

It is curious, is it not, how objects of but small significance assume importance in dreams? One of my earliest memories is of standing on the stairs at Streatham Park, holding a button up to the sunlight. I had found it in the garden and was much taken by the image of a leaping dog engraved upon it. My mother demanding to be shown what I held, I put it in my mouth, at which she boxed my ears for disobedience. Some years later, visiting Lichfield, I spied in the hall of the inn a painting of a man with a button missing from his coat, and persuaded myself it was his I had chanced upon in the garden of my childhood home. Is this not a strange confession, coming from one who professes to lack imagination?

You write of your wish to renew your friendship with my mother, but as you rightly observe, though you have seen and judged characters all your life instinctively, hers passes all calculations and combinations.

God bless you my dear Madame d'Arblay,
Ever yours,

H. M. Keith

On Harry's first going away to school, Dr Johnson composed him a prayer, after which recitation he stood in the drive to watch the carriage depart. Suddenly he turned to my mother and said, 'Make your boy tell you his dreams; the first corruption that entered my heart was communicated in a dream.' 'What was it, Sir?' she enquired. 'Do not ask me,' he replied, with such violence in his voice that she turned pale.

DISSOLUTION *n.f. (diſſolutio,* Latin)

1 Breach or ruin of anything compacted or
united
2 The art of breaking up an aſſembly
3 Looſeneſs of manners; laxity; remiſſneſs;
diſſipation

An univerſal *diſſolution* of manners began to
prevail, and a profeſſed diſregard to all fixed
principles.

Atterbury

Henry Thrale was a changed man. That reserve of
manner and good sense which had endeared him to
Johnson had evaporated. There was, for instance, the matter
of Sophy Streatfield, who had recently joined the Thrale
circle and with whom Henry gave every sign of having
fallen hopelessly in love. It was not a risqué liaison, for Miss
Streatfield was virtuous and he too ill to carry it to extremes,
but Mrs Thrale found his infatuation humiliating. It was as
though he deliberately courted disaster; though not yet fully
recovered from the effects of a second stroke, fortunately
mild, he insisted on standing for re-election to Parliament,

and lost. It was a blow to his vanity; he had represented Southwark for fifteen years.

Mrs Thrale and Johnson thought his defeat had been brought about by his altered appearance and demeanour. Upon the death of Harry something had broken within him, and in his lacklustre eyes and slurred speech the damage was apparent to all. He still hunted, rode about the countryside, gambled at cards, but his enjoyment of these pursuits had waned. His one passion – Miss Streatfield apart – was food, and now his appetite, always ferocious, increased to an extent that was truly alarming. As Johnson remarked one morning after counting the discarded shells of no less than seven eggs on his breakfast plate, 'Sir, you will soon surpass Falstaff in girth.'

A cause of more serious anxiety was the neglect of his business, which was exacerbated by a mounting extravagance. Once again the stables at Streatham Park were undergoing enlargement; a dozen peacocks had arrived to stalk the terrace; several marble statues had been purchased from Italy to stand along the drive, two of which had fallen to the dockside on disembarkation and now lay in halves in the shrubbery; to crown it all he was in the middle of negotiating the lease of a substantial property in Grosvenor Square.

Johnson, fearful of a financial collapse, spoke privately to Perkins, suggesting that the clerk should endeavour to persuade Thrale to place the entire running of the Brewery in his own, more capable, hands.

Perkins took his advice and wasting no breath on preliminaries came straight to the point, indeed, some way beyond it. He said, 'Mr Thrale, Sir, I have been thinking for some time in terms of a partnership in the business. What do you think?' Receiving no immediate answer from the astonished Henry, he continued, 'I would be willing to study the operative part of the trade and concern myself more with our exports . . . and as you are shortly to give up your house, my wife and our growing brood would be quite content to take up residence here.'

When Henry told Mrs Thrale what the chief clerk had said, she felt anger. Perkins had several healthy sons, and it was not tactful of him to refer to their sturdy growth. Nor, though for years she had longed to quit Deadman's Place, did she care to be edged out by a mere clerk. She too had suffered disappointment, for at the time of her husband's first stroke she had been delivered of a boy child, perfectly formed yet stillborn. Henry had scarcely noticed such an unfortunate outcome, and but for the sweet support of Mr Piozzi, Queeney's singing teacher, she herself might have gone into a decline.

'His insight into a woman's nature is almost feminine in its comprehension,' she confided, unwisely, to her eldest daughter.

'I allow he flutters his eyelids,' retorted Queeney.

'I have not noticed his eyelids,' countered Mrs Thrale, 'only his understanding.'

'Last year, and all the years before,' said Queeney, 'it was Mr Johnson who knew best what a woman felt.'

Mrs Thrale, endeavouring to extricate herself, found she stammered, even in her head. I have h . . . harmed Queeney in some way, she thought, not least by loving her too much . . . and must p . . . pay for it.

It was Johnson who finally convinced Henry it would be advisable to relinquish the management of the Brewery to Perkins, a function the clerk was already performing, in practice if not in name. He softened the suggestion by terming it a temporary arrangement. 'When you are fully restored in health,' he said, 'you shall take up the reins again.' Observing his Master's lips shiny with the grease of roast pig, brow dripping with perspiration, he reasoned such a time was gone for ever. Mrs Thrale was pleased at Henry's retirement; she had grown tired of her role as 'Lady Mashtubs', a title bestowed on her by the dead Mrs Salusbury. When she left the house in Deadman's Place she presented Mrs Perkins with its contents, save for Johnson's desk, sent on to Grosvenor Square, and the nursery furniture, which she dispatched to an orphanage in Greenwich. As she explained to Mr Piozzi, she had no desire to take with her that which would only serve as a reminder of irksome happenings.

Johnson was not happy at the thought of leaving his old rooms in the tower of the Brewery. He had reached an age when change was unwelcome, and beneath all the activity and talk of Grosvenor Square being more at the centre of things – Mrs Thrale held it was better for her husband to be closer to his doctors – he had the niggling premonition that he himself was being nudged further off. Anxious to avoid dwelling on such a dreadful prospect, he sought diversion. In involving himself in safeguarding the future of the Thrale business, he had neglected his critical essays on the poets, and now returned to the task, though without energy.

The Thrales had no sooner settled in town than Henry revived his notion of going to Italy. Worse, he said that the breach with Signor Baretti must be mended, for no one else was capable of arranging such a trip. Mrs Thrale was in despair at the thought of being united with a man she hated and one who had spread scurrilous stories about her. And how were they to drag Henry across the Continent, a man who could not keep awake for more than three hours at a stretch and who could scarce retain his faeces? When she turned to Piozzi for sympathy, he said Baretti was possibly not a bad man at heart, simply one whose earlier experiences had thinned his skin; the singing teacher's grasp of English was so convoluted that Mrs Thrale had difficulty in making sense of this.

Johnson, informed of the proposal, looked grave and said what Henry needed was more convivial company, more gatherings of like minds. So perturbed was he at his Master's deterioration that his knowledge of medicine deserted him; he was able to delude himself into thinking it was Thrale's mind that was the root of the trouble. It was a subjective diagnosis.

Thus a round of parties began, both in London and Streatham Park. Fanny Burney was now a great favourite of Mrs Thrale, and Johnson included her in his Latin lessons with Queeney. One morning when Sir Philip Clerke and Sophy Streatfield were visiting, Mrs Thrale persuaded Sophy to perform her *party piece* at the breakfast table. Fanny, who was not yet aware of Thrale's feelings for Miss Streatfield, but had heard of the young woman's ability to shed tears at will, was taken aback at the rudeness of the request.

'Sir Philip', Mrs Thrale began, 'has heard so much of your tears, Miss Streatfield, that he would give the universe to have a sight of them.'

'Indeed I would,' agreed Sir Philip.

'Well, you shall . . . you'll oblige, won't you, my dear?'

'No,' squealed Miss Streatfield, 'no, pray no—'

'Oh pray do, Miss Sophy! Pray let him see a little of it,'

coaxed Mrs Thrale. 'Consider, you are leaving tomorrow, and it's very hard on him if you won't cry a little.'

Suddenly, two tears came into Miss Streatfield's eyes and rolled in crystal pear drops down her cheeks; she was smiling quite beatifically. Mrs Thrale clapped her hands in admiration and cried out, 'Such tears manifest a tenderness of disposition while increasing a beauty of countenance.'

Fanny marvelled at Miss Streatfield's stupidity. Was it not obvious that Mrs Thrale was out to make sport of her? Then, at dinner that evening, Miss Streatfield proved herself not such an innocent after all. Mrs Thrale was sitting at her usual place at the table when Mr Thrale shouted out to her that she must change places with Sophy, for 'she has a sore throat and may be injured by sitting so near to the door'. Instantly, Miss Streatfield rose from her chair, at which Mrs Thrale cried out, 'Perhaps it will not be long before the lady is head of your table,' and burst into noisy tears, a display which, unlike that of the fair Miss Streatfield, did little to enhance her countenance. With that, she fled the room.

Much later, when Fanny and Mr Johnson went into the drawing room, they found Mrs Thrale composed but still smarting. The moment Johnson set foot over the threshold, she asked, 'Was I to blame for what happened?'

He replied, 'Why, possibly not; your feelings were outraged.'

'Yes, and greatly so,' she spat, 'and I cannot help remarking with what blandness you witnessed the outrage. Had this transaction been told of others, your anger would have known no bounds . . . but towards a man who gives good dinners and allows you the freedom of his library and home, you were meekness itself.'

After this tirade Johnson looked discomforted, and said not a word. He confided to Fanny the following day that it was Mrs Thrale's worry over her husband's breakdown in health, rather than his foolish cavortings with Sophy Streatfield, that had caused her outburst. When Fanny told Queeney what Mr Johnson had said, the girl observed it was merely what he wanted to believe. 'Mamma gives not a fig for Papa', she said, 'and is concerned only with herself.'

Queeney too was changing: she was neither so quick to take offence, nor so secretive. On occasions, in intuition and changes of mood, Johnson thought her very like her mother. One morning, when he was sitting drinking tea in the back parlour in Grosvenor Square, she rushed in from her singing lesson and proceeded to twirl about the room. She did not often give way to high spirits, and Johnson, who had caught snatches of her warblings, went so far as to liken the sound to the trilling of a songbird. Truth to tell, he found music intrusive, but Queeney's lightness of heart was infectious. He wheezed as he flattered, being more than usually troubled with his habitual asthma. Queeney urged him to stand upright and throw back his shoulders, something Mr Piozzi bid her do during instruction in breathing. 'It is important', she babbled, 'for the lungs to expand to their full extent.'

Captivated by her gaiety, he stood and adopted a military stance. 'Breathe in,' she ordered . . . 'deep . . . deeper.' He attempted to obey and was promptly seized with a fearsome attack of coughing. Some moments later, leaning back in his chair, he rebuked her for thinking the act of breathing was the same for all. 'It is as hard for me', he complained, 'to maintain a shallow intake of air as it would be for you to inhale a whirlwind.'

'Papa will not die, will he?' she suddenly asked.

'In time', he said, 'we all must die . . . but not yet.'

'Mr Garrick died before his time. I heard you say so—'

'That I did,' he said, 'and meant it, for we were young together and I miss him.'

'Do you miss Mr Baretti?'

'He is not dead—'

'No,' she agreed, 'but you do not see him, which is almost the same. You thought him worthy of friendship, did you not?'

Parrying her question, though understanding the reason for it, he said it was a good thing to hold people in affection, whatever the general and opposite opinion.

'Mamma was wrong, was she not, to forbid him the house?'

'Mamma did not forbid him. It was Mr Baretti who turned his own key in the lock.'

Queeney fell silent. Her face was so altered, its expression of animation quite wiped away, that Johnson felt pity. Thinking to distract her, he said, 'Mr Boswell considers himself a composer of songs. They have little in the way of melody, yet the words are catchy to those of a melancholy disposition. Last month he recited the beginnings of one. He has got no further than two lines, and those not good—'

'Tell me,' she said, albeit reluctantly.

'"Tis o'er, tis o'er,"' intoned Johnson, '"The dream is o'er, and Life's illusion is no more . . ."'

'Is there not more?' Queeney asked.

'No, Sweeting. What more could there be?'

She said, 'Mamma is good at turning keys in locks, is she not?'

He looked at her sharply, and replied in some agitation,

'Mamma is good at many things, not least at loving. You would do well to think of that.'

'I do not wish to think she loves Mr Piozzi,' Queeney cried, at which Johnson stood upright and, muttering to himself, head shaking from side to side as though to be rid of some stench beneath his nose, left the room. Queeney knew it was not rudeness on his part, more that being old he had doubtless remembered something previously forgotten.

'Tis o'er, tis o'er,' she sang aloud, and once more danced about the room.

Johnson was walking along Fleet Street, his gaze directed towards the ground, when his eye chanced upon the muscular tail of a rat protruding from a litter of old newspapers blown against the doorway of a pie shop. He was thinking at that particular moment of Dryden, of whom he had written, *The power that predominated in his intellectual operations was rather strong reason than quick sensibility*, a sentence he had reworked several times, for it seemed to him that he was dissecting himself rather than his subject. Had not Dryden been in possession of a mind stored with principles and observations? Were not his performances always hasty, either excited by some external occasion, or extorted by domestic necessity? Did he not compose without consideration and publish without correction? What his mind could supply at call, or gather in one excursion, was all he sought, for he had no love of labour . . .

Distracted, he stopped to observe the emergence of the rodent. Out it came, snout sniffing the air, forepaws raised. It saw, or sensed, him – and was gone in an instant.

Almost at once he was hailed by James Boswell, yesterday

returned from Scotland and on his way to Bolt Court hoping to find him at home. Puce with excitement, Boswell cried out, 'Sir, I am happy to see you,' and wrung his hand.

When they had tripped through the politenesses, Johnson said, 'The sight of an animal going about its business, seeking its food, foraging for its young – what a strange pleasure it affords us.'

'True, true,' Boswell affirmed, though he could see nothing but birds strutting the gutter.

'There is only one mendacious being in the world', continued Johnson, 'and that is man. Every other is virtuous and sincere.'

'True, true,' repeated Boswell, and begged to be allowed to walk with him, for, he said, he had now read a great proportion of the manuscript of *Critical Observations on the Poets*, and longed to have talk of it. Johnson replied that he was just now in a reflective mood, but, if it would please him, he would be welcome that evening at Bolt Court.

As they parted, he said, 'The main reason we take so much pleasure in looking at the lower animals is because we like to see our own nature in a simplified form.' This observation appeared to him so apt that he began to chuckle at his perspicacity, an outburst that got the better of him and developed into full-throated laughter, upon which the pigeons rose in a disordered flock and swirled about his head.

Mrs Desmoulins opened the door to Boswell; she was somewhat flushed. Sir Joshua, Arthur Murphy and Mr Allen, the printer, were already in the parlour, but as yet Johnson had given no sign that he wished her to withdraw. The preferred Mrs Williams was there, and Levet too, the one sitting by the fire in her faded scarlet, the other in the far corner, holding a cup out of reach of the cat perching on his bony knee. Mrs Desmoulins sat down beside Levet, something she would not usually do, but then she and he were not often present when Samuel entertained visitors.

At once Boswell began to praise Samuel's manuscript of the *Poets*. He argued that two hundred guineas was but poor recompense for such a mighty work of genius. 'It was not guineas,' corrected Johnson, 'but pounds . . . and it was not, Sir, that I was paid too little, rather that I wrote too much.'

'It is a work of infinite scholarship,' gushed Boswell, and proceeded to recite whole passages from the essay on Pope. He spoke so long and so fulsomely that Johnson growled, 'Enough, Sir. I wrote it in my usual way, dilatorily and hastily, unwilling to work and working with vigour and haste. Say no more, for it is not yet in print and your recommendations, which arise from prejudice, are not to be trusted.' He then poured out brandy for his guest, which silenced Boswell for the moment.

Sir Joshua talked of having called upon poor Topham Beauclerk, who, he feared, was not long for this world. 'His habit of taking opium has wasted him,' he lamented.

'I have heard', Mrs Williams ventured, 'that after he stayed the night at Mr Langton's, his bed linen was so infested with vermin it required burning.' At this Samuel looked angry, but held his tongue. Had I spoken so cruelly, thought Mrs Desmoulins, I should have been shown the door to the cellar.

Boswell brought up the subject of a lecture he had recently attended at Coachmakers' Hall. It had dealt with the resurrection of the saints following the crucifixion, and with the accounts of those claiming to have seen such a phenomenon. Mrs Williams thought it an interesting subject and one she would like to hear discussed, at which Johnson argued that it could not be interesting because there could be no proof. He was not disputing the fact of resurrection – 'The question simply is', he reasoned, 'whether departed spirits ever have the power of making themselves perceptible to us; a man who thinks he has seen an apparition can only be convinced himself; his authority will not convince another . . .'

He was interrupted by an unearthly howl from the shadowy corner of the room. All were startled, fearing that indeed an apparition had appeared among them; it was only Levet, upon whose knee the cat had seen fit to sharpen its claws.

'There is, however,' continued Johnson, 'a not infrequent happening, one I have experienced myself, of being *called* . . . that is, hearing one's name pronounced by a familiar person, but one too far distant for the sound to have been uttered by human organs—'

'Sir, Sir,' cried Boswell, 'I have known somebody to whom this happened. An acquaintance of mine was walking home to Kilmarnock when from a distant wood his name was called in the voice of his brother, who for many years had been residing in America—'

'And I suppose', said Johnson, 'that some days later he heard news of his brother's death . . .'

'Why, yes. Exactly so.'

'The voice I heard', Johnson said, 'was that of my dear mother. I was at Oxford, turning the key in the lock of the college gate when she quite distinctly called *Sam*.'

'And did you then receive news of her death?' asked Mr Allen.

'No, Sir, simply a letter requesting the sum of two pounds.'

Soon after, they sat down to dinner. There was not sufficient room at the table for Levet, who ate in the corner, fighting the cat from his plate. The meal was not lavish yet the cold meats were well seasoned and Mrs Williams's apple chutney declared delicious. Some months before, Johnson had bought a silver pepper pot, which he now passed round the company with a degree of reverence more fittingly accorded to a rare manuscript. When Arthur Murphy made use of it, shaking its contents liberally on his plate, Johnson plucked it from him and, after wiping it on the skirt of his coat, placed it out of reach.

It was when the dishes had been cleared away, and a third bottle of port opened, that Sir Joshua mentioned his visit to Streatham Park a week before. He had, he said, found Mr Thrale much altered. His appetite was now so terrible that one could scarce bear to look upon him at table. 'At one end', said he, 'there were lobster, carp and oysters . . . at the other, hams, boiled chickens, turkeys . . . and in between a quantity of pies . . . all of which he helped himself to in abnormal quantities and fell upon as if any moment his plate might be snatched away . . . and all the while champing with such voraciousness that the veins in his nose turned purple and his eyes threatened to pop from his head.'

'To show one's concern,' Johnson said, 'or to try to stop him, does little good. Mrs Thrale and I have tried everything in our power to modify his eating, to no avail.'

Arthur Murphy said Mrs Thrale was now back in town and happy to be residing at the fashionable centre of things. He had called on her but yesterday and found her preoccupied with plans for a musical evening she was soon to hold at Grosvenor Square.

'It is curious, is it not,' Mr Boswell remarked, 'how fond Mrs Thrale has become of the human voice uplifted in song?'

An uncomfortable silence ensued. Mrs Desmoulins was not alone in noticing the sly smile that accompanied his words. Then Johnson stood and poured himself a large measure of brandy; every eye turned upon him.

'Sir,' Mr Allen exclaimed, 'I did not think you drank.'

'For many years I have not done so,' he replied, 'and have but recently returned to it, though not in society.'

'I once remember', said Sir Joshua, 'many years ago, shortly before you gave up the habit, you drank three bottles of port, whereupon you found yourself so unable to pronounce a certain difficult word that after trying three times to get it out you put down your cup and left the company.'

'The word was *villainous*,' Johnson said, 'and it was not the word that was difficult, merely that my lips refused to shape it.'

Mr Boswell was in such an inebriated state at the close of the evening that he was unable to walk. Mr Murphy was obliged to piggy-back him into the Court, where, raucously singing, he was tumbled into Sir Joshua's carriage.

Mrs Desmoulins would have liked to have stayed downstairs in the warmth, but Johnson said she must go to her bed. The wretched Levet was not asked to retire. Indeed, no sooner had Mrs Williams said goodnight than he rose unsteadily from his corner and took her chair by the fire. The cat followed instantly and leapt upon his lap. Mrs Desmoulins reckoned it was the odour of herrings about his person that made the animal so fond.

When I am alone and dying, she thought, Sam shall hear my voice calling his name, and weep at the sound of it.

Mrs Thrale was determined her musical evening would become the talk of London society. With the help of Mr Piozzi she had hired a score of musicians and performers, and instructed Henry to compose a menu of such variety and munificence that it would require twenty-four servants to carry the dishes from kitchen to table. This task, one dear to his heart, visibly appeared to restore the spirits of the Brewer.

Mrs Thrale would wear a gown fit for an appearance at Court. It was made from material copied from goods brought from the South Seas, of a striped Otaheite pattern, trimmed with crêpe, gold lace and foil, and ornamented with stones very little inferior in lustre to the most brilliant jewels; the trimming alone had cost sixty-five pounds. When she tried it on for the benefit of Queeney, the girl declared it too *loud*.

Mrs Thrale had coaxed Mr Piozzi into beginning the concert with a song of her own choosing. Its words, she said, were particularly apt in regard to her husband. On the opening line, Piozzi must look directly at him –

> *If the heart of a man is depressed with cares,*
> *The mist is dispelled when a woman appears.*

– and then at Sophy Streatfield.

> *Roses and Lilies her cheeks disclose,*
> *But her ripe lips are more sweet than those.*
> *Press and caress her;*

With blisses her kisses
Dissolve us in pleasure and so repose.

– at which it would be provoking if Miss Streatfield did not
oblige with an imbecile display of tears.

Mrs Thrale persuaded Johnson to be present at one of
Mr Piozzi's rehearsals; she said she would appreciate his
comments. He sat astride a chair and endeavoured to look
pleasant. When the Italian soared into the chorus and,
gazing calf-eyed at Mrs Thrale, sang of kisses and blisses, he
stomped from the room.

Later, Mrs Thrale rebuked him for such ill-mannered
behaviour. 'You may not like music,' she chided, 'but you
have hurt Mr Piozzi's feelings,' to which he savagely
retorted that he did not recall her being so conscious of *feelings*, Piozzi's or those of anyone else, the night they had
been guests of Dr Burney. She stared at him with genuine
astonishment. She does not remember the past, he thought,
for the present is now all important.

On the night of April 2nd, Thrale ate so much that he
became comatose and collapsed with his head in the mess
on his plate. Mrs Thrale sent for the physician, Pepys, who,
after examining the sick man, said either he must be put
under legal restraint or else suffer certain death. Mrs Thrale
could not agree to the remedy. She declared that as it was
Henry's money that was spent on such gastronomic
excesses, it was his right to throw it away – but if his mouth
could be sewn up, she would pay for the thread herself.

The following morning, at breakfast, Henry again
stuffed himself so full that Johnson cried out, 'Sir, such
eating is little better than suicide.' An hour later Thrale
went out, left visiting cards at various houses, rode his horse

twice round the Square, and slept until roused for dinner. They now dined at eight rather than four in the afternoon as had been common at Southwark. Fanny Burney was present, Mr Langton, Queeney, Johnson and Mrs Thrale.

There was an attempt at chat, though it was difficult to shift Mrs Thrale from talk of her concert on the morrow. Mr Langton started to recall his knowledge of the Reverend Mr Hackman, who, two years earlier, had gone to the gallows for shooting the mistress of Lord Sandwich, but he was so distracted by the behaviour of Thrale that he soon trailed into silence.

The Brewer's appetite was beyond sensibility – he consumed four bowls of broth, two dozen oysters, two lobsters, three game pies, seven lamb chops and three stuffed capons, the whole washed down with numerous bottles of strong beer. Those around him put down their forks and stared at him aghast; even the servants looked frightened.

He rose before the puddings were laid out, and belching loudly and frequently quitted the room. Mrs Thrale followed him to the foot of the stairs. She called out to him, but he merely raised his hand in a dismissive gesture and continued upwards.

Five minutes later Fanny Burney entered his chamber and found him apparently none the worse for wear. 'Go, Miss Burney,' he bade. 'I have a desire to be alone.'

'He is less red now', she disclosed on her return to the table, 'and perfectly lucid.' A half-hour after, Queeney went upstairs. She found her Papa sprawled upon the floor, stockings and shoes removed. Terrified, she asked why he was lying there and received the reply, in slurred tones, 'Because I choose it . . . I lie so on purpose.' She noticed the dark skin of his bare legs, and the opaque quality of his milky toenails; he has the feet of a savage, she thought, and attempted to pull him upright.

'Leave me be,' he ordered, and placing one trembling hand to his livid lips blew her a kiss. She ran downstairs, emitting small screams.

Pepys was sent for, but could do nothing; it was too late. The dying man was lifted on to his bed, still murmuring that there was nothing to fuss about. Soon after he suffered a rupture of the lungs. Johnson held his hand and wiped the bloody froth from his mouth. On the morning of April 4th, as a rosy dawn leaked above the chimneys in the Square, Thrale died. He uttered no last words, merely let forth a prolonged expulsion of wind.

Johnson had never thought himself capable of self-deception. Hadn't most of the miseries of his life arisen from too close a scrutiny of actualities? Yet, upon the death of Henry Thrale he had every expectation that his friendship with his *dear mistress* would continue as before. Were they not so joined by affection and past experience, so in accord one with the other that the lift of an eyebrow or the droop of a lip rendered words unnecessary? He was not alone in making such an assumption. Indeed, Thrale had scarce grown cold before the gossip columns of the *Herald* hinted at the likely union between his widow and a certain lexicographer and poet. He did not tell anyone that he had read this scandalous tittle-tattle, nor did he care to acknowledge the vibrant leap of his heart on the reading of it. Once, at night, perusing a letter recently sent him by Mrs Thrale, her signature dissolved away and in its place he read, *I remain, Faithful & Obliged, H. L. Johnson*. Such a displacement of names caused him considerable agitation, and he flung the letter from him. The mourning period for Henry Thrale had scarce begun – it was not seemly to dwell on such an alteration of circumstances. Later he persuaded himself he had been thinking of dearest Tetty.

As an executor of her husband's will, he was of great service to Mrs Thrale, who turned to him for advice and support, and although he sincerely mourned the loss of his Master – *the continuity of being is lacerated* – he took pleasure in dealing with the practical details concerning the future of the Brewery; it freed him from the drudgery and solitude of writing. Thrale's five surviving children being but daughters, and Mrs Thrale loath to burden herself with the business, it was decided it should be sold. Mr Barclay, the Quaker banker, having made a substantial offer – it was agreed his nephew and the estimable Perkins would be in joint charge – the transaction was concluded with satisfaction to both sides.

Thereafter, life continued as of old, Johnson spending the better portion of his existence at Streatham Park and, in between, making his forays to Ashbourne, Oxford, Lichfield and Bolt Court. Mrs Thrale had now moved to a house in Harley Street, where, as always, a room had been allocated for his use.

And yet circumstances were not quite as before. Several times she had gone against his wishes in the matter of expenditure and once, at dinner, when he ventured the opinion that the sauce accompanying the goose was not as flavoursome as at Mrs Langton's, she had rebuked him in the harshest of terms, and in front of company. Some few days later, at Streatham, when he had ordered the carriage to be brought to the door, she had told him it was not convenient, as she would require the use of it herself later in the afternoon. As there were two carriages in the stables, he took this to be a sign that he was no longer of first importance. On seeking the opinion of Queeney and Fanny Burney, they assured him he was wrong in thinking so, but he detected a certain evasiveness in both.

He was poorly with stomach pains when he visited Lichfield and it did not help that Miss Porter also was broken in health. Worse, she was now very deaf, and it wore him out having to bellow into her ear. Such was his state of dejection that at last he allowed himself to express in words a fear long left unspoken. Hand unsteady, he wrote to Mrs Thrale – *Do not neglect me, or relinquish me. Nobody will ever love you better or honour you more.*

On his return, Mrs Thrale noticed a deterioration. She told Queeney that she wondered if he had not suffered a paralytic stroke; there was some drawing down of his mouth on one side and certain words were pronounced strangely.

'That of Italy, perhaps,' said the girl coldly, for Mamma was thinking of going there on an extended tour, Mr Piozzi serving as guide.

Sir Joshua also perceived a change in Johnson, not least in his outbursts of temper. As he explained to his sister, Frances, though his irascibility was nothing new, indeed an essential part of the man, he had always gone out of his way to ask pardon of those he gored in argument, particularly if they were inferior in intellect – but no longer. It was in his studio that Samuel had all but reduced James Boswell to tears. The conversation was of Bennet Langton, who through his extravagances at the card tables was now in serious debt and in danger of losing his property. Boswell said that, to save him, all his friends should call at his house and quarrel with him so fiercely that he would run from London and its temptations, to which Samuel savagely retorted, 'It would need but one caller, you, Sir, for if your company does not drive him out of his house, nothing will.' Though Boswell was undoubtedly a fool, he was sincerely fond of Johnson and it was not nice to see him treated so roughly.

Mrs Thrale came to a decision. It had become clear to her that Johnson believed he would reside with her for ever. While Henry had lived, he had conducted himself differently, for he was in awe of his benefactor. The Brewer removed, he had more and more taken to behaving as though he was her Lord and Master. As for her, what with his many illnesses and slovenly ways, she feared she was beginning to regard him much as one would an old and troublesome dog: smelly, wheezing, and constantly under one's feet. Besides, he shambled in the way of her future happiness. Something had to be done.

Searching him out in the summerhouse one afternoon, she announced she was letting Streatham Park to Lord Shelbourne for a period of three years. She intended, she told him, to retire in the autumn to Brighton and then perhaps journey abroad with her girls. It was for the good of Queeney, who had expressed a wish to travel. He must come too – to Brighton, that is.

He appeared to take it quite well, but then, he did not know what other changes she had in mind. When she left him, doves flew above her head.

On that dreaded last day at Streatham, Johnson rose from his bed far earlier than was his usual hour. His books had already been parcelled up and dispatched, but his desk was to remain, as was his chair, his bed and the little round table at its side. He trailed his fingers along the empty shelves and the surface of his desk in a final caress of farewell. Outside the window crows perched on the black branches of the winter trees. He gazed at the grey and sombre landscape and found it fitting, for it mirrored the desolation in his heart.

He used his chamber pot before going downstairs, for that too must stay behind; it had a blue border of flowers below the rim and a chip in the porcelain base where his stick had struck it by mistake. As he passed through the quiet hall he saw his reflection in the glass, that of an old, wobbling man, belly bulging, legs swollen with the dropsy. Lastly, he went into the library and gazed upon the books that had been his companions for nigh on fifteen years. '*Templo valedixi cum osculo*,' he said aloud, although he was not in church. On the walls hung the portraits of those once dear to him and now dead – Garrick, Goldsmith, Beauclerk, Thrale – and his own likeness hanging between the actor and the playwright. I am not yet gone, he thought, but might as well be.

He composed a prayer before leaving and, head bent, murmured its sentiments for the benefit of Mrs Thrale and Old Nurse. Queeney would not join in; she stood in the drive, pushing the gravel into small heaps with the toe of her shoe. When the carriage bore them away from the place he had called home, Johnson sat with a book open in front of him, though his eyes were closed.

During one of Mrs Thrale's dinner parties at Brighton, Johnson behaved with such rudeness to her guest, Mr Hamilton, that the poor man was driven from the house. Mr Hamilton made the innocent remark that he considered claret to be a very fine drink. Johnson said it was not fine, and that a man would be drowned in it before he got drunk. It was possible Mr Hamilton was not praising claret in general, but simply complimenting his hostess on the wine provided that evening. Anxious to avoid a confrontation, for Johnson was already hissing like a kettle coming to the boil, Mr Hamilton promptly agreed with him, observing that having drunk three glasses he was beginning to suffer from a headache. 'It is not the wine that makes it ache,' Johnson shouted, 'but the sense I am endeavouring to put into it.'

'How so, Sir?' asked Mr Hamilton, much puzzled. 'A head cannot ache from sense—'

'It can, Sir,' roared Johnson, 'if the head in question is not used to it.'

Two nights later, at a ball in the old Malthouse, he complained so loudly and so bitterly of boredom that Mrs Thrale told him to his face that he ought not to have come, 'as I am sure not one among us gains any pleasure from your company'. With respect to Mr Hamilton's lack of sense, Johnson had spoken no more than the truth, but she was tired of his bullying ways.

Afterwards, he attempted to apologise, but she brushed him aside. She had other matters on her mind, indeed was so disordered by the contemplation of them that she could no longer keep silent. The passion she harboured for Piozzi was now out of control – the mere mention of his name sent her pulses racing – and one morning, dressing in her bedchamber, she made a full confession to her eldest daughter.

She began hesitatingly enough, and with frequent assurances as to the enduring affection in which she held her children. 'Nothing I may feel for the man who has captured my heart', she said, 'detracts from the love I bear for you.'

'How could it?' said Queeney. 'Your heart is so big, Mamma.'

'My regard for your dear papa', continued her mother, 'was of a different degree . . . when he and I met I was ignorant of the world and of that whirling of the senses that betokens p . . . p . . . passion. He was a good man, a fine man, one who treated me with kindness and had an understanding of my—'

'Fickleness,' supplied Queeney.

'Fickleness', Mrs Thrale retorted, 'arises from a feminine need to fix one's soul to another. If that is denied, a woman may never know the reason for a deep and inner dissatisfaction.'

'Now that you know of it,' said Queeney, voice chill in tone, 'what will you do?'

Mrs Thrale's plans for the future were comprehensive. She would marry Mr Piozzi and take Queeney, Susannah and Sophy to live in Italy; Cecelia and Harriet, for the time being, would board with Lady Lade. There was much to be settled. She could not take the children out of the country without the permission of the guardians appointed by Thrale, in particular, Mr Crutchley.

Queeney went and stood at the window, so that her mother could not read her expression. She looked out at the shore and watched two bathing machines lumbering into the waves. We are all about to be sucked under, she thought, and blinked the angry tears from her eyes. Mamma's feelings for the Italian had not come as a surprise; the soft glances, the signs and smiles that passed between them were the subject of gossip in the drawing rooms of both London and Brighton, and had been for many months. The mention of marriage, however, was unexpected and shocking.

'You will like Italy', said Mrs Thrale, 'and, in time, dear Mr Piozzi.'

'I like him now', said Queeney, 'as a singing teacher. I would like him less if I was required to think of him as a father.'

'His mind is so attuned to the discipline of music', argued Mrs Thrale, 'that a knowledge of harmony precludes any desire for fatherhood.'

'Are you asking for my opinion on the matter,' asked Queeney, turning from the window, 'or simply telling me?'

'I would value your opinion,' cried Mrs Thrale, eyes full of hope.

'Well then,' said Queeney, 'if you must abandon your children, you must. You may turn us out to fend for ourselves, like puppies in a pond, to swim or drown as Providence pleases. I myself shall look out for a place as a servant and will never look upon your face again—'

'Nor write to me,' said Mrs Thrale, half smiling, in spite of herself, at such a childish outburst.

'I shall not easily find your address, Madam, for you do not know where you are going—'

'Dearest girl,' coaxed Mrs Thrale, and held out her arms.

'Mr Piozzi hates you and has told me so,' her daughter shouted. 'He is only after your money,' and with that she sped from the room and out of the house.

She was running down West Street towards the seafront when she saw Mr Johnson coming towards her. He had been swimming, and plodded barefoot, his bathing wrapper dripping water; a strand of seaweed clung to his ear. She would have fled past, but he caught her by the arm and peering into her tear-stained face asked what was wrong.

'Nothing,' she said. 'Nothing beyond the ordinary tussles with Mamma.'

He marched back with her to the shore and persuaded her to perch on the rocks below the cliffs, hoping the gentle lapping of the waves might calm her. The day was so limpid that sea and sky merged. A dog came by and sniffed at the girl's ankle, at which she dropped to her knees and endeavoured to hold the animal in her arms. It backed off, kicking up sand, and trotted away.

'You should be less trusting, Sweeting,' he admonished. 'The beast could have proved savage.'

'I am not in the least trusting, Sir,' she retorted, 'and every day grow more conscious of savagery. There are worse injuries than the bite of a dog.' The cynical force of her words, accompanied by a hurt defiance of manner, so disturbed him that he looked about for a distraction, and finding a species of lignite in the sand proceeded to give her a lecture on its properties. He explained it was strombolo, or sea coal, a composition of sulphur and salt, and recalled an experiment he had once attempted in the hall of Streatham Park, in which he had mixed it with a quantity of iron filings and heated both in a retort.

'To what end?' enquired Queeney.

'I forget,' he said, 'for there was no end. Your dear Papa feared I would blow up the house, and you along with it, and ordered me to stop.' Queeney giggled. Pleased he had lifted her spirits, he accompanied her back to the house.

Mrs Thrale received visitors that afternoon, first Mr Crutchley and then Miss Burney, though only she had been expected. Mr Crutchley disappeared into Mrs

Thrale's chamber and descended within the hour grim of
mouth and short on words. Johnson tried to question him;
beyond a terse comment on the perfidy of women, Mr
Crutchley refused to be drawn and soon departed.

Miss Burney too went upstairs, even before she had
removed her bonnet, and stayed there until dusk. At
intervals, those in the rooms beneath heard shrieks,
whether of laughter or dismay none could tell, followed
by protracted periods of silence. The younger children
ran upstairs and came back wide-eyed, complaining that
Mamma was not herself. Then, as the candles were about
to be lit, Miss Burney appeared on the landing and called
for Queeney.

Mamma was lying face down on the bed, moaning. Miss
Burney, eyes sparkling with excitement, said Mrs Thrale
was demented at the thought of giving up Mr Piozzi. Mr
Crutchley had told her she would not be allowed to take
her girls abroad and would most certainly forfeit eight hundred pounds a year in income if she so persisted.

'What do I care about the money?' cried Mrs Thrale,
voice muffled against the pillow.

'She does not care about the money,' interpreted Miss
Burney.

'She does not care about most things,' responded
Queeney, 'least of all her children.'

'That is not true,' Mamma spat, sitting up on the bed,
nose red and hair disordered. 'It is not my fault that I
adore Mr Piozzi. I did not set out to do so, I did not plan
it . . . he is so amiable, his abilities so above his station . . .
am I to abandon the hopes that I have cherished, let go the
happiness within my reach—'

'You must,' cried Miss Burney, and turning to Queeney

in some agitation, sought her support. 'She must, mustn't she?'

'There is nothing she need abandon,' said Queeney, 'save her children.' At which Mamma flung herself backwards and writhed about like an inmate of Bedlam. 'How am I to choose?' she wailed. 'Had I two hearts I might survive. Having but one, it will break between you.'

'Had you but one heart', pronounced Queeney, 'you would not think there was a choice.'

On going downstairs she encountered Mr Johnson loitering in the hall. She told him that Mamma, tired of London, was anxious to live abroad, and that Mr Crutchley had advised against it. 'Knowing Mamma, as you and I do,' she said, 'it comes as no surprise she is disturbed at being opposed.'

If he knew what she was keeping from him, he gave no sign. Indeed, that night he was in such good spirits that he diverted the company with the tale of a Newfoundland dog who had behaved like a bird on the nest.

Johnson was asleep in his bed at Bolt Court, or rather thought he slept, when he was startled by a flash of light striking the side of his face, a light so luminous that he was blinded. A moment later, sight restored, he was aware that he had lost the power of speech, not from a testing of his ability to utter words, rather that in his head he knew the facility had left him. To prove such a calamity, he opened his mouth and dumbly recited, 'I wasted time, and now doth time waste me.' Hearing nothing, he reached for his stick at the side of the bed and gathering what little remained of his strength banged it repeatedly upon the floorboards.

Some minutes later, Frank Barber, fortunately engaged in seeing to the fire in the parlour, heard his knocking and came upstairs. By means of sign language, Johnson instructed the alarmed Frank to bring him paper and pen, and laboriously wrote, *Fetch me a doctor*. His handwriting, though inclined to wander on the page, was legible.

Soon after, Mrs Williams rushed into the room and demanded to know what ailed him. Scoring out the words *Fetch me*, he replaced them with *I need*, at which she, hearing the scratching of his pen, ran demented about the room. In spite of his dilemma, the thought of the mute and the blind conjoined in such a catastrophe struck him as so comical that he succumbed to a convulsion of silent laughter.

He was laid low for four months, during which period, in spite of letters sent informing her of his illness, Mrs Thrale made no attempt to visit him. It was true she wrote back, effusively wishing him well and emphasising her concern, but she did not come in person.

He remembered the last time he had seen her, some weeks after her return from Brighton, when she had informed Mr Crutchley and the guardians that she had given up her intention of residing abroad and would retire instead to Bath, where, she vowed, she would establish a household, live economically and devote herself to her daughters. Samuel, of course, would be assured of a room in her new home.

He had visited her house on the eve of her departure and presented Queeney with a Latin Grammar and a Virgil. 'Dear Mistress,' he had addressed Mrs Thrale, 'God go with you,' and gazing long and intently into her eyes, kissed her cheek. On his way home to Bolt Court he had been obsessed with the dismal notion that he would not see her again.

Now, frail and pining, he reasoned it was not death that would part them, rather her withdrawal from his life.

Mrs Desmoulins was dusting the parlour when she heard him shout out in the room above. She ran to the foot of the stairs, but no further. He was become so uncertain of temper that it was not wise to disturb him unless summoned. He shouted again, but this time it was a string of words, none of which she understood, followed by a thud, as though a book had been thrown to the floor. As he had been learning the Dutch language for some months, she concluded it was proving difficult.

The anguish Johnson felt was so extreme that he beat his head against the wall. Above him hung a miniature of Mrs Thrale; snatching the likeness from its peg, he flung it to the floor. The recognition of his gullibility, his stupidity, struck him like a hammer blow. That he, who prided himself on his knowledge of human nature, of the vanity of human wishes, should have been so blind as to mistake the hope for the reality put his mind in turmoil.

When he had partially recovered his senses, he sat down at his desk, and, writing in the grip of such rage and emotion that the quill bent beneath the pressure of his angry fingers, penned a reply to Mrs Thrale's shameful communication:

Madam, if I interpret your letter right, you are
ignominiously married; if it is yet undone, let us once
talk together. If you have abandoned your children
and your religion, God forgive your wickedness; if
you have forfeited your fame and your country, may

your folly do no further mischief. If the last act is yet
to do, I, who have loved you, esteemed you,
reverenced you and served you, I who long thought
you the first of human kind, entreat that before your
fate is irrevocable, I may once more see you.

She wrote back, rebuking him for failing to acknowledge that she was in search of happiness, a pursuit he had
once considered laudable. His reply was less heated, in that
he wished her well and said he would not forget the kindness that had soothed twenty years of his wretched life.

Fanny Burney visited him some weeks later. She was
apprehensive as to how she would deal with the subject of
Mrs Thrale, should that lost lady's name enter the conversation. Dr Burney said she need not be anxious, as he was
sure Mr Johnson had shifted her from his mind, and
besides the name was now Piozzi, not Thrale.

Her father was wrong; no sooner had she entered the
room than Johnson began to interrogate her on the events
of those last months in Bath, for, he said, frowning thunderously, he himself had been left in the dark.

Miss Burney did her best to shed light on the matter.
'Mrs Thrale – as she then was – bending to the wishes of
Queeney and Mr Crutchley, exiled Mr Pi—'

'Do not mention that name,' Johnson roared, striking his
breast with his fist.

'She told him', continued Miss Burney, storing in her
mind, for future fiction, Johnson's countenance and ges-
tures, 'that he must return to Italy. Before he left he called
on Queeney and thrust into her hands letters previously
written by Mrs Thrale. Apparently he wept, but she, brave
girl, coolly accepted them and showed him the door. Mrs

Thrale shut up the house in Brighton and retired to Bath, but she was not herself.'

'Not herself indeed,' growled Johnson. He adopted a curious stance, arms spread wide and hands upraised, as though to stop the walls from closing in.

'Soon,' said Fanny, 'Mrs Thrale began to show signs of disorder – after midnight she took to roaming the garden singing of love and kisses. Once, she would have wandered out naked had not Old Nurse prevented her. Frequently she cried out, *"My heart, my soul, my Pi . . . my singing teacher."* She lost her appetite, her delight in company, her temper, though Queeney claimed the last had always been unstable. From pecking at her food, she progressed to eating nothing at all. If she was forced, she vomited, and at last was in grave danger of wasting away. A doctor being summoned, and grudgingly acquainted with the reasons for her decline, he urged that . . . *the man* . . . be sent for at once. He vowed he would not be responsible for the life of his patient if his advice was ignored.'

When she reached the end of her sorry narrative, Johnson no longer frowned. Now, his expression was so pitiful, his brow so etched with misery, that Miss Burney wished herself invisible. He sat down and studied his feet; she could not help noticing that though his chair was missing a leg, he maintained his seat without effort. Perhaps, she thought, he has always been accustomed to imbalance, though again, it could be the dropsy in his legs that sustained his equilibrium.

The silence becoming oppressive, she searched her mind for diverting topics. She was about to mention the restoration of estates forfeited by Jacobites, when he suddenly cried out, 'Did she dwell on me?'

'That she did,' Fanny answered, and hesitated.

'Speak out,' he cried.

'Frequently she spoke of her break from you and declared she hoped you would forgive her—'

'I asked for the truth,' he said.

'She thought your expectations too high.'

'Madam, she was right,' said he, and rising from his broken chair, eyes full of tears, gestured for her to leave.

Tiptoeing down the stairs she was waylaid by Mrs Desmoulins, who enquired of her whether she saw a change in Mr Johnson.

'No,' she lied, for she was past talking.

'Did you not notice his eyes?' persisted Mrs Desmoulins. 'They have grown larger, and now carry the gaze of a child.'

'I saw no alteration,' she protested, though indeed she had.

'He has burnt all her letters,' Mrs Desmoulins told her. 'He took them out into the side yard and hacked down the branches of the poplar tree to feed the fire.'

'It is perhaps advisable', said Miss Burney, 'to consume memories.'

'The poplar came as a sapling from Streatham Park,' cried Mrs Desmoulins. 'These past ten years he has tended it like a father his son.'

Miss Burney pushed past her and made her escape. As she trotted down the steps and into the Court, she could not help smiling, for Mr Boswell had told her that Mrs Desmoulins had long been in love with Mr Johnson; she found it comical that an old woman, plain of features and red of complexion, should harbour such a misplaced passion. But then, was it not a conceit common to another member of her household?

She did not see Johnson again for several months. When he next received her he boasted he was now much recovered in health. He said Dr Heberden's bleeding of him had given relief, and the prescribed doses of opium he daily took now enabled him to move about as formerly. Only two nights ago he had gone to his Club with Mr Boswell and walked home without distress. She said she was delighted at finding him so well, though it seemed to her that his asthma was worse and his dropsy advanced.

'I will not capitulate,' he cried, and next instant brought up the name of Mrs Thrale, demanding to know what news there was of her. She told him she had been informed by Queeney that her mother and the Italian were at present in Milan. 'She writes to Queeney,' she said, 'but Miss Thrale does not reply to her letters and scarce bothers to read them.'

'Poor Sweeting,' he murmured. 'She has lost her mother.'

'They were not close—'

'On the contrary,' he said, 'they were too close,' and added, 'A strange thought strikes me – we shall receive no letters in the grave.'

'Mr Boswell', she said, 'once told me that upon asking if any man had the same conviction of the truth of an afterlife as he had of common affairs, you replied, "No, Sir . . ."'

'I do not recall the statement,' he replied, 'but perceive the sense of it. If you mean am I serene at the thought of what awaits, the answer must be "No", for being rational I regard salvation as conditional. As I can never be sure I have complied with the conditions, I remain afraid of death.'

'Why, Sir,' she was foolish enough to protest, 'you who love God have surely nothing to fear,' at which, thumping

his stick against the floor, he shouted, 'Madam, it is the fear
of God that keeps me alive.'

When she had gone he sat for an hour or more staring
into the flames. Presently, Mrs Desmoulins stood outside
his door complaining that Frank Barber had given the cat
the supper cheese. 'It will do the dear creature more good
than either of us,' he bellowed, 'for both of us have trouble
with our bellies.'

He got up and going to his desk took out a sheaf of
papers. After no more than a cursory examination he flung
them on to the fire. A page fell to the hearth; he was about
to thrust it back into the coals when he glimpsed Queeney's
handwriting –

Southwark
November 24th, 1772

Sir,
Mamma knows I would have written sooner, but she
said you would be troubled no more with my stuff –
I left Susan and Sophy well yesterday but poor
Grandmamma was bad. Socrates is dead and old
Puss like to die. Papa is well and has bought a new
horse. Mamma is well too, if cross. I am very much
obliged to you for the honour of your letter.
Your most humble servant,

Queen Hester

He wept, and strove to analyse the cause. Age, he reasoned, weakened the emotions owing to a realisation that

the light was fading and nought but darkness lay ahead. Suffering, which fell to one's lot in the course of nature, by chance or by fate, did not, *ceteris paribus*, seem so painful when imposed by the arbitrary will of strangers; it was the wounds inflicted by those closest to one that drew blood. In the curling of the burning papers he saw the face of Mrs Thrale and, seizing the poker, stamped her image into the everlasting flames.

To Miss Laetitia Hawkins,
2 Sion Row,
Twickenham

January 5th, 1811

Dear Miss Hawkins,
Your accusation that I told Miss Burney that your
papa stole Dr Johnson's journal and watch is
unfounded. Nor can I be accused of spreading
rumours concerning my mother's relationship with
Dr Johnson, for their closeness during my childhood
was the cause of much unhappiness. An excluded
child has no wish to provide proof of a bond greater
than that which is supposed to exist between mother
and daughter. I can only believe that Miss Burney,
her latest fiction not attaining the approbation
afforded to *Evelina*, has resorted to a regrettable wish
for fresh notoriety. It could not have been she who,
on plumping up the Doctor's pillows and asking if it
would do, received the reply, 'It will do . . . all that a
pillow can do,' for I have a letter from her giving an
account of a visit she made to Bolt Court on
December 8th, in which so many people were
already gathered in his chamber that he sent word
down he was too tired to see more. Nor was your
father present that final night, nor Sir Joshua or Mr
Langton, the last two being his dearest friends. The
account of his end, which you ascribe to Miss

Burney, is erroneous. The seizing of a lancet, and the cutting of his leg to release excess fluid, was committed in the presence of Francis Barber, who sent for Dr Cruikshank to sew up the wound.

When death came the Doctor was alone save for Francis and Mrs Desmoulins. His stertorous breathing having stopped, they went to his side and observed he had gone.

I have no recollection of a padlock and key which you say my Mamma employed to confine Dr Johnson in his room when the madness came upon him. I regret I shall not be answering any further letters. It is not only the dead who need to be left in peace. I pray you, do not write more.

Yours,

H. M. Keith

1784

 PILOGUE

Twenty-four coaches followed the funeral carriage
to Westminster Abbey. It being a Monday and the
streets crowded, several officials of the abbey went
ahead to clear the way. Snow fell, but gently, as
though to draw a veil across the heavens.

Sir Joshua Reynolds was chief mourner, followed
by Francis Barber; the exalted importance afforded
to the latter caused Sir John Hawkins considerable
irritation.

The burial service was conducted by Dr Taylor of
Ashbourne at one o'clock in the south close.
Edmund Burke and Mr Langton were among those

who bore the lead coffin. James Boswell was not present.

Dr Taylor lost strength of voice on two occasions, upon which he dabbed at his eyes with the cuff of his gown. He had drunk heavily the night before and was conscious that his own end could not be long delayed.

A hole had been dug close by the remains of David Garrick. The coffin lowered into the damp darkness, a flagstone was set in place inscribed with the words:

Samuel Johnson, L. L. D.
Obiit XIII die Decembris
Anno Domini MDCCLXXXIV
Ætatis suæ LXXV

The expenses for the funeral amounted to forty-four pounds six shillings and seven pence, excluding the sum of thirteen shillings and fourpence paid separately to the bellringers.

Mrs Desmoulins sat alone in Bolt Court, roasting chestnuts in the fire.